THOSE
Girls

To mum and dad—you're the best,
and to Cazza—my muse

1

Jinx Slater lay in bed listening to her pal Chastity Max-Ward shagging the handyman. She wasn't so much listening, mind you, as accidentally overhearing, for the paper-thin walls of the sixth-form boarding house had been built with no regard for aural abstinence.

Nor, for that matter, had the supposedly squeeze-through-proof ground-floor windows been built with any regard for a girl with escape on her mind and a miniature screwdriver kit in her tuck box.

And escape, as it so often was, was on Jinx's mind. She leaned out of the window handily placed at the head of her single bed in her room at Stagmount, the imposing girls' boarding school that sat atop Brighton's cliff face, and looked toward the town. Despite it being only the second week of

September and unseasonably warm, there was a definite promise of the winter to come in the air outside. As she breathed in a lungful of sharp sea air, she glanced at the twinkling lights of the gin palaces moored at the marina to her right. She looked past these toward the fluorescent flickering of the funfair beyond and held her breath as long as she could.

She turned her face to the left as she exhaled, relishing the cool breeze. She stared at the navy expanse of calmly rippling sea set against the darkening sky, and thought of what lay beyond. She thought of freedom, of dancing, of drinking, and of laughing until you thought you could breathe no more. She also thought that even a spot of ear-bashing drum 'n' bass—which she *hated*—would be infinitely preferable to the noises emanating from next door.

Chastity's moans grew louder as her fluffy blond head beat rhythmically against the wall. The handyman was obviously handy in more ways than one, but the only reason Chastity liked him so much—or so she said, anyway—was because he'd had a bit part in some cop show as a teenager.

Jinx relinquished her duvet, got out of bed, leaned across her desk, and knocked three times on the poster-covered opposite wall: Liberty's wall. Liberty and she had slept in the same single bed for the last three years, but tonight Liberty was—halfheartedly, no doubt, with much huffing and puffing and shaking of her half-Persian head—working on her A-level art coursework. All of them had to turn in five pieces, in any medium, on "reflection and refraction."

The entire thing was due tomorrow, quite a big project considering the amount of weed Liberty smoked. Jinx had already done most of the work for her. Bless Liberty. She wasn't the cleverest girl in the school, but she was certainly the crudest. She was fantastic company and Jinx's best friend at Stagmount.

In summer, visitors professed astonishment at the Gothic building's warm beauty; in winter, they invariably likened Stagmount to a prison. The stone seemed to absorb the sun—golden and welcoming from May to September, it quickly turned gray and foreboding in winter. The weather made such a difference that the bursar—always with one beady eye on the holes in the roof—had decreed last year that prospective parents were only to be shown round during the summer term. He'd been right. Enrollment at full price went through the roof, and the waiting list was longer than ever.

It was small bother for Jinx to dash off a couple of expert-looking sketches, but they took Liberty weeks. Liberty mostly spent those weeks moaning, groaning, pulling her long dark hair, and chewing on her bottom lip until it bled.

Jinx sighed and resigned herself to a morning spent finishing Liberty's "The Sea" project. Thankfully, Jinx had insisted on Liberty taking the same project as her; three years' experience had taught her that if she wanted Liberty as a partner in crime, she would have to do her work as well. Frankly, it was a small price to pay for high jinks and hilarity all term long, and Liberty was the perfect buddy.

At the tap on her door, Jinx carefully placed the half-smoked cigarette she'd just re-lit on the windowsill, burn end facing out, and removed the cautionary hard-backed chair she'd wedged beneath the handle.

A wild-haired Liberty threw Jinx's door open and then threw herself onto the bed. Wearing a lime green velour track-suit, an ostentatious gold cross—somewhat bizarrely, for one who professed herself an orthodox Muslim, although she mainly did this to avoid the daily chapel service—and huge gray rugby socks that had Jinx's brother George's name sewn onto the heel, she curled herself underneath Jinx's duvet, plumped both pillows behind her back, leaned her head against the wall, and made a face intended to convey abject misery. In fact, she looked stunning, as per usual. "Hey, Jin," she mumbled from her prone position, eyes closed. "Sorry about the socks. Been meaning to give them back for ages, but they're so comfortable."

None of the girls cared much about what they looked like running about the school—there was no one to see apart from the teachers and one another. They didn't have to wear uniforms in the sixth form, so they mostly slobbed about in an infinite variety of pastel-colored tracksuits—with ubiquitous Ugg boots in winter and cool trainers in neon green, pink, or yellow in the summer. Sure, they dressed themselves up to the nines when they went out on the town, but it made it more fun, somehow, that they weren't doing it every day.

"Jin, I've been drawing that fucking crab for three hours now, and it's starting to freak me out. I keep looking into its dead, staring eyes and thinking it's trying to talk to me. And that bloody racket coming from next door isn't helping either. I really fancy a few drinks." Liberty made a grab for the half-smoked fag, took a long drag, looked at Jinx properly, and brightened considerably. "It's the second week of term and we haven't escaped once yet, *and* we've never been out at night, just the two of us. Please say we're going out!"

"Liberty Latiffe! Are you stoned?" Jinx laughed. Did Dolly Parton sleep on her back? Probably, yes.

Chastity's handyman resumed his pounding, and Liberty's head began to beat gently against the wall in time.

"Fuck it. Is there any male within a twenty-five-mile radius she *hasn't* shagged? And I'm fucked if I'm going to be made to join in by proxy. Come on, Jin, it's ship-out time."

Jinx grinned. She pulled off her match regulation navy blue tracksuit bottoms with the red stripe ("go faster," Chastity called it) down the side, unbuttoned her not-so-crisp white shirt, lay down on the floor, and reached behind the messy desk for her favorite pair of skinny black jeans.

Jinx eyed them and prepared to breathe in. Disco punk was all well and good, but really, jeans like this would probably render her infertile. Which actually, she mused, wouldn't necessarily be a bad thing.

She lay on the floor and quickly turned bright red as she struggled to pull the jeans over her knees. Jinx was not fat. "Christ," she gasped, as she finally got the fuckers over her ass, "I am *dying* down here."

Liberty bounced up and down on the bed, laughing. "Jin,

you look so, like, stupid doing that."

"Piss off! Now shut up and get ready—and don't smoke any more of that skunk. It would really mess up our first term in the sixth if you got caught doing that."

Liberty giggled as she tripped out of the room, and Jinx began surveying the wreckage atop her chest of drawers. Squinting into the dirty mirror, she applied Benefit peach blusher, YSL navy mascara, and a smearing of sticky, vanilla-flavored gold Lancôme lip gloss before running industrial quantities of Frizz-Ease through her curly blond hair. She slipped on a hot pink T-shirt with a black skull-and-crossbones motif stenciled on the front and smiled at her dusty reflection as she wound ropes of black beads around her neck.

She squirted about half her bottle of Chanel perfume in front of her before stepping into the voluminous cloud, simultaneously spinning around as she sought out the partner to the retro gold Nike trainer—metallic sportswear, very hot right now—that was swinging by its laces in her left hand.

At the same time that she spied the missing shoe, one of the myriad Blu-Tacked photos adorning the inside of the open cupboard door caught her eye. A black-and-white Polaroid taken by Jinx's mum, Caroline, who obsessively documented every single thing that ever happened to any member of the Slater family—including snapping dead pets in their shallow graves while the rest of the family sobbed at a respectful distance—it showed her and Liberty on the first day they'd met. It was three years ago but seemed like twenty. They both looked so small and afraid, tiny first-years on the first day at school. Jinx loved that picture. "Oi, Lib," she yelled, thrilled that they were going out, and thumping on the wall between them. "Hurry up!"

Ms. Patricia Gunn sat on the navy blue sofa in her small staff flat, one of her fat hands clutching a tumbler that contained slightly less than an inch of whisky.

The other hand, its mottled and liver-spotted flesh spreading with furious strain, pressed down atop the globe that lived on the occasional table next to the sofa.

She looked cross as she spoke the word of God and tried to feel as drunk as possible. It didn't work.

"Those little bitches, those little bitches," she murmured over and over again, her stranglehold on the entire continent of North America tightening.

Ms. Gunn stood six feet five inches tall in her flat, stockinged feet, and was almost as wide as she was high. She was wearing what she called—horrifically, as far as those in the know were concerned—her "lady suit." This was a now-threadbare, once-luxurious ruby red velvet dressing gown over a massive pair of stripy blue men's pajama bottoms, held up with the sort of red-and-white string butchers use to tie joints of meat together, with scuffed, beige, faux-leather slippers. She looked, frankly, hideous. "Those little bitches," she repeated, her face turning puce as she thought about how furious Jinx Slater and Liberty Latiffe had made her that morning. She found herself permanently cross this term—since Jinx Slater had moved to Tanner House she was no longer under her official jurisdiction and therefore no longer eligible for her very worst punishments.

Most of the girls were terrified of this sour-faced harridan, with her booming voice and military approach to discipline. The naughtiest girls in the school, however, took a sheer, some would say perverse, pleasure in provoking the loss of her legendary temper.

Ms. Gunn reached for the bottle of aged Talisker by her feet. She usually drank the famously naff Famous Grouse, but one of her charges' fathers had bought her this expensive drop hoping to sweeten relations. Despite the fact that she was universally hated by the girls, most of the other staff, and the parents, Ms. Gunn always got the best end-of-term presents. It was amazing, actually, that the parents would not only cough up the extortionate and ever-increasing fees that helped pay Gunn's wages without ever daring question her skewed authority, but that they would also try to butter up the old witch with costly gifts from Harrods and Fortnum's.

That very afternoon—*and it's only the second bloody week of term*, she thought bitterly—Ms. Gunn had suffered a nasty surprise. Traversing the brick-paved path that ran from house to house behind the main building with so many offshoots it was like an extremely complex rabbit warren, hoping to catch one of the many illicit smokers having a crafty fag before tea, she'd heard shrieking and laughing and a clattering mechanical sound coming from near the nurse's office.

Shuffling as fast as her huge bulk and flat feet would allow, thoughts of dishing out a hefty punishment warming her insides, Ms. Gunn rounded the corner. She stopped, dumbstruck, at the sight that greeted her.

She saw a curly blond head, and a straight dark one on top of it, whizzing past her at the speed of light in some kind of silver chair. It passed so quickly that she didn't at first realize that the silver chair was, in fact, the wheelchair belonging to her own dear mother.

Gunn kept the chair in one of the numerous bike sheds for when her ancient mother visited. It must be said that her mother was not *technically* disabled, but rather one of the earliest victims of Britain's obesity epidemic. The wheelchair was very much needed because of too many pies (and crisps, boxes of very expensive white chocolate champagne truffles, very cheap chicken Ginsters slices, and Scotch eggs—mmm, skeggs: the fat man's fruit—from that nice deli in Hove, in Ms. Gunn Senior's case) spoiling the old woman's legs. And why bother to walk, the old Ms. Gunn thought, when she had that big, sturdy daughter always ready and willing to push her about the place like a queen?

Everything became clear—it always did for Ms. Gunn, eventually—and a hot flush of anger spread from her vast chest up her turkey neck, before growing livid vermilion across her furious face.

It had to be those two she-devils Jinx Slater and Liberty Latiffe. The girls had lived in Ms. Gunn's main house as recently as the last day of last term, and although she had tried to rule and rile them with her rod of heavy wrought iron from day one, they had continually managed to give her the slip. She turned puce just thinking about them.

If truth be known, Ms. Gunn had actually felt the first stirrings of something akin to relief when she'd snarled her good-byes and handed over those terrible final house reports, safe in the knowledge that next term the girls were to be in the charge of that useless popsy Brian Morris.

Upon reading the reports, the Slaters had laughed heartily over Ms. Gunn's descriptions of Jinx as a "cold fish" with a "positively criminal mind-set." Amir Latiffe sadly never had the opportunity to consider his daughter as "Nicole Richie to Slater's Paris Hilton" or "thick, thick, thick—*not* likely to get *into any* university." This was because Liberty had carefully unsealed the envelope, removed the offending page, and calmly burnt it in the back of the chauffeur-driven Mercedes that always took her to and from Heathrow Airport at the beginning and end of term.

Now Ms. Gunn sat on her hard-backed sofa, tightened her stranglehold on America, guzzled her expensive whisky, and thought furious thoughts.

"How *dare* they!" she suddenly screamed, shocking Myrtle, the rake-thin ancient whippet that had been left, orphaned and homeless, at Wollstonecraft House when her predecessor had finally kicked the bucket, and followed her everywhere, into a severe fit of the shakes.

"Not only did they steal—*steal!*—my property," she continued, ever redder in the face, as poor Myrtle attempted to cover her long face with her bony paws, "and make light of my mother's disability by joyously careening down the slippery stone pathway in her wheelchair—thereby, if one looks closely enough, scratching one of the wheel trims—they've gotten away with it!"

She finished, panting, on a long crescendo of rage. Myrtle, shivering with terror, slunk behind the back of the sofa. She stuck her head under a cushion that had fallen down there, but there was no getting away from The Gunn's vicious invective. "There's nothing I can do this time," the housemistress mused in a quieter, almost reflexive tone, one that Myrtle recognized as particularly evil. Ms. Gunn just hated not being able to mete out terrible punishments and dire threats of expulsion, particularly where those two were concerned. "No," she carried on, her voice rising once again as she thought about Mr. Morris, "that useless . . . *man*, Brian bloody Morris, had to intervene. Not only scuppering my chance of revenge—and oh, how sweet it would have been to have the cretinous reprobates copying out, word for word until it was finished, *twice*, the entire Maastricht Treaty in my study every Saturday and Sunday for the rest of term—but calling into question my authority!"

Ms. Gunn fell silent. Myrtle desperately looked around for an escape route, but the kitchen door had been slammed shut in an earlier fit of pique. The vast woman sat there and thought about how she hated those girls—more, much more than she hated the others. She didn't like any of them particularly, but the black hatred she felt for Jinx and Liberty had taken on almost as great a depth of feeling as her forty-year passion for Icelandic literature and ancient Norse mythology.

Her scowl grew heavier and her forehead almost disappeared as she thought about how she'd half shuffled, half run (such as she could) to the staff room, panting all the while, to call for help. The few staff lounging about on the sofas inside, drinking lukewarm teas and voraciously reading the *Sun* hidden inside copies of the *Times*, barely looked up as she breathlessly explained her torture.

Eventually Brian Morris, realizing that his colleagues were not about to act swiftly—if at all—put down the English teacher's well-thumbed copy of *The Prime of Miss Jean Brodie* he was rather disbelievingly reading the back of, took pity on the hideous Gunn, and offered to assist her. He'd felt he should, really, especially when he realized that two of his girls were involved—the two fun, pretty ones. Yes, he liked them! He had especially enjoyed meeting Mr. Slater when he'd dropped Jinx off at the start of term. It was rare to find someone who obsessed about his beloved football team, Southampton, as much as he did.

Gunn shuddered as she recalled what had happened next, and poured herself a restorative refill.

She'd insisted the two of them visit the lockup bike shed where she stored the chair to confirm it had been broken into and the contraption stolen. She hadn't liked it *at all* when Morris suggested she calm down, and told her that under no circumstances whatsoever was she to telephone for the police. A very stern look passed across his usually smiley face, and Ms. Gunn had suddenly felt the tiniest bit stupid.

"How dare the man tell me to 'calm down,'" she yelled, looking around for Myrtle, not realizing that her petrified dog was hiding behind the sofa, "as if it were I who was being ridiculous. Bah! It wasn't him who'd had his authority called into question, or him whose disabled mother's wheelchair had been made an object of hilarity, was it? No! It bloody well wasn't." She hadn't liked it when he'd enquired too closely about her mother's disability, either—if she hadn't known better, she'd have sworn he was mocking her.

When she'd finally managed to turn the hefty key in the rusty padlock and wrench the shed door open, she'd been appalled to see the wheelchair sitting in front of them, glinting almost aggressively at her in the shaft of sunlight illuminating it. Morris, of course, had smirked and told her she must have been mistaken. And she was sure that if she hadn't stomped off in the most massive tantrum he might have gone so far as to give her a piece of his mind. Bah! Either way, she had been made a laughingstock.

Gunn sat on her sofa, staring unseeingly at the tube of her portable black-and-white television, and thought that this really was the straw to break the camel's back. This time she would get revenge. Slater and Latiffe had better watch their slim, young backs, she resolved, for she, Ms. Patricia Gunn, was not going to take this final breach of her erstwhile unblemished authority lying down. Oh, no. She was going to be looking out for them, make no mistake.

"Where's that bloody useless dog? Myrtle . . . *Myrtle!*" she screamed, wanting a witness—however witless—to her next threat. Myrtle slunk along the wall, her back toward the television, and stared at her with sad, wary eyes. "One day," whispered Ms. Gunn, staring right back at her, spittle oozing out the corner of her dry mouth and drooling down her whiskery chin, "they're bound to slip up. And I will be waiting."

Jinx unscrewed the safety catch on her double-glazed window and giggled to herself as it swung wide open. The whole process had taken less than two minutes—whichever fellow had put these in should have been taken outside, blindfolded, and made to take his chances with the scary security man's lion-size Alsatian.

Jinx, who spent an inordinate amount of time daydreaming up new reality TV formats, was jolted out of her "Man Fights Dog: Who Wins?" reverie as Liberty came crashing through the door, clutching handfuls of wispy tops, her face so sparkly it looked like she'd come off worst in a fight with a giant glitter machine.

Liberty dumped the twinkling mound of fabric on Jinx's bed, obviously completely undecided as to what to wear, and began rummaging through Jinx's dirty-laundry basket.

"Liberty! That's all dirty. Leave it alone, for God's sake—why don't you wear one of these?" Despite having been best friends with Liberty for years, Jinx never failed to be impressed by her pal's seemingly limitless wardrobe. Jinx held up a shimmering gray vest covered in tiny sequins and checked the label. "Stella fucking McCartney? Jesus, Lib, you've kept this one quiet. It's gorgeous."

Liberty was busy applying the remains of Jinx's Frizz-Ease to the ends of her long- -and always absolutely frizz-free—dark locks. "Oh, Dad's assistant bought me a load of stuff in Riyadh last year. I've never worn it. You can have it if you like."

Jinx also never failed to be amazed that Liberty's terrifying father, despite his massive and oft-professed devotion to Islam, would buy these clothes for his daughter, not seeming to see anything incongruous in the fact that the majority of the girls who bought bags and bags full of stuff from the smart parades of designer shops in Riyadh staffed exclusively by men were forced to hide them underneath oppressive burkas. Liberty loved her dad but went home as little as possible. She spent most weekends and half-terms with Jinx, and usually accompanied the Slater family on holiday.

The Slaters loved Liberty. The first time she'd come to stay, two weeks after the girls had started at Slagmount on their first official exeat weekend, Caroline and Martin had warmed to the beautiful and charming girl who offered to help clear up after their characteristically huge Sunday roast, but had to be shown how to load and operate the dishwasher first.

And Liberty loved the Slaters. She'd never really experienced family life as they lived it. At her dad's house in Riyadh, there were too many servants to mention, a veritable army of people to wash, cook, clean, drive, garden, everything.

At Jinx's rambling house in the Hampshire countryside there were dogs, cats, brothers, sisters, and numerous friends and relatives constantly dropping in to join the jostle for space and attention. Whatever it may have been, the house certainly wasn't quiet, but the noise seemed to affirm the place's inherent warmth.

The chintzy sofas covered in dog and cat hair, the colorful, threadbare rugs that covered the red stone of the kitchen floor, and the almost-too-hot-to-touch oven were truly a world away from the white lines and black marble floors of the oppressively silent mansion on the outskirts of the oppressively silent city of Riyadh.

Liberty looked stunning in the glittery Stella top—which Jinx insisted she wear—above skintight indigo jeans and bright white trainers, and the pair grinned at each other's self-satisfied reflections in Jinx's dirty mirror as they simultaneously applied a last-minute slick of lip gloss.

"How *is* your dad, Lib?" Jinx asked as she blotted her lips with a tissue. "You've hardly told me anything about your holidays." Jinx kept one eye on Liberty as she waited for her response—she knew what a nightmare time Liberty often had with him in the holidays.

"Much the same—I do love him, but you know what he's like." Liberty sighed as she carefully drew a fine line of glittery silver eye shadow underneath her lower lashes. "We were getting on fine until he caught me waxing my bikini line by the pool."

"What?" Jinx burst out laughing. "Why the hell were you doing it by the pool? What's wrong with using the bloody bathroom? I bet the poor man had the shock of his life."

"Yeah, well, it was a hot day and I didn't want to miss any rays. And if anyone had the shock of their life, it was me, when he came running round the corner ranting and raving and shaking his fist about 'common prostitutes,' all that 'you're no daughter of mine' crap, and his boring bloody broken record stuff about taking me away from Stagmount. And then he started on about Mum—said if I wasn't careful I'd end up as Americanized as she is. Not that I think that's a bad thing, naturally. You know what he's like about her."

"But . . ." Jinx was always shocked by the things Liberty's dad said to her. She knew damn well that whatever she might do wrong—and there was plenty—her dad would never say stuff like that.

"I know, I know," Liberty groaned. "He refused to speak to me for two weeks and wouldn't let me out of the house. Not that there's anywhere to *go* there, anyway, but it totally sucked. Anyway, he's over it now and I can't be bothered to think about it—I want to have fun tonight. Let's go!"

Jinx returned the screwdriver to her tuck box and put the

tiny window screws in the pink ceramic pot on her desk for safe-keeping—although she liked to go *out* illegally, she didn't much fancy anyone uninvited getting *in* the same way. Liberty balanced precariously on the windowsill before lowering herself the couple of feet to the cigarette butt–strewn grass below. God, the fight they'd put up to get these rooms had been so, *so* worth it.

Liberty was rooting in the depths of her tan Mulberry Roxanne bag for her mobile phone as Jinx carefully placed her battered copy of *The Handmaid's Tale*—assigned books did have their uses—between the window and the frame, before turning off the strip light and swinging her legs over to join her pal.

She hated that light—made the place look like a bloody prison cell. Not that she'd ever been in either a prison or a cell, you understand, but she *was* an avid reader of the *Sun's* crime pages and now considered herself an expert on all aspects of incarceration at Her Majesty's pleasure. She'd tried draping a sarong over the lamp, but it had caught fire and Mr. Morris, Stagmount's geography teacher and head of the lower-sixth-form house, had begged Jinx to leave it be.

She and Liberty liked Mr. Morris a great deal—all the girls did. He was an incorrigible old flirt who encouraged them to call him Brian, but he let them smoke in his garage so long as they swept up the butts on a weekly basis, and he allowed his girls to keep alcohol—"Wine and beer only, girls!"—in their rooms.

Best of all, as far as house rules were concerned, he was remarkably laissez-faire about them tripping off into Brighton on weekends, so long as they were back by 11:30 P.M. Which, considering most of the pubs they loved shut at this time anyway, was more than reasonable of old Brian and certainly left the girls well disposed toward him and therefore less inclined to break the rules.

Apart from tonight, of course. But as far as Jinx and Liberty were concerned, it was a rule that they go out, just the two of them—illegally—in the first week of term, and this bore no reflection on Mr. M or his relatively easy to keep rules. Indeed, if all went according to plan, and there was no reason to think it would not, he would be none the wiser.

With Liberty still rummaging about, the two began walking round the back of the white-painted lower-sixth house and toward the perimeter fence. A muffled "yesss" escaped Liberty's lips as her right hand emerged from the bag clutching her perennially elusive mobile.

As always, Liberty waited until they were halfway across the dark lacrosse pitch closest to the road before ringing for a taxi. Also as always, where these late-night escapades were concerned, she asked that the driver meet them just outside the school's huge ornate main gates.

They bent low to the ground as they traversed the side of the pitch closest to the real world, but stood up straight again as they reached the cover of the line of wind-bent trees that shielded their progress from any prying eyes watching from the school.

The escapees grinned smugly and gave each other

congratulatory high fives as they spied freedom, waiting patiently in his familiar green-and-white striped car like the benign fifth member of Dürer's Four Horsemen of the Apocalypse.

The driver winked at the girls in his rearview mirror as he asked them where they wanted to go. Brighton taxi drivers were used to picking up Stagmount's finest at odd times and places, and would no sooner squeal on their charges than they would change lanes without indicating.

Hell, they should be used to ferrying the girls about. They'd been at it since 1865, when the formidable Tanner sisters had founded Stagmount. While education for upper- and middle-class boys in the nineteenth century was seen as a passport to success in public and professional life, girls were educated for the drawing room, if at all. In one of the earliest feminist experiments, these three bluestockings intended their charges to have the same educational opportunities as boys, and the dear old place was still going strong.

Huge oil portraits of the three hung in the imposing library; wherever you stood or sat in that grand, oak-paneled room, it was absolutely guaranteed that at least one pair of those ancient eyes would be fixed upon you. You couldn't help but be impressed by their drive and determination—those ladies were clearly of the "less chat, more action" school of thought, and by God, they'd done it.

David Bowie's "Changes," Jinx and Liberty's totally number-one favorite song, was booming out the cabbie's stereo, and the girls asked him to turn it up. "Time may change me / but I can't trace time," they sang as they drove along the white-stuccoed seafront toward the Sea Life Centre and the start of the pier.

After Liberty had dished out such a generous tip the driver's eyes bulged, they jumped out and joined the throng of tourists, suits from London with their dates, and locals pushing through the metal gates. Jinx looked around lovingly. She was obsessed with the pier. FREE ENTRY, ENTERTAINMENT, AND DECK CHAIRS: OPEN 365 DAYS A YEAR. Was there *ever* a more welcoming sign? Jinx was sold on sight.

Surely no girl with drinks money in her pocket, poppers in her handbag, best friend in tow, and a night of drinking, dancing, and laughing ahead of her had ever had a bad time there.

Jinx and Liberty clutched the plastic pint glasses brimming with lurid pink Sex on the Beaches they'd bought and settled into a companionable silence on a bench facing Stagmount, intent on slurping up their cheap vodka mixes as quickly as possible. The building loomed out of the cliff face, and besides an occasional light twinkling, was strangely austere in the dark.

A gang of spotty, sportswear-sporting lads, shouting, pointing, and pushing one another, interrupted their reverential downing.

"Oi, sweetheart!" shouted one, standing behind his friend and pointing at Jinx. "Wanna sit on my face?"

Christ, she thought, *what an invitation! Please* do *excuse me while I strip off right here, right now, delighted by this obviously not to be missed, once in a bloody lifetime opportunity.*

"Why?" Jinx drawled, in her very best "I am ever so bored by you" voice. "Is your nose bigger than your dick?"

Liberty creased up, spraying a mouthful of sticky pink drink in front of her in an impressive arc.

While his three mates jeered and laughed, the lad looked as though his parade had been well and truly golden-showered on, and not in a good way. "That's fucking gratitude for you," he sneered, fingering the deliberately frayed sleeve of his bright white hoodie. "Ugly slags."

Jinx tilted her head to one side. "I'm confused," she said, arching a disbelieving eyebrow. "I am supposed to be grateful to *you* for what, exactly?"

"Yeah," Liberty joined in, "and how come you want her to sit on your face if she's so *ugly*?"

"Ugly fat *slags*!" chanted Prince Charming, failing to see any incongruities and warming to his theme. "Ugly fat *posh slags*!"

"Much as it saddens me to leave such fine conversational-ists," Jinx said to Liberty, "I feel we've wasted quite enough time on these cretinous fuckwits. Alcopop, sweetie?"

The boys seemed to melt away as the pair stood up, linked arms, and headed toward the fairground, but they were only hiding round the other side of the sheltered seats.

"*Lesbians!*" came the insightful parting shot. "*Dykes! Rug-munchers!*"

"Why is it, Lib," asked Jinx, genuinely perplexed, "that some guys think it's perfectly okay to shout out unasked-for sexual invitations, and then they can't take it when—pretty fucking reasonably—the invitee declines their kind offer, only to fall back on the 'ugly slag' thing? "My brothers would never do this, nor would their friends—would they?"

"I can't imagine it, sweets," Liberty answered, before nudging Jinx hard in the ribs and sniggering, "and especially not that lovely Jamie we met last half-term."

"Shut up, Lib." Jinx blushed, remembering how absolutely gorgeous she'd suddenly, unaccountably found her brother George's best friend and how she'd hardly been able to talk to him without swooning all over the place.

"I mean, it's pretty fucking obvious," she continued, back on track, "that they don't think you're ugly, or they wouldn't have asked for it in the first place." Jinx shook her head. "And it's also pretty fucking obvious—because you *said no*—that you're not a slag, either. Why does this lot think it's okay?"

"I dunno, Jinx," said Liberty, eyeing up the roller coasters. "Fancy a go on the Crazy Mouse?"

The enforced separation of a long summer holiday, combined with flying through the air at high speeds after having consumed buckets of cheap vodka is a potent mix, and Liberty and Jinx's heads were spinning as they crunched their way from the edge of the promenade across the pebbles and down to the waterfront.

Jinx stuck out a leg to trip Liberty, and her friend shrieked and collapsed inelegantly—but not face-first—onto the stony beach close to the water's edge. Jinx landed on top of her. Despite being almost the middle of September, the air was warm and the girls lay where they fell, squealing and shoving each other like pigs at a trough, mobiles, jumpers, and handbags strewn around them. Summer was clinging on to Brighton with all her might, and these two could not have been more delighted with her efforts.

Jinx lay with her head on Liberty's stomach, facing the midnight–blue-and-white expanse of softly gurgling sea.

"Hey." Liberty sat bolt upright, knocking Jinx's head unceremoniously from its comfy pillow onto the sharp beach below. "I can't believe I forgot to tell you—guess what I've got!"

Jinx, who'd found herself suddenly eyeballing some particularly gritty stones without any notice whatsoever, raised a jaded eyebrow.

"The freaking disco biscuits, that's what!" Liberty had her pale green Chanel wallet out of her bag and open before Jinx had a chance to right herself.

"Here, chuck us that vodka lemon, J." Liberty removed a pink, heart-shaped pill from a tiny plastic Ziploc bag, popped it in her mouth, took a great glug from the proffered bottle, and swallowed masterfully.

She held out the remaining E before jumping up and down triumphantly as Jinx necked hers. "I can't believe I forgot them—remembering forgotten drugs is, like, the best thing *ever!*"

"Liberty Latiffe . . . I *knew* there was some reason we were best friends forever," said a properly impressed Jinx. "Well done, angel, but where the hell did you *get* them from? You've been in Riyadh all summer, and I'd bet a whole lot of money these discos did not come from there. . . ." She paused, a look of sudden horror on her face. "Please—*please* tell me you didn't get them out there and bring them back with you."

Jinx couldn't put her finger on exactly what it was about

Liberty's dad that bothered her, as Amir Latiffe had always been the perfect gentleman where she was concerned. He frequently sent stunning Persian carpets, magnums of vintage Krug, and tins of delicious Beluga caviar to Caroline and Martin Slater, accompanied by beautifully handwritten thank-you notes on stiff Smythson cards for their hospitality toward his eldest daughter.

Whenever he was in London on business—thankfully, such an occurrence was pretty infrequent—he would hire the Harrods helicopter to fly him to Stagmount, where he'd pick up Liberty and invariably Jinx and whisk them off to amazing places. On Liberty's birthday in the first year he'd flown them to Cornwall and back in a day, and in the second year he'd taken them to the George V in Paris for dinner.

Liberty loved her dad and Jinx loved Liberty, but for all his largesse—in fact, partly because of it—Jinx knew he was not the same as her dad. She also knew, instinctively, for this was one topic that she and Liberty had never discussed, that the second he became disillusioned by Stagmount or—worse, much worse—disappointed in his daughter, Liberty would be gone, no questions asked. And once Liberty was gone, Jinx had a terrible feeling she would never get her back.

"Don't be an idiot all your life, Jinx." Liberty staggered to her feet and started pulling off her jeans. "I got 'em from Dad's new driver, Raoul, on the way back to school from the airport. We had a great chat about house music, and he is proper *hot*, too. Come on, we've *got* to have one last swim of the summer."

Jinx frowned as Liberty peeled off her pink glittery socks

and stuck one in each toe of her bright white trainers. Jinx couldn't work out whether Liberty's bravado in the face of Islam and her dad was stupidity or denial. Either way, she didn't much fancy her chances if she had to go head-to-head with the man on anything.

After all, Sofia, Liberty's mum, had never stood a chance. Jinx had heard this story many times, yet it seemed so alien to her, she still sometimes felt it couldn't be really real.

Sofia and Amir met and fell in love while at the same MBA course at Harvard in the '80s. They got married in the States, and Sofia told Liberty she was conceived under an American flag quilt in a hammock at a wild house party in Martha's Vineyard. According to Sofia, who was Persian but had mostly grown up in the States thanks to her dad's job with the UN, the pair of them had been absolutely head-over-heels, passionately, wholeheartedly, madly in love.

Sofia insisted their baby be named Liberty, after the country she'd been born in, but also in the hope that she would be as free to make her own decisions in life as the girls she knew in America.

When the time came for Amir to take his soul mate home to meet his family in Saudi, however, his parents were visibly appalled by his liberal, American wife and insisted he either divorce Sofia immediately and send her home, or be disinherited forever. Brave Amir had—sobbing all the while, apparently—packed his wife and young daughter onto the next plane out of there. Much as he loved them, he'd wailed, he was powerless to resist his parents' wishes. And, presumably, the thought of losing all that cash was just too much to bear.

Liberty didn't see him again until, when she was eight years old, he sent a particularly brutal henchman to Iran to kidnap her away from her beloved mother while they were on holiday and take her to him in Saudi. She had never met her father, didn't speak his language, and had to contend with the focused hatred of a stepmother who was reminded, every time she looked at the beautiful Liberty, that although she was the first-choice wife of Amir's family, she was very much the second choice for him. None of the girls could work out why he'd suddenly decided he wanted his daughter back by his side, and he'd never explained himself other than to repeatedly avow that it was his "right" to have his daughter at home with him.

The last anyone heard of her, Liberty's mom had been working as a live-in reflexologist at an extreme detox center just outside of L.A. but had fallen in love with one of her clients, a republican politician from Alabama, and was thinking of relocating. Liberty occasionally received packages from her, filled to bursting with scented candles, wonderful organic face masks and naturally sourced massage oils.

Liberty ran toward the water in her matching lacy pale green boy shorts and bra, squealing and jumping when the sharp stones bit into the bottom of her beautifully pedicured feet. She stopped dead at the waterline.

If Liberty had had her way she'd have been teetering on the edge for hours—she never could just jump straight in. Sadly for her, though, Jinx had other ideas. Jinx struggled maniacally to get her extra-tight jeans off. Liberty was going in, straight in. The jeans were off.

As Jinx performed The Ultimate Waterside Rugby Tackle, taught to her with great precision in Mykonos that summer by her brother George, Liberty's piercing shriek must have been heard all the way to the marina.

They came up for air coughing, giggling, and splashing a few feet from the shore, neither able to touch the bottom, and rolled onto their backs, kicking gently to keep themselves afloat, delirious at the sheer brilliance of a midnight swim in the Christmas term.

Jinx stretched her neck back and felt the familiar waves of Ecstasy-induced euphoria rolling over her. She grabbed Liberty's hand and the pair floated beneath the stars, nattering about how much they'd missed each other over the summer and loving the feeling of the salty sea against their skin.

"Jinx," a wrecked and emotional Liberty spluttered from beneath a breaker that had rolled gently over her skyward-turned face, "I've never had a friend like you. I missed you so much over the summer, I can't imagine what life would be like without you in it."

Jinx squeezed Liberty's hand. "I'm the same, Lib, and you know it. I've got loads of friends, but no one like you. You make boring things seem exciting, and exciting things, well—*brilliant!*"

"And anyway, darling, it's freezing." Jinx squirmed underwater. Even under the influence of what was turning out to be some particularly great E, she preferred to *be* a great friend rather than to endlessly discuss it. "I think we should head in. I urgently need to be dancing right about now."

They sat on a low stone wall, shivering in the night air and pulling on their clothes. Liberty flung her arms around Jinx and squeezed her tight. "I. Love. You. So. Much." She didn't let go the whole way up the beach, as they stumbled—Liberty way more unsteady on her feet than Jinx—past the fish-and-chip shops and carousel under the promenade, and up the steps in front of the Royal Crescent.

Pausing to slip her shoes on, apply some emergency mascara—she'd once read a piece in *Style* magazine saying the only sin with mascara was not to wear any, and had never knowingly been seen out without it since—and wring out her wet hair, Jinx jumped as if she'd been shot when she heard someone call her name. Yes, she and Liberty were devil-may-care in the face of rules, but the absolute last result they wanted from an illicit night out was a load of tricky questions and the series of dull lockdowns that would inevitably ensue.

Both of them bent low behind a handy phone box. Liberty swore softly as one of Jinx's golden heels ground the soft brown leather of her Roxanne bag into the grimy pavement.

"Shut up," hissed Jinx. "In case you hadn't noticed, we're supposed to be keeping a low profile here, so quit your moaning!"

"Oh my God, if it isn't Stagmount's very own dumb and dumber." A beaming Chastity, clutching handyman Paul's hand tight in her own, ran across the road, oblivious to the volley of beeping horns and muffled curses as cars swerved to avoid them, narrowly escaping a nasty accident. "Have you been swimming? You're fucking mad, both of you. It's September for Christ's sake!"

"Thank God it's you!" exclaimed Jinx, teetering on one foot as she laced up her other shoe. "We pissed Gunn off earlier, and it wouldn't surprise me if the old witch was on the warpath. Not that she's been seen to leave the Stagmount boundaries for the last, oh, at least three years."

"Yeah, you wouldn't want that," sniffed Chastity, flicking her long blond hair. She'd been in a different lower-school house than the others, had never had an altercation with Gunn, and was consequently nowhere near as obsessive about her as Liberty and Jinx were. "Anyway, what are you guys up to? One of Paul's mates is deejaying at the Church, and we'd love you two to come with us, wouldn't we?"

"Course we would," said Paul, who was only a year older than them and spent a lot of time hanging out with Chastity's friends. "More the merrier."

Liberty linked arms with Paul, Jinx linked arms with Chastity, and the foursome bounded up Ship Street away from the seafront, delighted by the turn of events, happy as Labradors. If they'd had tails, they'd have been wagging them like mad.

Unfortunately, the bouncer at the head of the snaking queue had a very different take on how their evening would pan out. He waved Chastity and Paul through with barely a second glance, but grimaced menacingly when Liberty wobbled in front of him. Clocking her glazed eyes and damp hair, the balding man-mountain turned to glare at Jinx. She gave him a jaunty wink, but he was having none of it.

"You two, no way." He enunciated his strictly one-syllable sentence slowly.

"Oh, please let us in," Liberty begged. "It's our best friend's birthday party, and we absolutely *promise* to be on our very best behavior." Stagmount girls were famed the world over for playing their impeccable manners alongside a mild flirtation—with man, woman, or beast—to get what they wanted in any situation, no matter how drunk, wrecked, or cross they might be. She was batting her eyelashes as fast as she could when he relented.

"All right, girls, I'm going to do you a favor, but this only works one way—and that's my way." He paused, clearly pleased with such incontrovertible evidence of his power and status, and determined to enjoy every second of it. "You're too drunk for me to let you in now—you need to sober up. Go to McDonald's, have yourselves a Happy Meal, and make damn sure I don't see you two again for at least half an hour."

"Fine." Jinx smiled amicably. "Thanks a lot. See you in half an hour, then."

"I'm not hungry at all," moaned Liberty as they headed back toward the seafront, "and I *hate* fucking McDonald's anyway. And if I *was* going to go there, I'd have six chicken nuggets and an apple pie."

Jinx shook her head—sometimes Liberty was so basic it was painful. "Shut up, Lib. All we've got to do is amuse ourselves for half an hour, and McRon's—*obviously*—is not going to feature."

"In fact," said Jinx, stopping abruptly and gesturing toward a deep purple door set back from the pavement, "this is where we're going to wait it out. Perfect."

This bar was so cool it didn't have a name, only the purple door signifying its existence to Brighton's great and good—or drunk and drugged, more like. Either way, having left Liberty chatting with a boy at their table, Jinx propped up the bar with a large tumbler filled with more bright blue absinthe than tonic in one hand and a flaming sambuca in the other, and reflected that the sixth form was getting off to an excellent start.

The first thing she saw when she turned back toward their seats, however, was Liberty, facedown on the small round table, surrounded by an admiring throng of very trendy boys. Jinx was confused. Where had that bright yellow ring around her head come from? Was it a hat? An oversized scrunchy? What? And what were those guys doing, nudging each other, pointing and laughing at Lib? She sighed. Jinx was well used to rescuing the totally clueless Liberty from potentially sticky situations like this.

Mumbling about lightweights and ruined evenings, Jinx shoved her way past the boys, put their drinks on the table, and unceremoniously yanked her friend's head back. Liberty, coughing and spluttering, opened her eyes. Jinx, who was also having trouble focusing by now, peered intently at her pal, marveling at how bright the whites of Liberty's eyes were. They looked so blingtastic, albeit a bit bleary, and kind of rolled back. She couldn't believe it had taken her three years to notice how *white* they were.

It was only when a cigarette butt fell out of Liberty's feathered fringe that Jinx realized what the yellow circle was. A huge, filthy ashtray, that's what. No wonder, then, given the dirty great load of fag ash blacking up her face, that Liberty's eyes looked so luminous, and no wonder the boys had all been giggling like morons at her. Jinx would never trust Liberty to cope on her own on a night out. She had zero concept of personal protection and was an absolute sucker for every charmer, flatterer, slimeball, and wide boy in town—most of whom were mesmerized by her beauty and would do anything to try and get her into bed. Not that Liberty—in her right mind, anyway—would have acquiesced. Whatever her dad might think, she did have some standards. She'd only been chatting to them to be friendly.

Jinx released her grip on her friend's ponytail, dipped a napkin thoughtlessly into her lurid blue drink, and handed it to Liberty. Without support, Liberty's head lolled, and her outstretched hand brushed the side of the low table before coming to rest, monkeylike, on the floor. And, as if in slow motion, she face-planted right back into the middle of the ashtray with a resounding thwack.

"Christ," muttered Jinx, swooping their mobiles, fags, and wallets into her oversized brown bag with a white leather Pegasus stitched on the side while staggering to her feet, one sad eye on the fit barman she'd been hoping to chat up later. "Most people wouldn't put up with this. You're a fucking disaster area, Latiffe. You're lucky I'm here to sort you out—what if your dad found out about this? Jesus, let's get you home."

Since Liberty was completely incapable of standing unsupported, Jinx propped her against a whitewashed wall outside and rang for a cab.

After an arduous evening spent filing parental letters
in what she—hilariously, she thought—referred to as her
"circular file" (otherwise known as the wastepaper bin in her
study) and scoffing bourbon creams, Ms. Gunn was enjoying
her customary midnight snooze in front of the telly before bed.

Lying on her back on the sofa, cushions plumped behind
her huge head, mouth open wide, and a cup of lukewarm tea
perched precariously between her vast thighs, Ms. Gunn was
also in the midst of the best sex dream she'd ever had.

"Oh . . . oh . . . oooooh . . . *Susan*," she moaned, somewhat
incoherently, gnashing and grinding her stumpy teeth, "don't
wait another second, take me now, I beg you, the pleasure is
almost too intense. . . ." Ms. Gunn began writhing around, such
as she could, and a desperate smile lit her sleeping face as the

tea appeared in danger of slopping about all over her lap.

"Dick, dick, dick, dick," muttered Ms. Gunn in staccato, gurning impressively as she threw her head back in a paroxysm of ecstasy. Sleeping Beauty she was not.

Ms. Gunn was close to dream-induced climax—the only kind she was ever likely to get these days—when she was suddenly, *rudely*, awoken by a muffled yell followed by a lot of giggling coming from the open corner window that looked over the drive and the ice ceam shop.

"Argh!" she screamed, sexually frustrated and furious, as she jumped up.

"Argh!" she screamed again, doubly furious now as cold tea disported itself gaily about her lower person as if it were all part of a personal vendetta.

She rubbed ineffectually at the great expanse of her lap, cursed vehemently, and peered out the window. She frowned so hard at what she saw that she gave herself an instantaneous migraine. Clutching her throbbing head in her fat hands, she drew back as if shot and gingerly lay back down on the damp sofa.

Ms. Gunn screwed her piggy eyes tight closed. She felt so thoroughly done over in so many ways, she worried she might actually break down and weep and wail right there.

But no, thoughts of potential vengeance put her back on an even keel, and she made up her mind to deal with the miscreants here and now, once and for all. As she slammed the door to the small flat behind her, Ms. Gunn reached into her pocket and withdrew her aviator sunglasses. The lenses were scratched and the frames twisted, as she never bothered with a case, but she always wore them when on one of her many detective missions—even in the middle of the night.

She fancied they lent her the girlish air of Nancy Drew, her favorite literary detective. Nancy, that attractive young super-sleuth, could solve any mystery in eighty pages: braving white-water rapids in a sinking canoe on one page, and whipping up a gourmet meal for fifteen on the next. She was wealthy, yes, but not afraid to get her hands dirty. Why were none of the Stagmount girls like her? In truth, the silly glasses made Ms. Gunn look even stupider than normal.

She rammed them over her eyes and shouted for Myrtle.

Half blind and short of breath—caused, or so the girls insisted anyway, by Ms. Gunn sitting on the poor beast by mis-take during a particularly racy episode of the six o'clock news one evening—Myrtle slunk along the outside wall and fell into her customary step, three paces behind her adoptive mistress.

They made a queer sight, the overfed mistress and her skinny dog shuffling through the dark night, but Stagmountians were used to Gunn and her odd practices.

Gunn, her migraine refusing to go away and pounding in her head like a million angry wasps smoked out of their nest, stomped her way across the verdant quadrangle with no regard for the KEEP OFF THE GRASS signs she had campaigned so offi-ciously for.

Slater and Latiffe, Slater and Latiffe. The words hammered into her brain with every flat-footed step she took. She'd looked out the window just in time to see Latiffe careering off the side of one of those wooden benches by the ice cream shop, and was under no illusion whatsoever that those two weren't drunk as skunks. "Pah," she spat at Myrtle, who cowered away from her but was too terrified of the consequences to attempt to run away, "that dark one probably couldn't even walk a straight line *sober.*"

"Those little bitches are going to get it this time, make no mistake." Gunn slapped a vast thigh for emphasis, causing Myrtle to jump at least a foot in the air. "They've made a fool of me once too often, and"—she did an impromptu little jig at the thought of this, but immediately regretted it as the unscheduled movement rocketed the unceasing migraine up a step—"this time they are going to regret it. Oh, yes.

"How many times has Slater been suspended already?" Gunn demanded of her dog, forgetting that the whippet did not have the gift of speech, and aiming a bad-tempered kick at the beast's flank when no answer was forthcoming. "You really are useless, aren't you? Man's best friend my arse. Anyway, it must be at least three. Bah."

She remembered Mrs. Slater—Gunn was furiously jealous of most of the parents, and especially the mothers, but Caroline Slater's easy grace, fabulous wardrobe, loving husband, and convertible silver Porsche Boxster Turbo drove her even wilder than usual—actually laughing the last time she'd phoned to inform her of the suspension, before saying, "Oh, how wonderful, Ms. G. The weather's lovely—she can ride her pony and come skiing with Martin and me." Gunn had slammed the receiver down in disgust and bitterly regretted not making the spawn of the devil sign the special lockdown register in her study every fifteen minutes during all her free time for the next two weeks instead.

Gunn knew the girls would have to reach the safety of Tanner House via the circuitous games pitches route, whereas she could stride down the drive with impunity. So by her reckoning, even though she was no Olympic athlete, she'd reach the front door and Brian Morris before they'd have a chance to walk all that way and climb in whichever window they'd hijacked for their evil purposes. The despicable slugs!

Gunn arrived at Mr. Morris's door in record time and out of breath. She leant on the buzzer and was gratified to see his tired face at the window almost immediately.

"Wass up?" the poor man groaned at the huge bulky outline blocking out his porch light. "Patricia? Is everything okay?"

"I am sorry," intoned Gunn pompously, "to wake you, Mr. Morris, but I have a very serious matter to discuss with you, and it absolutely cannot wait."

"Right," mumbled a shattered Mr. Morris, who was never tip-top on first awaking. "Let's have it then. What's the problem?"

"The problem, my dear man, is that two of your girls are not in their rooms. I was woken—in the middle of the most excellent dream, I might add—by yelling on the drive. I looked out my window and saw the reprobates staggering about. Clearly"—here she stuck her huge nose even higher in the air than seemed possible—"inebriated."

Mr. Morris shook his head and sighed, but was too tired to do anything but lead the way to the lower corridor. He made a big show of switching on the lights, kicking the wall as if by mistake, and coughing loudly as he did so. Frankly, he didn't give two hoots if the girls had been out or not, but he was damned if he was going to be shown up in front of this terrible woman.

They stopped outside Jinx's room, but before Mr. Morris had a chance to knock, Gunn burst in like a fat stoat released from a hunter's trap.

The room was in darkness, but the teachers could clearly make out a few blond curls on the pillow, and a decidedly Jinx-shaped hump under the duvet. She emitted a tiny perfect snore and rolled over. Mr. Morris spied a wet, mud-splattered golden heel peeping out from under the end of the bed. He smiled to himself as he quietly pulled the door closed and turned to Ms. Gunn.

"Well, Patricia." Mr. Morris drew himself up to his full five feet seven inches and pulled his pale blue towelling robe tight at the waist. For a somewhat diminutive and wrinkly man, he cut an imposing figure standing there in the middle of the night in the shadowy lower corridor. "I trust this will be the end of the day's accusations." Ms. Gunn, champing at the bit to interrupt, was dumbstruck when Mr. Morris raised an authoritative hand to stop her.

"It's late, and I, for one, am going back to bed. I am sorry, Ms. Gunn, but you must leave immediately. I won't hear another word against those girls." He raised his hand again and was sure he heard a muffled snort of laughter, quickly turned into an elaborate coughing fit, from the other side of Jinx's door. "Nope. I'm not listening. If you feel you must discuss this matter any further—although I sincerely hope you will not—you'll find me in the staff room tomorrow."

Chastened and appalled, Ms. Gunn trudged down the drive, slowly, furiously. *If it's war they want*, she thought while grinding her teeth impressively loudly once again, but for a much less happy reason, *it's war they're going to get*. "And," she whispered to a very frightened looking Myrtle, summing up, "there's only going to be one winner."

"Jinx, Chastity, Liberty! How marvelous of you to join us," Mrs. Susan Dickinson, aka The Dick—the second-most-hated teacher in the school after Ms. Gunn—growled at the girls as they slunk in through the back door of the cavernous, wood-paneled assembly hall. "It's always the back door with you three. You'll never make anything of yourselves with that attitude. For goodness' sake, hurry up and take your seats. . . ." She paused, her beady bird's eyes scanning the room. "Over there—back row but one to the right. And look sharp—Mrs. Bennett is waiting to address the school."

"Yes, miss," mumbled Jinx, before whispering to Chastity, "I bet *she* always takes it in the back door. Who'd want to look her in the eye for any sustained period?"

Chastity snorted, earning them all a furious glare from The

Dick, but Jinx's fuzzy head was pounding and she was beginning to feel distinctly sketchy and shady and could really do without any more of The Dick's feeble sarcasm. "Sorry, miss."

The Dick raised a thinning ginger eyebrow and turned her back. She was head of Stagmount's excellent, world-renowned modern-languages department, and had bright orange hair that contrasted horribly against her incredibly pasty skin. She'd worn the same terrible Prince of Wales–check green-and-brown skirt every day for the last five years and stank of awful body odor. She would tolerate no talking in her lessons, no laughing, no loo stops, no questions—unless asked in perfect French, or whichever other language she was ruining forever for the girls—no late arrivals, no gags, no lip gloss, no mobile phones, no chewing gum, no fun. She did, however, speak French, German, Urdu, and Mandarin Chinese like a native, which was presumably how she'd gotten her job in the first place.

The Dick also had a son, Brendan, regularly held up to her classes as a god amongst men, the perfect son and student who managed to combine astonishing levels of religious fervor in one so young with a classics degree at Oxford, a place from which he would—naturally—graduate at the top of his class. Brendan's very existence was, of course, a source of constant fascination to the girls, who found it equally hilarious and horrifying that someone had had the temerity to impregnate The Dick in the first place. He was also the only subject on which The Dick could ever be drawn out, and his many merits were therefore especially discussed on the dreaded vocabulary test days.

The three sixth-formers collapsed onto the end of one of the old oak pews that had been co-opted from the chapel at the end of last year due to some highly successful PR tours of Russia and the Middle East that had brought in two hundred more girls, necessitating more seating space for school meetings.

While every girl was expected to attend the biweekly assemblies, not every girl could be forced to attend the daily chapel services in the Byzantine Chapel, with its beautiful marble floor and stunning stained-glass windows.

Privately, Stagmount's headmistress, Mrs. Bennett, thought this was a shame. She couldn't help but wonder why, exactly, these highly educated and affluent parents from all over the world bothered to send their daughters to Stagmount and then insist upon measures that would inevitably exclude them from main-school life.

Privately, Mrs. Bennett thought a lot of things. The thought that popped into her head most often these days was that theory is not the same as practice. But she was always very careful to toe the politically correct line in public.

Jinx unzipped her tight purple hoodie and wriggled out of it. She was sitting between Chastity—who'd been up all night shagging Paul—and Liberty, and was beginning to feel extremely hot and claustrophobic as her hangover set in. "For Christ's sake, Lib, move up. I'm dying in here."

Liberty gave a theatrical shuffle that moved her ass about a centimeter further up. "I can't. That's as far as I can go or I'll be on the fucking floor," she hissed. "You're not the only one feeling shady—lighten up, for God's sake."

Being told to "lighten up" when teetering on the precipice of a potentially furious mood always tipped Jinx over the edge and Liberty knew it. She knew how to push all of Jinx's buttons, although she rarely pressed the anger ones. Today, though, she would have pushed NUCLEAR DESTRUCT without a care in the world had it been in front of her. She hated Jinx's bad moods. They were like a black storm coming out of a clear blue sky with no warning at all.

Jinx ground her teeth, clenched her fists, and stared determinedly at the back of the head in front of her, a furious scowl twisting her usually smiley features.

Liberty decided she'd had enough. "Temper, temper," she half whistled, in a merry singsong voice specially designed to drive Jinx up the wall and onto the ceiling.

Jinx reached across and pinched Liberty's thigh, hard. Liberty emitted a high-pitched squeal and stamped her spike-heeled sling-back onto Jinx's Ugg boot–clad right foot. At the exact moment that Mrs. Bennett took her place behind the eagle-shaped carved maple lectern, Jinx cursed loudly in pain and jumped up.

Mrs. Bennett stopped shuffling her papers, lowered her reading glasses, and fixed Jinx with a gimlet eye. "Everything all right at the back there?" she enquired, a decidedly icy tinge to her usually warm voice. "Hmm. Jinx Slater, perhaps you would come and see me in my office at the end of school notices?" This was a rhetorical question, of course—come hell or high water, the entire school knew Jinx would be there.

"Oh God, Jin, I'm really sorry," Liberty whispered, immediately repentant. "That was so my fault—I'll come with you and explain."

"No, don't worry about it, Lib. I shouldn't have pinched you, and anyway, it's not going to be as bad as last time, is it?" They both grinned, remembering the last time Jinx had been called to Mrs. Bennett's office and the resulting weeklong suspension.

Drunk as a lord, Hermione Dennis had nearly drowned swimming naked off Shoreham Beach and, since the girls had been partying there to celebrate Jinx's fifteenth birthday, she'd felt it was only fair that she take the flak. She hadn't minded much, especially since her mum and dad had been in the Caribbean at the time and she'd spent the week in London having a riotous time under the care of her hilarious eldest brother, Damian. Liberty had been just as involved as Jinx, but Mrs. Bennett had taken the executive decision not to inform her father.

Even the staff knew never to telephone or fax through the usual letters detailing gatings, punishments, or bad behavior that other parents received with monotonous regularity. Jinx's mum had told her that soon after meeting Mr. Latiffe for the first time, Mrs. Bennett had pinned a notice about it in the staff room and sent round an e-mail to make sure they all knew never to contact him unless about strictly academic matters.

In the middle of their first term, Liberty had failed to hand in her science project on time. Mr. Moore, the junior-school biology teacher, had faxed his standard parental letter to Amir detailing Liberty's failings. Whereas most parents would have phoned their daughter and given her a good ticking off at best or grounded her for a couple of days at worst, Amir had hit the roof and threatened to take her out of Stagmount then and there.

After that, Mrs. Bennett had extended her blanket ban to encompass all direct contact unless first passed by her. This didn't stop Amir from flying off the handle with unvarying regularity.

At the beginning of the second year he had tried and failed, for three days in a row, to get hold of Liberty on her mobile phone. Convinced she had either been murdered or, worse, was ignoring him, he chartered a private helicopter to fly him straight to Stagmount. When he arrived he was appalled to find Liberty not in situ. The fact that she was in Stratford on an educational English trip to see A *Winter's Tale* and had accidentally dropped her mobile down the coach toilet did nothing to appease his rage. It was only after an hour in Mrs. Bennett's office that he'd come to his senses and decided against flying on to the theater, forcibly removing his daughter, and taking her home with him to Saudi.

"No, you're right. No one in the hospital this time, eh?" Liberty slung her arm around Jinx's waist and the two sat in companionable silence as they waited to hear Mrs. Bennett's revelations.

"Good morning, girls." Mrs. Bennett's voice echoed around

the hall, an unmistakable air of authority and gravitas attached to it. "Firstly—and it does pain me to have to start on such a low note so early in the term—I would like to remind you all that smoking is strictly forbidden. Quite apart from being a revolting habit, it poses a serious fire risk. Mrs. Dickinson and Ms. Gunn tell me they have seen girls—senior girls, they believe—smoking in the passages behind main school. This must stop. From now on, anyone caught smoking can expect a twenty-pound fine, to be donated to a cancer charity, and a weekend's gating. Do I make myself clear?"

Six hundred and fifty girls rolled their eyes and murmured their assent.

"Good. Let's hope that's the last I shall have to say on the topic." Despite knowing exactly what she was going to say next, Mrs. Bennett reshuffled the sheaf of papers on the dais in front of her.

"Secondly, as many of you know, I spent the last two weeks in the States, attending the Global Association of Private Schools annual conference in New York." Here Mrs. Bennett paused and looked around the room, thinking how excellently her keynote speech about the importance of multicultural integration in schools had been received.

"It might please you to know that Stagmount's reputation remains unsurpassed amongst both our domestic and international colleagues, and that we came top of the girls' school league for the third year running."

As the girls began to clap and cheer, Mrs. Bennett permitted herself a tiny smile of self-congratulation. They were good girls, really, all of them. They seemed to get a lot of enjoyment out of life, and so they should. She couldn't bear mopers and whiners. This lot were thoroughly *nice* girls, and certainly a lot more fun than the ones she'd left behind at Benenden.

"However," she continued, "this is no excuse for us to sit on our laurels. I want you all to work—and play—as hard as you possibly can this term. I'd like to see us win the tennis and lacrosse tournaments I know the sports staff have entered us in, and I expect the house plays to surpass last year's brilliant efforts.

"Lastly"—she smiled around the room—"you will all no doubt be delighted to hear that the plans for the new swimming pool complex have been finalized, and it should be operational by the beginning of next term."

Mrs. Bennett always liked to leave her assemblies on a high note, and the girls—and their parents—had been lobbying for a new pool for two years. She swept triumphantly off the stage, through the middle of the auditorium, and out of the door as, like a cageful of spider monkeys, girls of all ages began chattering and cackling at her news.

7

Jinx slouched against the wall outside Mrs. Bennett's office, halfway down the main corridor. She was halfheartedly kicking one Ugg-booted heel against the skirting board, thinking about how much she actually liked and, you know, *respected* Mrs. Bennett, and how it was thus really doubly unfair that she should be called to see her in her office like this in only the second week of term.

Jo, Mrs. Bennett's titian-haired secretary, looked up from the latest *Heat* magazine she was avidly devouring at her desk and smiled at Jinx. "Gosh, you've got a face like a wet weekend! Don't fret, love, Mrs. B is a real pussycat underneath that tiger-like exterior—and anyway, she really likes you." Jo winked. "Won't be long. She's just on the phone to that *Guardian* journalist. He's called at least four times this morning already, can't seem to find his way here from the station." Jo sighed, shook her head theatrically from side to side, and began reading "Hot or Not."

Jinx smiled and stood up straighter. Jo was right—Mrs. Bennett did like her, and she liked Mrs. Bennett. She'd hardly done anything too bad anyway. What was a kicking between friends? More interesting was the journalist. She wondered what he wanted. Mrs. B did have a hefty media profile and was always to be found in the weekend broadsheets, having provided pithy copy for "I Couldn't Have Got Where I Am Today Without," "A Day in the Life Of," and "Best of Times, Worst of Times" et al, but the girls had read too many of them to be much interested.

Just as Jinx's wild imagination was running riot with a tall tale involving one of the very beautiful and very rich Russian fourth-formers, the mafia, and a foiled kidnapping, the heavy door creaked open and Mrs. Bennett popped her short dark-haired head through the gap. "Jinx? Ah, good, nice to see you. Do come in."

Jinx grabbed her book bag and extra-long scarf off the floor, swept through the open door into her headmistress's lair, and seated herself in one of the red velvet hard-backed chairs opposite the vast mahogany desk.

Mrs. Bennett's office was a peaceful place, Jinx decided, as she gazed round the high-ceilinged room. A group of wicker chairs sat in front of the marble fireplace, and the varnished oak floor was mostly covered with a bright red, orange, and yellow patterned Bokhara rug. Three bronze sculpted racehorses stood on a low glass coffee table underneath the large picture window looking over the playing fields down to the sea, and a huge oil portrait of Penelope Tanner, the eldest of the three sisters who'd founded the school, smiled down at interviewees and miscreants from the opposing wall.

As Jinx leant forward to dump her bag on the floor, a ten-pack of Lucky Strikes fell out of her coat pocket. Fuck! Mrs. Bennett was seated behind her huge desk by now and couldn't see the floor, but really—what shit luck Jinx was having at the moment. She twisted her neck as if stretching out a kink, at the same time pretending to touch her toes and ramming the offending fag packet deep to the bottom of her textbook-laden bag. "And bloody well stay there!" she hissed, before sitting up and smiling winningly at Mrs. B.

Mrs. Bennett cocked her head to one side, pursed her lips in a puzzled fashion, and peered at Jinx through her black-framed Prada spectacles.

"Is everything all right, Jinx? You seem to be having some—ah—physical problems today. Have you got a bad back? If so, you really must make an appointment with the physiotherapist—we need you fighting fit for all the lacrosse matches this term!"

"No, no, Mrs. B. Everything's fine, thanks—really!" Jinx said in what she sincerely hoped was a breezy voice, as the absolute last thing she wanted was a session of torturous physio when there was nothing wrong with her. She also neglected to point out that she'd been kicked out of the lacrosse team halfway through her first term for smacking Daisy Finnegan round the head with a stick. She'd asked for it.

"I think I slept a bit funny, that's all. I'll have a good stretch before bed tonight." Jinx made a big show of sitting up ramrod straight, crossed her ankles in imitation of Princess Diana, clasped her hands demurely in her lap, and smiled reassuringly at Mrs. Bennett. "How are *you*, Mrs. Bennett?"

"Ah." Mrs. Bennett sighed. "*In media res*, you know." Jinx stifled a giggle and thought that it was a good thing Mrs. B had the terribly pretentious habit of dropping Latin words and phrases into ordinary conversation, as otherwise Jinx would no doubt have had the most almighty crush on her. And whichever way you think about it, a crush on the headmistress is never a good thing.

"Now Jinx," Mrs. Bennett continued, her usually serene face looking ever so slightly flustered, "you're probably wondering why I called you in here." Jinx squinted and nodded in what she hoped was a scholarly fashion and leant forward slightly. So she wasn't going to be told off for her breach of the peace in assembly? Bloody teachers. Of *course* she was wondering what she was doing here.

"Well, the thing is . . . most irregular at this stage, of course." Mrs. Bennett paused, looking uncharacteristically perplexed. "Thanks to"—she paused to purse her lips before carrying on—"the bursar, we've got a new girl starting tomorrow, in the lower sixth, and I thought you would be an excellent person to take her under your wing a bit. You know, show her the ropes and where everything is."

Jinx sat up straight for real. A new girl? Two weeks into the term? Wowser, this was great gossip for sure!

"Naturally, Mrs. B," Jinx simpered. "I'd be *delighted* to help her—and you—out. What's her name?" Of course, Jinx didn't give two figs what the new girl's name was, especially when there were about a million other more important questions she wanted answered, but experience had taught her it was best to start off innocuously, especially where sharp old Mrs. B was concerned.

"Her name is Stella Fox." Mrs. Bennett leant her elbows on the desk and linked her fingers, her forearms making a pyramid shape.

"She's coming here from Bedales." Jinx raised an eyebrow. "She's been at Bedales since the third form, and so may find Stag-mount's ways a little—erm—tougher than she's been used to."

Mrs. Bennett hesitated, pondered Jinx's "helpful" face in front of her, and brightened considerably. "But, thanks to your very kind offer of help, Jinx, I am sure she'll settle down in no time at all. You really are a very warmhearted girl, and I am counting on you to make Stella feel right at home."

"Of course, Mrs. B. Stella will be fine with us—we're a very friendly lot in the lower sixth, you know." Jinx winked, then blushed when she registered Mrs. B's surprise. Inappropriate facial expressions were like a disability with Jinx—she despaired of ever mastering the poker face.

Mrs. Bennett smiled and leaned back in her chair, thinking that really, whatever Patricia Gunn had to say about her—and she had plenty—Jinx Slater was a thoroughly nice girl and turning into a real Stagmount success story.

Jinx, meanwhile, was thinking about the two girls she'd known at prep school who'd gone to Bedales and what absolute slags they'd turned into. Clever academically, yes, but stupid beyond belief when it came to boys. Yuck, just thinking about the positively whorish Jennifer and Josephine, who'd had such rectitudinal attitudes toward sex until they'd been targeted by the Bedales brainwashing stun gun, made her feel sick.

She shuddered as she recalled Jennifer earnestly trying to explain to her during one Easter holiday that actually it was *empowering* to sleep around, and that the three guys she'd shagged at the same party had, like, *respected* her for it. Ha! *She wishes. Why not have some respect for* yourself, *Jennifer, and just not do it in the first place*, thought Jinx then and now. She'd not seen her since.

Mrs. Bennett stood up and opened the door. As Jinx prepared to stride purposefully gossip-ward through it, Mrs. B patted her shoulder and said, "Jinx, I want you to know that I'm really proud of you and the lovely young woman you are becoming. You are a real credit to this school. Don't forget that."

"Aw, thanks, Mrs. B." Jinx blushed again, pleased this time, and smiled her way out, bobbing in the doorway like a Victorian parlor maid before pulling the door closed behind her.

She was surprised to find Mr. Morris standing by Jo's desk, in almost the exact same woebegone position she'd vacated those few minutes earlier. She really did like the dude a great deal. "Hey, sir," Jinx exclaimed. "How are you? Seeing Mrs. B? Is it about the new girl?"

"Ah, if it's not my favorite pupil." Mr. Morris grinned, although the wide smile did not seem to reach his wrinkly eyes. "Sadly, Jinx, Mrs. B and I must discuss some rather boring issues regarding the new geography curriculum. Nothing likely to interest you, I'm afraid. You're not in trouble yourself, I hope? I've got quite enough gray hairs to be going on with, thank you very much!"

"Nah, sir, Mrs. B just wants me to extend the warm hand of friendship to the new girl—Stella Fox her name is—coming from Bedales, of all places. I, of course, said I'd be delighted to help so everything's sweet. She'll be in our house, I guess? How come you didn't say anything?"

"Mrs. Bennett wanted to tell you herself, and yes, Stella will be in our house." Mr. Morris looked suddenly uncomfortable again, causing Jinx to reflect that the teachers sure were being weird today. "And I didn't say anything because I am a professional and have my reputation to consider." He smiled another sad smile and looked positively relieved when Mrs. Bennett popped her head out and motioned him inside. He wiggled his fingers at Jinx and disappeared through the oak door.

Jo was on the phone with the man from the *Guardian*, telling him that *no*, he couldn't attend his appointment two hours late, or indeed tomorrow, and rescheduling him for five weeks down the line. Jinx could hear him begging in a squawky voice for an earlier appointment, but Jo was firm. Mrs. Bennett, didn't he know, was a *very* busy woman. She put him on hold, started cackling to herself at celebrity fashion disasters, and didn't look up as Jinx turned left and began walking, slowly, thoughtfully, down the deserted corridor in the direction of double English.

Jinx slunk into her back-row seat in classroom 4b and immediately turned her attention to the blackboard, which was covered in Dr. Brown's scrawling handwriting. *Gender, space, and identity in early eighteenth-century literature*, she read, and smiled beatifically as she stretched her legs in front of her and sank down into her seat. The eighteenth century was easily her favorite period. She loved those gothic novels, and especially enjoyed the satirists. Dr. Brown was also easily her favorite teacher—such an inspiring man, but Jinx resisted the temptation to punch the air. After all, she did have a reputation to uphold.

The lower-school dining room was teeming with girls of all shapes and sizes by the time the sixth-form gang made it down from the English room for lunch.

A disgusting smell of beans and cabbage rent the air, and in clear preparation for her daily speech about the extortionate fees and the disproportionately terrible food, Chastity wrinkled her rather large nose.

"Fuck's sake, Chas," said Fiona, a geeky-looking girl in their art class who'd been in Friedan House before she joined Tanner with all the others, and was turning out to be surprisingly, pleasingly chippy. "Don't start on them." She gestured toward the dinner ladies who'd been there at least as long as they had and long before that, probably. "It's not *their* fault—they just serve the food."

"All right," said Chastity, clearly in a huff. "It's just that my mum says—"

"We all *know* what your bloody mum says and thinks and does—about everything, and frankly, we don't care," shrieked Fiona, frustration making her more vociferous than usual. "You don't hear us quoting our mothers every five minutes, and if your mum's so bloody marvelous, why don't you just fuck off home?"

Chastity stared at Fiona, furious. "If you ever speak about my mother like that again, I'll fucking have you." The telltale red spots high on her cheeks proved that Chastity meant it. "And you'll wish you'd never been born. End of."

Jinx and Liberty watched this fear and loathing in the canteen, amused. Fiona looked downright scared.

With her long blond hair extensions and jangling Tiffany bracelets, Chastity might look fluffy, but once riled she took no prisoners. She also adored her mother above all else, especially since her media-mogul father had fallen—missing, presumed dead—off the side of his yacht in 1993, right after she was born.

Chastity never talked about him; there was some mystery surrounding his death that Jinx's dad had once explained to her that was now long forgotten, but Jinx and Liberty knew enough never to question Mrs. M-W's pearls of vicarious, and slightly skewed wisdom.

"Best leave it, yeah," Jinx sniggered into Fiona's ear as they piled their plates high with tired-looking tomato salad and soggy quiche Lorraine and headed away from the service stations into the dining room proper. "You don't want your face ending up on the wrong side of Chas's fist."

Chastity paused by the end of a long table and flicked her hair. A group of second-years immediately squeezed them-selves as far down toward the end as they could, while the sixth-formers arranged themselves around Liberty at the head of the table.

The younger girls' chatter became hushed and self-conscious as Jinx pointed at them, pretended to slit her throat with her pathetically blunt knife—Mrs. Bennett was intent on having no self-harming slasher clubs at *her* school—and gestured for the others to lean in close as she prepared to spill all about her meeting with the head.

Jinx elbowed Liberty—who was staring out the window—in the ribs before hissing, "New girl coming tomoz—into our year, called Stella Fox, from Bedales!"

"Nooo! Why so late in the term, Jin?" Liberty asked, all her attention fixed on Jinx.

"Dunno. Mrs. B wasn't very forthcoming. She seemed a bit off, if you ask me."

"What do you mean, 'off'?" Liberty was a strict black-and-white girl; she never could grasp subtleties or gray areas.

"You know—not like normal. Bit distant. Nice enough, but seemed to have something on her mind." Jinx glanced at Liberty scratching her head. "Christ, there's only so many ways I can say it!"

"Right," nodded Liberty, clearly none the wiser. "But," she whispered, looking for all the world as if she were seriously thinking about how, exactly, the atom was split, "there must have been some kind of problem with her, right? If she's leaving Bedales to come somewhere new, two weeks into term?"

"Bingo. My thoughts exactamundo, Mademoiselle Marple."

Liberty frowned, a clear sign she was engaging her brain, but Jinx stepped in before she could open her mouth. "And don't, please don't, ask me who Miss Marple is. I'll tell you later."

Jinx groaned and pressed her face into her pillow as the radio-alarm went off, but opened her eyes when she recognized Bonnie Tyler's husky voice. God, she loved BT passionately, shamelessly: her very own not-at-all-guilty pleasure. If ever there were a sound more conducive to getting a girl up and about in a morning, then Jinx hadn't heard it.

"I don't know what to do, I'm always in the dark!" Jinx sprang out of bed and shouted along at the top of what Stagmount's choir master termed her "musically retarded" voice. "Living in a powder keg and giving off sparks!"

Good radio, thought Jinx, *would be playing this twice in a row. Three times, even.* No such luck—she grimaced as the opening strains of Madonna's sexed-up take on "American Pie" came on. She'd never understood all the fuss about the dreary original, and had gone right off her erstwhile heroine since she embraced tweed and chickens and became what Jinx, rather often and loftily, referred to as "yet another casualty of marriage."

She grinned as she imagined Her Madgesty sitting in her countryside pile fighting with her mockney bloody husband over the remote control—*nature program or a documentary, dear?* Yes, it must be tricky trying to be down with the *kidz* when your most pressing concern was your own kids.

Jinx wasn't against marriage per se—her own parents had been together for a mostly happy twenty-five years after all, and she'd have been properly gutted if they split up, as so many of her friends' parents had. In fact, she had a sneaking suspicion that Caroline and Martin's regular furious rows were what kept them together.

She'd long learnt not to pay any attention as one or the other yelled about divorce before screeching off in a cloud of burning rubber. It never came to anything, and they were usually all smiles in the morning. Far worse was the studied indifference she'd noticed in other people's parents. The ones that didn't seem to give a shit what the other one was doing or saying were inevitably the ones who ended up splitting the proceeds from the sale of the family home.

But thinking about getting married herself made her feel all trapped and claustrophobic. Caroline always laughed and said she'd been exactly the same and that Jinx would grow out of it. "We'll see," Jinx always replied snidely, before flouncing off upstairs, flinging her bedroom windows open, and shocking the ponies outside into sudden gallops with a burst of top-volume DJ Sammy.

She'd rather have eaten Ms. Gunn's stinking old shoe than change her name, and she never could understand why otherwise right-thinking people got all hot under the collar about a load of bitter bureaucracy. "Officer, I'd like to report a theft." Jinx yawned. "An identity theft."

Anyway, thought Jinx, as she scraped her hair back from her face, pulled on her ratty pink dressing gown, and grabbed her palest blue Anya Hindmarch wash bag with a black-and-white photograph of Marilyn Monroe on the side, *is it even possible to be a feminist and have a big white wedding?*

As she wandered toward the bathroom at the end of her corridor, Jinx realized she was still thinking about weddings and scowling. She smiled at Fanny Ho, a boyish Chinese girl given to wearing sharply tailored Paul Smith suits, who'd been in the year above but had had to stay down due to a nasty bout of glandular fever, and who was on her way to the library, where she read the trickiest business pages of the FT every day before breakfast. Fanny, looking fabulous in a lilac trouser suit with a bright pink tie and white open-necked shirt, gave her a shy wave and hello in return.

"Get a grip, girlfriend," Jinx said to herself in her best comedic California accent when Fanny had run up the stairs. "Where's Ms. School-is-useless-but-for-pranks this morning?"

"Jinxy baby, are you talking to yourself?" Liberty breezed out of her room, followed by a sharp gust of freezing cold air.

She'd beaten up her radiator to stop it working, permanently, and slept with the window wide open summer and—weirdly, according to Jinx—winter. "It's the first sign of madness!"

"Actually, Lib, euphoria, delirium, and wanting to be freezing cold all the time are the first signs of madness," Jinx said, flicking her towel. "And I should know, 'cos you exhibit all three. Ooo, look—if it isn't Miss Hoity-Toity herself, our esteemed head girl." Jinx made a mock bow as Daisy Finnegan exited her room three doors up, wearing pale pink pajamas and her despicable pair of Garfield fluffy slippers.

"Just our luck having that sneaky suck-up on our corridor," Jinx said loudly, making sure Daisy could hear.

"Yeah," agreed Liberty. "She's so far up Ms. Gunn's butt, I'm surprised she hasn't disappeared up there."

They giggled as Daisy stuck her nose in the air and swung round, giving them the full benefit of her "shocked" face.

"I simply will not hear a bad word against Ms. Gunn," Daisy intoned, her squeaky yet strangely monotonal voice raised in anger. "She is a pillar of Stagmount society!"

"Pillar of salt, more like," smirked Jinx, always delighted by any opportunity to wind up her old nemesis from Wollstonecraft House. "Lot's wife had nothing on that lying old bitch."

"Mmm, nice slippers, Daisy," said Liberty, always horrified by what she saw as Daisy's crimes against good taste. "Where did you get those—the dollar store?"

Daisy sneered, flicked her mousy rats' tails in a poor imitation of the beauty ads, spun on her yellow-and-black stripy heel, and flounced off to a chorus of peals of laughter.

"Lib." Jinx grabbed Liberty's free hand. "That new girl's arriving today. I'm going to have to take her about a bit—you'll help, won't you?"

"Course I will—you're my best friend, aren't you? It's quite exciting, actually, someone new coming in." Liberty winked at Jinx. "I've been feeling a bit bored lately: same old faces, same old chat."

Jinx frowned slightly and let go of Liberty's hand as they shoved through the swinging door into the bathroom at the end of their corridor. Liberty never could resist a bloody gimmick.

They were the only ones in there, as all the others were down at breakfast. It was sauna-hot from an hour's solid showering, and the windows and mirrors were all steamed up.

Jinx had once been into George's school bathroom at the end of the boys' shower time, and it had *stunk*. Thankfully, being a girls' school, this place smelt wonderful—mint shower gel, lemon shampoo, Aveda rosemary conditioner, and Vera Wang body lotion jostled for prominence in the hot air.

Liberty could be naff as hell quite a lot of the time, and was obsessed with musical theater. They'd sung "Copacabana" in the showers early on in their first term and made a tradition of it. Chastity's mum always told them—the truest thing she'd ever said—that a show tune a day keeps the doctor away, and these two were in possession of positively rude constitutions.

"Don't get me wrong, I only want to know / Who are you?" Liberty's Christina Aguilera tones rang out over the dividing wall. "What have you sacrificed? / Jesus Christ Superstar, / Do you think you're what you say you are?" Jinx, who couldn't stand having change foisted upon her and much preferred Rodgers and Hammerstein to weirdo Andrew Lloyd Webber, didn't join in as loudly as usual.

10

Jinx, Chastity, Liberty, and Fiona exited the side door of Tanner House clutching toast-and-Marmite triangles, and began the trek up the winding drive to the main school building and the classroom where they had their daily tutor group meeting.

Fanny Ho dashed past them, in the direction of the library. Jinx waved at her again and wondered—not for the first time—how anyone could spend so much time in there. "I saw her wearing something totally different earlier on," whispered Liberty, who kept a close eye on everyone's wardrobes. Fanny's lilac trouser suit had been ditched in favor of a bright orange tulip skirt, white T-shirt, and cowboy boots. "That girl's got more clothes than *me!*" Liberty sounded incredulous. "And she's changed her hair."

Despite having always studied together, the sixth form had been split amongst the four main-school houses for their first three years at Stagmount, and this was the first term they'd all spent sleeping under the same roof.

Each of the junior-school houses was named after a famous feminist: Wollstonecraft, where Jinx, Liberty, and the dreaded Daisy had lived—somewhat paradoxically, they'd always said, given the great Mary's arguments against the subjugation of women—under Ms. Gunn's oppressive thumb; Pankhurst, where Chastity had been kept in line by Hammerhead, of whom she was actually very fond; Steinem, where all the sporty red-stocking girls—so named because of their bright red hockey socks—lived, and which had won practically every single house match in the history of the school; and Friedan, where Fiona had lived, and which was considered "creative."

The lower sixth, on the whole, consisted of girls who were more interested in having fun than anything else. Bullying was considered very non-U, and the girls who didn't get on pretty much ignored one another. The girls were always astounded by tales of eating disorders at other schools; they loved their food, ate huge meals and often entire packets of custard creams in front of their beloved *Days of our Lives* and *Jerry Springer*.

It was nice, walking up the drive. Despite it being the second week in September the sun was shining and the sea was calm. The girls meandered along, their faces turned to the sky, thinking there was no greater place on earth than Stagmount in the sun.

Jinx bent the ring pull back on a can of Diet Coke and took a long swig. She was addicted to the stuff and could never contemplate finishing an essay, tidying her room, or making an important phone call without an icy can in her hand. In fact, if she hadn't known that her mum would kill her if she ever found out, she'd have had it on her cornflakes every day.

The peace was shattered by a sudden volley of loud beeps. Someone was clearly pressing down hard on their car horn, repeatedly making the most horrendous noise with no regard whatsoever for the sanity of those trying desperately to cram their brains with fiendish French vocabulary or murderous maths theories in the last few minutes before lessons began.

"Christ alive," shrieked Chastity, who'd been muttering biological terms to herself under her breath. "What the fuck's going on?"

"I don't know," said an anguished-looking Fiona, whose train of thought had also been ruinously interrupted, and who was pointing at the steps that cut through the gently sloping hill by the ice cream shop. "But it's definitely coming from over there."

They legged it to the scene of the crime, all intent on giving the perpetrator a piece of their mind, but stopped short when they saw what lay beneath them.

Just to the right of the ice cream shop, a small red car was lying on its roof. They could see a pale-faced, ginger-haired man calling for help and waving with one hand out of the half-open driver's-side window, and honking the horn as hard as he could with the other.

Jinx was vacillating between taking a picture of him on her mobile phone for posterity and calling for a fire engine to cut him free when she saw Jo sprinting from the main house toward the steps. "Damn it," she muttered to a fascinated Liberty. "Here comes Jo. That's a ruined opportunity. I definitely can't snap him now—she'd kill me."

"What the—?" Jo was breathlessly exclaiming as she drew near. "Oh." She folded her arms as she peered through the window, stepped back, and said witheringly, "It's you."

The girls were agog with excitement on the first couple of steps. Who the bloody hell *was* this man, and why was Jo—normally an oasis of smiles and chats—so cross with him?

"I distinctly recall telling you to make another appointment. I imagined you would use the *phone* to do so."

"I'd just reached across for a jelly baby," whimpered the man, as if that explained everything, "when out of nowhere I found myself skidding down the hill and landing upside down like this."

"I know who it is," Jinx whispered excitedly to the others, whose shoulders were heaving with barely contained laughter. "It's that journalist who keeps trying to interview Mrs. Bennett. It's hilarious—he keeps fucking up his dates and times, and now he's driven over the cliff. This is brilliant—look how cross Jo is!"

Jo was in the middle of one of the best tickings-off they'd heard—especially as the upside-down man's pale face was growing redder by the second—when she spun round and noticed the gaggle of girls hanging onto her every word at the top of the steps. "Girls!" she said, throwing a very cross look indeed in their direction. "Don't stand there gaping. I'm sure you've got lessons to go to. I'll sort this out, don't you worry about that!"

The girls reluctantly picked up their bags and turned back up the path toward the main school.

As they swung through the arched porch built of heavy, rough-cut stone and through the huge Romanesque door at the sanatorium end of the corridor, still snorting and laughing about the fate of that poor man, Daisy Finnegan caught up with them.

"Hello, girls," she said, sounding exactly like one of the freaking teachers, and with a sideways warning glance at Jinx, who had really savaged her on occasion. "Just to let you know, there's a new girl starting today and she'll be in your tutor group."

"We know," said Jinx, wishing the bloody bitch would leave them alone. The sneaky, suck-up part she could deal with, no probs—worse was the fact that she never seemed to brush her teeth. They always looked furry and yellow, and Jinx could hardly stand to breathe the same air as her. "I spoke to Mrs. B about it yesterday. So thanks, and so long."

The quartet made to move away, but Daisy grabbed Jinx's arm above the elbow. Jinx flinched as she caught a whiff of Daisy's death breath. "The thing is," said Daisy, excitement making her even more revolting than usual, "I heard she was made to leave Bedales. And no one gets expelled from *there*, do they?"

"I dunno, Dais." Jinx was desperate to get away and so much nicer than usual. "We'll let you know what she's like later on. See ya!"

"Wouldn't wanna *be* ya," she muttered as Daisy headed off to the science labs, probably about to dissect a poor defenseless rat or frog or something, her straggly ginger ponytail swinging pathetically behind her. "Why doesn't she get a fucking haircut and try brushing her fucking teeth once in a while? Christ, she makes me want to puke."

The others nodded in pretend sympathy, trying to stifle their laughter. It was quite something to be "fingered"—as they described any encounter with Daisy Finnegan—twice before first lesson.

They crashed into classroom 4b and took their seats— Chastity, Jinx, and Liberty, in that order, in the very center of the back row; with Liv, who'd been in Steinem, next to Chastity; and Charlie, who'd been in Friedan, next to Liberty. The five of them had shared every back-row opportunity they could for the last three years and had no intention of changing anything just because they were now in the sixth form. Fiona—claiming bad eyesight, although she'd never once been seen to wear glasses— liked to sit at the front.

Just as Chastity was filling Liv in on the new girl, Mrs. Carpenter, their form tutor, strolled through the door. The girls liked stylish, friendly Mrs. C but were wary of igniting her legendarily schizophrenic temper and immediately fell silent. She was dressed in her customary all-black outfit accessorized with lots of silver bangles that jangled whenever she wrote something on the whiteboard, and her chunky-silver-ringed hands were gripping an ELVIS LIVES mug of black coffee so strong and lumpy it looked like oxtail soup.

Mrs. C placed the coffee on her desk, shrugged off her long black cardigan, and smiled around the room. "Hi, girls," she said, resting her forearms on the back of her extremely expensive ergonomic chair, the only one in the whole school. Legend had it she'd dashed screaming into the incredibly tight bursar's office, stripped off her skirt, and insisted on showing him the bruises on her bottom caused, she said, by her standard-issue chair, and that he'd been so embarrassed he'd immediately signed the order form allowing her this one. She was clearly in a good mood.

"How are you all?" she asked, beaming her megawatt, some would say manic, grin around the room. "No problems with timetables or anything, I hope? We spent days—*weeks*, it felt like—sorting it all out at the end of last term. I nearly dropped dead of boredom. The thing that saved me was planning out"—Mrs. C was given to long monologues about her life in all its fascinating aspects, and the girls were used to being asked answerless questions, quite happy to sit back and zone out—" . . . my new kitchen. I tell you, girls, it is fantastic. I've got an American-style fridge and freezer, black granite worktops— much better than wood, they'll never chip or stain, and one's got to bear things like that in mind, of course—a stainless-steel range and—come in!"

Mrs. C's full and thorough inventory of her new kitchen was, thankfully, interrupted by a knock at the door that heralded the arrival of Mrs. Bennett and one of the most attractive girls the class had ever seen.

The room fell silent, and Mrs. Bennett cleared her throat and coughed once before turning to Mrs. Carpenter. "Good morning, Mrs. Carpenter. Good morning, girls." Mrs. Bennett was using her extra-polite voice. Since it had many uses, the girls could never decide whether to be pleased or concerned when they heard it. "This is Stella Fox. Stella will be in this tutor group, and, of course, in the sixth-form house. Dave is taking her bags to her room, and . . ."

Whatever Mrs. Bennett had to say about Stella's baggage was lost on the girls as they stared at Stella. She was about five foot five, but looked willowy despite her height. She had wavy, dirty blond hair with an inch of dark roots that looked intentional, Sarah Jessica Parker style, tied in a side ponytail at the nape of her neck and falling over her left shoulder to just above her elbow. Big green eyes underneath long dark lashes liberally plastered with thick, dark brown mascara peered unabashedly around the room, and her big porno-mouth lips were painted a matte dusty pink.

She had cheekbones to die for and a smattering of freckles across her Saint-Tropez-tanned forehead and nose. She was wearing the tightest, skinniest gray jeans tucked into what looked suspiciously like Chloé black boots with a chunky wooden heel, and a skintight deep purple T-shirt emblazoned with the legend J'ADORE DIOR in red diamanté sparkles underneath a tight black tuxedo jacket. She carried an oversize pale green Balenciaga bag in one impeccably French-manicured hand and a sheaf of papers in the other.

"Jinx. *Jinx!*" Mrs. Bennett was staring at Jinx, who, feeling slightly dazed, quickly shifted her focus to the head teacher. "Perhaps you would be so kind as to find a place for Stella to sit, and take her to the canteen at break time?"

"Of course, Mrs. B, no problem." Jinx stood up, smiled her best, brightest, most welcoming grin at the newcomer, and marched to the front of the room, where she held out her hand. "Hi, I'm Jinx. Lovely to meet you."

"Hey." Stella took the proffered hand and shook it almost as languidly as she spoke. "Pleased to meet you."

At the same time that Jinx spotted a spare seat next to Fiona in the front row, Stella turned to Mrs. Carpenter, who was staring at the new arrival as if she'd never seen anything like her—and she probably hadn't: even Mohamed Al Fayed's daughter had never turned up at a lesson looking like *this*. "Hello, Mrs. Carpenter," she said, in her slow, accentless voice. "Would it be possible for me to sit at the back near Jinx? It's just that I'm a bit nervous about sitting on my own at the front."

"Come off it, Stella." Jinx laughed and nudged her in the ribs. "How old *are* you? Are you sure you should be in the lower sixth? These are the assigned seats for the year, and since you've come in so late, you're going to have to take one of the free ones." Stella pursed her lips and gave Jinx a very black look. She folded her arms, raised one eyebrow, continued to stare darkly at Jinx—who'd only been joking around, and who rarely noticed "meaningful" looks anyway—and didn't respond.

Mrs. Carpenter looked puzzled but nodded her acquiescence when Mrs. Bennett clocked Stella's expression. The teacher cleared her throat for the second time and scanned the back row. "Charlotte," she said, "perhaps you would come and sit next to Fiona."

Charlie looked appalled but didn't say anything as she gathered her books together, glared at Stella, and stomped her way to the front.

Miraculously recovered, Stella smiled sweetly at Mrs. Carpenter and followed Jinx to the back row, where she sat quietly down in Charlie's chair, folded her arms again, and gazed expectantly around the room. She didn't look even the slightest bit nervous.

"Right, girls." Mrs. Carpenter seemed somewhat uncharacteristically dazed. "There's no time left for tutor group business, but if any of you need anything, you know where I am."

"And"—she gestured toward Stella, still looking a bit bemused—"I trust you will all be as helpful to our new friend as you can be. Adios!"

The headmistress and the teacher disappeared through the door, leaving behind an eerie silence amongst the usually rowdy girls.

Liv was the first to break it. "Nervous my ass," she snorted as she scowled at Stella and jumped up to commiserate with Charlie, who'd been her best friend since they'd stolen the gardener's tractor two years previously and tried to do handbrake turns with it on the grass tennis courts. The sports staff had been furious, but Mrs. Bennett had eventually seen the funny side, and once they'd finished taking the tractor apart, oiling every cog and wheel until it gleamed, and putting it back together again, she'd initiated a schoolwide science project that involved building a sports car from scratch. The girls loved it.

The remarkably self-possessed Stella took zero notice of Liv and turned to Liberty and Jinx. "So, then, *girls*," she said, a slight sneer playing about her pink lips as she sarcastically imitated Mrs. C, "what do you do for kicks in this dump?"

Liberty giggled admiringly at her. "Me and Jinx had a wild time on the pier last week."

Jinx bristled, but remembering Mrs. Bennett's request that she look after Stella until she was settled in, she bit her lip and forced a friendly smile.

"Take no notice of Lib," she said. "The only thing playing in her head is fairground music on a constant loop." She winked at Liberty, who didn't notice, because she was busy staring admiringly at Stella's boots. Stella smiled to herself and then flashed a big grin at Liberty, clearly pleased that Jinx's best friend was all over her like a particularly nasty bout of hives. Jinx wanted to grab Lib and force some emergency antihistamines down her throat. Designer clothes and good looks often had that effect on her, and when they were combined with the kind of icy aloofness that Liberty usually mistook for coolness, she could always be relied upon to roll over like a freaking spaniel.

"So," Jinx said, "why did you come so late in the term, then, Stella?"

"So," said Stella, with another sneer, "why are you called Jinx?" Sure that Stella was being rude to her, Jinx was undecided as to whether to call her on it. She stared at the new girl, but decided to give her the benefit of the doubt.

The others grinned—they'd heard this story many times but never tired of it. "Well," began Jinx, smiling just thinking about it, "I've got two brothers, and we all loved the Famous Five books when we were growing up. Eventually, though, when I was about eleven, we decided that George and Julian and the others were actually boring, prissy little bastards who didn't even have very good adventures anyway, and so we decided we'd be our own threesome, but call ourselves the Fearsome Three instead and have code names to be, you know, cooler." Stella frowned. It was evident that she saw nothing cool about this at all, name changes or not.

"I was christened Jane, although everyone called me Jin, because I once drank a pint of it by mistake, but with a J because of the Jane bit, and then my brother Damian decided on Jinx and it stuck. We all had to have a special power as well, and mine was causing bad luck to my enemies using psychic waves of pink energy, 'cos pink was my favorite color. Still is, actually."

Stella looked confused. "What was Damian's name, then?" she asked.

"Oh, we called him Gaymian, because he's gay." Jinx laughed. "He's been gay for, like, forever. And his special skill was lighting a cigarette the first time he tried in any weather condition.

"It still is for him, too, alongside making the best spaghetti Bolognese in town," Jinx continued, on a roll now. "He keeps saying he's going to put it on his resume."

Stella smirked enigmatically at this but said nothing.

The girls spent the morning trailing from one lesson to another, watching Stella carefully, but she sat quietly at the back, not saying much and seemingly impervious to their curious glances.

Sister Minton, the cuddly school nurse with an unfortunate arrangement of thick black hairs above her top lip, whom the girls always fondly referred to as Mister Sinton, took Stella off at lunchtime to be weighed and measured and all the rest of the terrible things the school medical entailed, leaving the others a perfectly timed forty-five minutes in which to shovel down their customary carb-fest, watch half of *Laguna Beach*, and get changed for games. Although Liv snorted magnificently every time Liberty mentioned the new arrival's fabulous clothes, all the girls were too busy seeking out missing hockey socks and hunting down clean white T-shirts to discuss Stella.

11

Jinx and Liberty stood by the side of the hockey pitch in a straggly line with the rest of their class, watching Miss Strimmer and Miss Golly make their way down from the sports hall, past the swimming pool construction site and toward the pitches.

Strimmer wore a short navy tennis skirt every single day, winter or summer, and the girls were used to the faintly horrific sight of her mottled tree-trunk thighs glowing red with exertion as she ran manfully up and down the edges of the long pitches shouting praise and abuse in equal measure, although rather more of the latter where the older girls were concerned.

Where Strimmer was quite short and rather fat, Golly was tall and thin. Only the really sporty girls loved them, and the odd couple delighted in holding court in their office in the sports hall. So much for Mrs. Bennett's clique bashing—they ran the absolute worst one in terms of exclusivity, and all the sporty girls stuck together, which was just as well really, as far as Strimmer and Golly were concerned.

They were the only two people in the whole school who looked unhappy at the end of term. Neither had ever married, or was ever likely to, and it was hard to imagine them leading any kind of normal life. They both spent every waking hour lording over the girls, organizing interminable house tournaments of every conceivable kind and refereeing—or fixing, more like—matches against their rivals.

Golly was the cleverer of the two, but since Strimmer was an absolute bona fide, card-carrying moron, it is fair to say that wasn't saying much.

They glared at Jinx as they approached, and Jinx, glaring back, thought about how much she hated both of them, and had ever since they'd had a spectacular falling-out at the end of the first year. A neighboring farmer specialized in breeding and selling miniature farm animals at ludicrously inflated prices. His rather sound reasoning for charging whatever he liked was, who knew how much a petite pig should cost anyway?

Amongst the aging city boys and showbiz lawyers who snapped up countryside homes in commutable Sussex—making life very difficult for most of the normal farmers as property prices flew through the roof—it was a serious status symbol to have a couple of small sheep or a diminutive donkey keeping the grass down on the front lawn.

On the morning of a very important tennis match against Millfield, the reigning champions at just about everything, his entire flock of pygmy goats appeared—as if by magic—in the courts. They'd proved an absolute devil to catch and round up, and the match had to be canceled.

Strumpet and Gosh, as all the girls called them, had been so unreasonable and rude about the whole affair—swearing at the poor (actually rather rich since giving up dairy farming in favor of raising the lucrative miniature beasts) farmer and aiming futile kicks at the poor (actually highly delighted) little goats—that Jinx had simultaneously resigned from the hockey, tennis, swimming, and tennis teams, the last of which she'd captained.

They'd tried to get her back on side, but Jinx had refused. She'd tasted—literally—the benefits of match-free weekends and was not at all inclined to go, cap in hand, begging forgiveness. She'd still played lacrosse, but then there had been the hitting-of-dreadful-Daisy incident, so she'd jacked that in, too. It had wound Strumpet and Gosh up to the max, and they'd never forgiven her.

She grinned broadly as she stood there in the cold, thinking about how that tiny little black goat had seemed to smile so happily to itself as it bit deep into the seat of Strumpet's pants and refused to let go. *Goats are brilliant*, she thought to herself, smirking. *They really will eat anything.*

"Slater!" Gosh looked cross. "You can play in midfield, reds—and stop smirking." Jinx, smirking so hard her cheeks hurt, grabbed a red bib from the trunk, sauntered into the center of the pitch, pulled it over her eyes, and pretended to be blind, moaning and pointing about with her hockey stick.

"SLAAAAA-AAATER!"

Jinx could hear the rest of the class laughing, so she pretended not to hear Strumpet, dropped her hockey stick on the ground, and did five cartwheels in quick succession, still blindfolded.

She jumped up and pushed the bib up to her forehead, looking round in pretend shock. "Goodness gracious golly *gosh*," said Jinx, loving the fact that most of her classmates were creasing up on the sidelines, "I *am* sorry—I thought I'd gone blind for a second there."

Strumpet and Gosh bared their collective teeth at Jinx and resumed picking the teams.

Liberty and Fiona were stuck at either end in goal. Both of them hated sports, and Strumpet and Gosh had long ago given up trying to get them to show any interest.

Chastity, pleased because she thought blue looked lovely against her blond hair, was playing opposite Jinx in midfield. Liv and Charlie were on Jinx's team, on the wing, with Stella and Daisy opposite for the blues.

Jinx enjoyed playing the fool rather more than she enjoyed playing the game, but when she could be bothered, she was really very good at hockey.

Jinx won the first ball and tapped it past Chastity, watching Stella out of the corner of her eye, interested to see how she'd perform. Jinx dummied easily past Daisy and ran with it right up to the shooting circle, noting with interest how well Stella was playing. "Christ," she yelled back to Liv, "it's not exactly competitive out here, is it?" She did a little dance before aiming the ball straight between Fiona's shaking legs.

"*Red goal!*" shouted Strumpet, waving her black-and-white ref's flag, signaling a return to center.

Jinx winked at Chastity. "You have it this time," she said, and hung back. Chas flicked it back to Stella, who began running deftly down the left half toward Liberty, who was examining her nails, looking for all the world as if she was in Harvey Nichols's fifth-floor café awaiting her favorite chips and aioli and a glass of pink champagne.

"*Pay attention, Latiffe!*" screamed Strumpet. As Liberty looked up, bemused, Stella's ball smacked into the side of her head with a terrible thud. Liberty didn't make a sound as she collapsed in a heap underneath the white string of the goal netting.

"Fuck, *fuck!*" Jinx was sprinting up the pitch to Liberty and screaming at Stella. "*You fucking bitch!*"

"Slater! Stop this *now!*" Strumpet was also running toward Liberty and shouting at Jinx. "I will *not* have that kind of language on my hockey pitch. Accidents happen, we all know that!"

Jinx ignored her as she dropped down next to Liberty. "Lib." She shook her shoulder gently and bent close to her best friend's ear. "Lib, are you okay?"

"Urgh," Liberty moaned. "My head hurts, Jin. What happened?"

"You got hit by a hard ball, darling." Jinx spoke softly but her eyes turned black as she registered Stella close by, listening intently and seeming to smile. "You're going to have a sore head, but you'll be fine."

"Don't all stand there gawping—someone go and get the fucking matron, for Christ's sake." Jinx was apoplectic and hadn't regained her composure by the time Strumpet arrived.

"First things first—secure the scene." This was Strumpet's favorite saying. "Liberty—how are you feeling? No, don't get up, lie there for a bit longer." Strumpet turned to Jinx, grabbed her elbow, and frog-marched her away from where Liberty was lying underneath the goal. Stella seemed to smirk as they passed her.

"If I *ever*"—Strumpet was gearing up for a big one, Jinx could tell—"hear you use language like that again, it will be straight to Mrs. Bennett for you. Do I make myself clear?"

"Well, no, actually, you *don't*," Jinx hissed, furious and worried about Liberty. "I know you won't believe me, but you were down the other end and couldn't have seen it. That"—she pointed to where Stella was kneeling by Liberty and shuddered with impotent rage—"*thing* did it on purpose. I *saw* her aim the ball at Liberty's head."

Strumpet cleared her throat, not at all displeased at having Jinx Slater exactly where she wanted her for once. "Accidents happen, Jinx," she intoned. "And I am absolutely disgusted at you trying to pin the blame for an act of God on a girl who has been at the school for less than twenty-four hours.

You will apologize to me, and you will apologize to Stella, or you will be gated this weekend. And that will be the end of it."

"Miss Strimmer." Jinx ground her teeth, frustrated. "I am trying to be reasonable here. I will happily apologize to you. I'm sorry—I really am—but I will *not* apologize to Stella. I won't, and *that's* the end of it. I know what I saw." Jinx forced what she hoped was her most reasonable, adult smile, but it came out as more of a bared-teeth scowl.

Golly bounced up to the pair of them as they were facing off and said, "Strimmers, a word please."

The two teachers huddled to one side, no doubt gleefully plotting her demise, while Jinx stared straight ahead, refusing to look anyone in the eye, arms crossed, bristling with rage and indignation. Fucking teachers.

She spun round as if she'd been shot when Stella touched her arm. "Just don't touch me or you'll fucking wish you hadn't." Jinx's most menacing voice sizzled with fury.

"Jinx, I really don't understand why you're . . ." Stella paused and flicked her expertly dyed hair for emphasis. "You're going off on one like this. I mean, I'm *flattered* that you think I'm so good at hockey and everything, but I certainly didn't aim the ball at Liberty's head. I guess she wasn't"—Stella looked ostentatiously at her nails for emphasis—"*concentrating* so hard."

Strumpet and Gosh reappeared, and Stella weighed straight in before Jinx had a chance to say anything. "Oh, there you are Miss Strimmer and Miss Golly." She smiled at the two of them as if they were all the best of friends, in such a smarmy fashion that Jinx thought she would projectile puke right there and then. "We've been having a good old chat, and you just missed Jinx apologizing to me. I must say," she simpered, "I'm delighted she thought I was good enough at hockey to aim the ball so well!"

"Well done, Jinx," sighed Gosh, clearly disappointed by what she saw as a missed opportunity for revenge, "but you really must learn to control that temper of yours. It's most unseemly."

"Stella, you may as well take Liberty up to the san, and you must come and do a trial for the first team this weekend. You looked great out there, you really did." Gosh turned to a shell-shocked-looking Jinx. "And you can take Liberty's place in goal for the rest of the lesson."

12

Liv and Jinx were leaning out the changing-room window, thinking and smoking furiously. Chastity—who couldn't stand smoking but didn't want to miss out on the postgame chat—was sitting on a nearby bench. Charlie was washing her hair at the same time that she was valiantly shouting out suggestions for hastening Stella's demise over the wall of the shower cubicle.

Liv had a wicked look in her eye. Jinx saw it and couldn't stop a tiny smile from crossing her enraged face. If Liv was going to go all out, no one would be able to stop her, least of all Jinx, who was equally set upon payback.

"Hmmm," Liv mused, clearly deep in thought. "What would Tyra do?"

"GET LOST!" they suddenly shouted in unison, as a

scared-looking fourth-former poked her head round the door.

"Jesus *Christ*," said Charlie, emerging from the cubicle wrapped up in a huge purple towel. "I'm only trying to help."

"Not you, moron," said Liv, turning round and winking. "I've got it. I know what we've got to do."

Three faces looked up expectantly. "She's playing us for fools. She thinks that by playing the new-girl card she can do whatever she wants and get away with it." Liv smiled triumphantly and played her trump card like the Vegas pro she would become. "And we're going to let her."

Jinx scratched her head, Chastity flicked an imaginary piece of lint from her spotless black cashmere V-neck, and Charlie dropped her towel. "Whaaat?" she shrieked, jumping up and down, not bothering to retrieve her sodden bath sheet. "Liv! This time you've really lost it. Are you seriously suggesting we let her get away with being, like, the biggest bitch in the world?"

"Yes." Liv flicked her fag butt into the bottom of the air vent on the outside wall of the ballet studio directly opposite the open window, turned round to face the rest, folded her arms, and smirked. "Don't get it twisted, sister." This was Liv's favorite phrase in the world—"What would Tyra do?" came a close second. She used both almost continuously since having heard them on her favorite TV show of all time, *America's Next Top Model*. All the girls loved ANTM, but Liv was properly obsessed with it. The British version, the American one—she loved the Australian show, too. Hell, she'd even been found avidly peering at the German version one wet afternoon at the end of the previous term, and *no one* wants to watch that.

"We're going to sit back and give her exactly as much rope as she needs to hang herself," she carried on, evidently pleased with herself. "We know what she's like, and I bet you all a night out at Ricky T's it won't be long before everyone else does. All we're going to do is *facilitate* their realization." Liv's dad was a big cheese in a communications company, and she loved to impress her friends by dropping his marketing-speak into normal conversation.

"Evil ge-ni-us," said Jinx, slowly, thoughtfully. "But what if you're crediting the others with more brain cells than they've actually got?"

"Stella's not stupid," she continued. "Far from it. I know we've only known her a day, but look how she scammed Charlie's seat off her—*in front of* Mrs. Bennett—and got away with it. Look what she did to Liberty—and *me*—just now, and got away with it."

"Yeah." Chastity leant back and began twirling a long blond strand of hair around her index finger, always a clear sign to the others she was thinking deeply about something. "What if she just gets worse and worse and no one but us sees it?"

Jinx looked skeptical, too. "Hmmm. I see what you're saying, Liv, I really do, but don't you think we should do something more, like, immediate? Or *violent*? I don't want her going around thinking we're easy targets or that Stagmount's full of pussies compared to that slag heap Bedales."

Liv banged the window shut, jumped down off the bench, and reached for her Asics. "Case closed. Trust me, ladies, she's going to regret fucking with us. We'll show her who's boss round here."

As the foursome swung through the sports hall's double doors, they bumped straight into Stella and Liberty, who were heading, arm in sycophantic arm, in the direction of Tanner House.

Liv, placing a warning arm around Jinx's waist, smiled sweetly at the high-fashion twosome, and enquired after Liberty's head.

"Oh, it's fine," she said, a slightly wild look in her dark eyes, the angry bump on her forehead glowing red like one of the beacons they saw shining out to sea from the marina every night. "Mister Sinton gave me two paracetamol and told me to have a nice lie-down."

They all laughed, in spite of themselves. No matter what was wrong with her, whenever a girl went to the Stagmount san, she was fobbed off with two painkillers and—depending on the severity of the complaint—a promise of a nice afternoon in bed.

A year earlier, Stefanie Blake—who none of them had much liked on account of her aggressive warts—had been carried, weeping and wailing, into Mister Sinton's lair with a twice-broken thighbone. Dear old Mister S had prescribed her usual, and Stefanie had lain in bed in terrible pain, hallucinating and slipping in and out of consciousness, until one of the cleaners had seen fit to phone for an ambulance.

Things had taken a slight upturn for a couple of weeks after that, but the san was obviously now back to business very much as usual.

"The exact same thing happened to me in my first year," sniffed Stella, "and I was in an ambulance and on my way to Winchester hospital before you knew it. Bedales took this kind of thing very seriously, you know."

Jinx raised an involuntary skeptical eyebrow at the same time as Liv, her face a study in solicitousness, and shook her head.

"What a terrible thing," she murmured, placing a conciliatory hand at Stella's elbow. "It must have been awful for you. I bet all your friends were *really* worried."

Chastity, who'd tried to turn a high-pitched squeal of hysterical laughter into an ill-timed cough, started choking. But before Stella had a chance to register any suspicion, Liv started again.

"You did come out the other side okay, though, didn't you? I mean, you weren't, like, disfigured or anything?" Liv was peering intently at Stella's face. "Is that your original nose, Stella? I didn't like to say anything before, but now you've told us about your terrible accident I thought it was safe to ask. . . ."

"Of *course* it's my original nose," an obviously irritated Stella cut in. "And the accident wasn't terrible—I had a tennis ball in the face, that was all. I was just making the point that Stagmount leaves a *lot* to be desired."

"I see," said Liv, with what the others recognized as her

most dangerous smile, tightening her grip on Jinx's arm. "I guess, coming from such an amazing place as Bedales, Stagmount must be a real disappointment to you."

"If there's anything we can do," she continued, "to make things more . . . bearable for you, then you must let us know. We simply couldn't *stand* to think of you miserable and not coping."

Chastity, never known for steely control in the face of hysterics, began mumbling under her breath about saxophone lessons, grade-eight exams, and not enough practice, and legged it toward the music school, emitting high-pitched squeals of glee as she bounded off up the hill.

Stella stared suspiciously after her, before glaring from beneath her gently curling fringe at the rest of the girls gathered around her. She rocked back and forth on a pair of this season's must-have patent turquoise heels and, flashing a row of pearly white Hollywood-style teeth, licked her lips with a very pink and pointy tongue.

"Well," she drawled, shoving one hand in the back pocket of her navy, skintight Seven for All Mankind jeans and placing the other on her hip, "that's very kind of you all. I'm sure I'll get used to Stagmount. Eventually."

"So when are you going to do your first team trial, then, Stella?" Charlie smiled encouragingly at her. "You did look *amazing* on the pitch."

"Oh . . ." Stella shook her head as if she were trying to communicate with a bunch of half-wits. "I won't be doing that. I certainly don't want to spend all my Saturdays sweating in the freezing cold for that pair of tossers. Of course, if I did try out I'd definitely get in—I was on all the teams at Bedales, but I certainly don't have anything to prove *here*."

She smiled thinly at the group, tossed her hair, and gestured for Liberty to follow her back to Tanner. "Liberty, why don't you come and check out my handbag collection," she called over her shoulder.

Like a parody of a little lemming, Liberty grinned weakly at her pals and trailed off in Stella's Chantecaille-scented wake.

The girls watched them leave in spaced-out silence, until Charlie snorted magnificently and spun on her heel.

"This is a fucking disaster area. Come on, Liv—how much longer are we going to play this game before we let her really have it?"

Jinx, who was actually leaning toward the same conclusion but wanted to give Liv's theory a full and proper testing, swung her bag at Charlie's turned back.

"Come on, Charl. Liv's never let us down in the past and we've got to give this a go—can't fall at the first freaking hurdle, can we?" Jinx grinned. "Surely you haven't forgotten the deliciously delightful downfall of dreadful Tiffany Bigsworth at the end of the first year? Or cheerily waving bye-bye to Claire "In the Community" Kemp at the end of the second? Our Liv has seen off far worse than that tramp."

"Yes." A self-satisfied Liv paused and smiled serenely. "And we're going to get rid of Stella, too. But in the meantime, we've got to be as nice as pie to the witch. Let's take her out for a friendly 'getting to know us' dinner later in the week. We'll invite all the others. She's bound to fuck up somehow. The only thing I don't understand is what the *fuck* Lib sees in her. Her tongue is practically forked."

"I know," Jinx said, glancing in the direction of Tanner House and narrowing her eyes. "I've been thinking that myself. You know what Lib's like—she's totally clueless and she's always loved a gimmick. And then there're the clothes . . . and the makeup . . . and the bloody handbags. And no doubt Ms. Fox has been filling Liberty's head with tales of dishy boys and derring-do at Bedales. Lib probably thinks she's, like, really sophisticated."

"You're so right, Jinx," Charlie said. "I heard them talking earlier and it was practically enough to make me lose my freaking lunch all over the quad. Sucking up doesn't even cover it. I've never seen anything like those two hanging onto each other's every word. And the snake wasn't mincing any when it came to her own accomplishments, that's for sure!"

"Anyway," Liv continued over her shoulder, sauntering off to the main school, "while you two have a cushty afternoon of sweet fuck-all to worry about, I'*m* about a million hours late for maths—and remember, ladies: don't get it twisted!"

Jinx and Charlie giggled, agreed to make the reservation, linked arms, and went off toward Tanner, thoroughly overexcited by the prospect of an afternoon spent mostly watching music videos.

13

Eight of the lower sixth-formers were sitting around a smallish square table with their knees touching in their favorite restaurant in town. Blind Lemon Alley served the best burgers, wings, and ribs—their number-one favorite foodstuffs—they'd had anywhere. And since it was tiny and practically invisible from the road, there was little chance any of the Stagmount staff would chance by on the prowl and catch them filling themselves to the brim with piña coladas, just the kind of sickly, creamy drink they loved.

It was such a small place, there was no room for any other customers on the top floor when they were there. This suited the girls down to the ground—they could be as noisy and offensive to each other as they liked without annoying any other diners. And because they always left such fantastic tips, the staff left them to their own devices up there. Since the drinks menu featured so many sticky cocktails and their favorite beer, Corona, it was inevitable that their chat would take a lewd downturn at some point in the evening, but they wouldn't have wanted to ruin anyone else's meal. This arrangement suited everyone.

Jinx was squashed in between Chastity and Chloe Thompson, with Liberty and Charlie opposite. Stella and Liv were at one end, and Amelia "Mimi" Tate had—as per bloody usual—space for both her elbows and her handbag at the other. Wherever they went, she always got the best seat. Even at really packed and scummy house parties with no beds anywhere to be seen, Mimi would skip downstairs the next morning stretching happily, looking fresh as a freaking daisy, having found a spare double complete with clean sheets and goose-down pillows.

Baskets of spicy chicken wings, mounds of deep-fried onion rings, and plates piled high with sticky barbecued ribs jostled for space amongst the beer bottles and cutlery alongside a token green salad sitting in front of Stella.

In between knocking back great gulps from her bottle, Chloe was holding forth. Because she was desperate to study medicine at Cambridge, Chloe had started working toward earning the Duke of Edinburgh's gold award that term in an attempt to beef up her application. Part of it involved community service, and she had to spend every Wednesday afternoon for the rest of term working in a local care home for the elderly. She was telling the girls what an absolute dump the place was, and had already christened all the people who worked there "granny bashers."

"So," Chloe said, giggling, "when I got there this incredible hulk of a woman—I swear she was butcher than Gunn—grunted, threw an overall at me, and told me to put it on before helping her clean all the bathrooms."

Chloe picked up a rib and gnawed on it reflexively before continuing. "So I'm down on my hands and fucking knees scrubbing shit off the wall—no, Jinx, I don't know how it got there and I don't bloody well want to know, either—when Butch Woman suddenly goes, 'What you doin' this for, then?' So I say I'm doing community service, and before you know it, the overall's been ripped off my back and I'm ensconced in a lovely little sitting room with a cup of tea, helping this sweet old dear with the *Telegraph* crossword."

"No, Liv, not the fucking cryptic." Chloe rolled her eyes. "She wasn't a day under eighty-five and probably suffering from Alzheimer's. Anyway, it suddenly occurs to me that the butch bitch thinks I'm in there to do *proper* community service—you know, like I've been arrested for something—and she's obviously scared I might lose my rag and run amok if she keeps giving me all the shitty jobs. I'm going to let her keep thinking that until the bloody thing's finished, too."

They all laughed. With her sleek brown bob, big green eyes, and flawless alabaster skin Chloe looked less like a criminal than Little Bo Peep.

Mimi was helping the waitress stack up all the empty

plates, and Charlie was down at the bar ordering one of the sickly sweet piña coladas that came in huge, fishbowl-type glasses complete with parasols and sparklers when Liberty asked Stella what the magazine poking out of her bag was. "It looks cool," Liberty said. "Chuck it over."

The girls were allowed to place orders for newspapers and magazines with the newsagent down the road from Stagmount, and Liberty's weekly stack of deliveries was so heavy Mr. Morris had to carry it inside for her. Probably as a result of all those long, boring holidays in Riyadh with no one to talk to, there wasn't a fashion, celebrity, or music magazine she wasn't intimately acquainted with.

Stella, who was looking very pleased with herself indeed as seven pairs of eyes focused on her, pulled the glossy mag out of her oversize Balenciaga and tossed it across the table to Liberty.

Pretty much the whole school was whispering about the mysterious new arrival's fabulous clothes, and every day she walked down the corridor as if she were striding down a Parisian catwalk—fully aware of the many pairs of envious eyes checking her out as she did so. She loved the attention.

"It's something we started at Bedales," she said, smug as hell. "One of my best friend's parents is in publishing and sorted out the computers and printing for us. We started it a couple of years ago. In fact, I edited this issue."

The girls craned over the table to peer at the front cover. In big letters at the top they could see the word CLASS, in smaller capitals underneath was SCHOOL HOLIDAYS: WHERE TO GO AND

WHERE TO AVOID, underneath that, even smaller, was WHO'S WHO: YOU AND YOUR PARTIES. The cover image was a picture of a blond girl wearing a ball gown, lying on an England-flag towel on what looked like a Cornish beach.

"Is it a fashion thing, Stella?" asked Mimi, who was reading the cover lines upside down. "I love that girl's dress."

"No," Stella sniffed. "It's about what it says—class."

"What?" Mimi smiled at her. "Actual classes? Lessons? What a great idea—was it just for Bedales? We've never had an in-school magazine."

Liv winked at Jinx as Stella frowned and recrossed her slim legs. "No, Mimi," she said, reaching for the magazine and stroking its glossy cover lovingly. "It's about *class*. Social class. We tell our readers where to go and who to be seen with and, more pertinently"—she paused to smile evilly around the table before letting her gaze linger on Chastity—"how to avoid coming into contact with common chavs."

Liberty looked confused, Mimi appalled, and Chastity and Jinx disgusted. Liv, who'd gulped down her entire White Russian during Stella's short explanation, suddenly started laughing so hard she slid down her seat and landed in a heap under the table.

"I'm sorry." Liv was snorting so raucously under there she could hardly get the words out. "But that is the most *ridiculous* thing I've ever heard. And you're telling us you had readers for this schlepp? Who were they—your mum and dad? Ha! Stop, it's too much."

Chloe had grabbed the magazine and was flicking through it, laughing and pointing out the worst headlines and photos. "*Class*? You should have called it *Ass*! Although I wouldn't wipe mine with it."

"Come on, guys." Liberty looked totally unsure of what was going on.

But Chloe's comment had sent Liv into further paroxysms. The others were smirking and giggling at Stella, too, by now. Only Chastity sat ramrod-straight in her seat with a face like thunder.

"You can't be serious," she said, with what the others recognized as her most furious expression on her face. "You're telling me someone—a proper publisher no less—actually paid for you idiots to print this shit? I think it's *disgusting*."

Chastity pointedly turned her back on Stella and said to Charlie, just back from the bar, "Thank God my parents sent me to Stagmount." She twisted back round to glare at Stella. "I'd probably be banged up for murder by now if I'd gone to Bedales."

Liv extricated herself from the tangle of legs, and when it became obvious that Stella wasn't going to help her up, Chloe stuck out a hand to pull her to her feet. Jinx leapt up to help their favorite waitress as she came smiling up the stairs bearing a huge tray loaded with delicious calypso coffees, and asked for the bill. "Come on, guys," she said, downing her coffee in one. "We'll be late back if we don't get a move on!"

Stella grabbed her magazine and stuffed it back into her

bag. Chastity threw some money on the table, said goodbye to everyone except Stella, and raced off to see Paul. *Class* wasn't mentioned again, although Liv and Chloe couldn't stop themselves from emitting the odd involuntary snort.

They made it back to Tanner House with a minute to spare, said good night, and disappeared off to their rooms. Jinx, who'd paused to check the telephone message register, held the swing door open for Fanny Ho, who was wearing Hello Kitty pajamas with green haviana flip-flops and standing outside signing a credit card receipt for a motorcycle courier from Feng Sushi. He handed over a huge bento box, and she made her way back in.

"Thanks, Liberty," said Fanny, grinning shyly at her.

"Er, I'm *Jinx*." Jinx was pretty pissed, but still surprised Fanny had got her name wrong, given how long they'd known each other and how different Jinx and Liberty looked. She squinted at Fanny. "You look different," she said. "If I wasn't so pissed and probably not seeing straight, I'd say you were someone else entirely."

Jinx shook her head, confused. "Anyway, we played tennis together about fifty-five times last term, remember? I can't believe you forgot my name!"

"Oh God." Fanny looked confused. "Sorry, Jinx. I've been doing . . . calculus . . . for hours—it's obviously turned my brain to mush."

"Hey, don't worry about it. I kept calling my friend Davina 'David' last Christmas. She wasn't amused, but I did have the most almighty hangover. I'm glad I don't do maths anymore," Jinx said as she gestured toward the food. "I'd be the size of a house if I ate all that."

"Yes," Fanny said, giggling bizarrely as if this was the best joke in the world. "All those, erm, equations have made me absolutely starving. Good night!"

14

Two weeks later, Jinx, smoking a covert cigarette during chapel time in the garage one morning, was less than delighted to overhear Stella and Liberty talking round the back. "The thing *is*, Liberty," Stella had said in a disgustingly patronizing voice, "you're seventeen years old. You should have had at least five boyfriends by now. I've had loads."

"Yes." Liberty sighed, obviously desperate to impress her new friend. "But I just haven't had the opportunity. And my dad would kill me if he thought I was seeing anyone. And then them, probably. Actually, make that definitely—and he'd definitely take me out of Stagmount. He's really hot on stuff like that."

"Fuck him," Stella retorted nastily. "It's none of *his* business what you do. And how would he even know? Don't worry, Lib, I'm going to take you under my wing. Show you a good time."

Jinx ground her teeth and stubbed out her cigarette as she listened to the two of them walk off, making plans for a wild night out to rectify Liberty's boyfriendless situation and giggling about something or other. Fucking Stella! All the rest of them knew exactly what Liberty's dad was like and did their best to protect her—especially when he flew into one of his psycho rages. They'd even gone so far as to write lists of things she should say to calm him down when she was expecting one of his regular enraged phone calls.

Jinx was thinking about the latest call—Amir's fury when he'd spotted a year's subscription to *Marie Claire* magazine on his bill. He wasn't cross about the cost—hell, no. He had been concerned about the "slutty" stories and "practically porn-star" photo shoots his daughter was obviously being corrupted by. Liberty had been so upset that Jinx had posted a copy of the magazine to Amir, with a letter pointing out all the campaigning journalism it contained. He'd calmed down almost immediately.

Jinx, staring at the floor and chewing the side of her thumbnail, was thinking about how she could never imagine Stella doing the same or even caring much, when Fanny Ho strolled in clutching a packet of Marlboro Reds. Fanny looked almost as startled to see Jinx as Jinx was to see her.

"Since when did *you* start smoking, Fan?" Jinx enquired, looking confused. "I thought you hated it!"

"Um." Fanny seemed to blush before quickly turning round to grab one of the upturned milk crates the smokers sat on.

"Yes, you're right. I *did* hate it but . . . now I don't."

"Well," Jinx smiled at her, "I can't argue with that. Welcome to our humble home."

"I'd love to stay and chat," she added, getting to her feet and grabbing her bag, "but if I don't dash up the drive right this second, I'll be seriously late, and judging by her deeply unreasonable behavior yesterday, Mrs. C is in one of her nut-job moods. See ya!"

Fanny—who Jinx thought was looking very relieved about something or other, only she didn't have the time to stay and find out what it was—smiled and waved as Jinx bent down and crawled out from underneath the half-shut garage door. Jinx shook her head when she got onto the drive and rubbed her eyes. Fanny looked different again, but Jinx couldn't put her finger on how. Jinx looked at her watch and did a double take. "Shit," she muttered. "I'm going to be late if I don't get a move on."

Jinx flew down the drive to tutor group, half an eye on the time and the other on the decidedly stormy-looking sky above her. Christ, she just couldn't stand it when the weather began to change for the worse. Every single year about this time, when the swallows started preparing to fly away, she felt miserable and moody and wanted to join their flight.

She made it into her seat seconds before Mrs. Carpenter swept through the door. Mrs. C was still in one of her furious moods, and all the girls groaned like mad when she informed them that now was the time to start seriously preparing for their mock exams next term.

Between those, lessons, matches, and house plays, they could find no spare time for anything much at all.

Jinx was on her way to lunch when she spotted Liberty and Stella way ahead of her in the queue. She couldn't help but think that Liberty, much as they all loved her, was not the sharpest tool in the box and still had zero idea as to how much Jinx and all the others disliked Stella. Jinx felt weird about it.

15

First thing Monday morning after a particularly boozy half-term holiday, Stella and Liberty—who had been bonding steadily ever since the hockey-ball incident and really were joined at the hip by now, and who were ridiculously delighted to see each other after only a week apart, having only known each other for three weeks—were both slouched on an overstuffed beanbag in the common room, flicking through the papers. Jinx and Chastity were lying top-to-toe on the best sofa, watching MTV *Dance*, staring enviously at Brittany Murphy dancing around in Oakenfold's new video, and shoveling down Coco Pops.

Jinx was also mulling over how she'd tried to speak to her old friend Jennifer from prep school to ask her what she knew about Stella. None of them had any idea why Stella had left Bedales: they'd all asked, but she always coyly replied that as

Stagmount was far higher up in the league tables, her parents had wanted her to move so that she would have a better chance of getting into Oxford.

Jennifer was the only person any of them knew who'd gone to Bedales, and so it was left to Jinx to find out as much as she could over half-term. This detective mission wasn't helped by the fact that Jinx had ignored all of Jennifer's friendly overtures for the last three years since their row about slaggy behavior, but Jinx had been trying her best to re-extend the hand of friendship to get the answers she wanted.

She'd telephoned Jennifer's house and gotten her mother. Damn it, she'd never liked the woman much. When Jinx was growing up, she'd been famous for sending her daughter to birthday parties clutching a Tupperware box filled with tofu pieces, grapes, and carrot sticks, and instructing the other mothers not to let Jennifer have any of the jelly and ice cream the others so happily tucked into.

"Oh, hello, Mrs. Lewis," she'd said in the politest voice she always used on parents. "It's Jinx. Jinx Slater. Is Jennifer around at all? I'd like to invite her to a small party at my house tomorrow night."

Mrs. Lewis broke down in tears—not the best response Jinx had ever gotten.

"Gosh," she'd said, desperately holding back the nervous giggle that was threatening to leap out of her throat, "I *am* sorry to have called at such a bad time Mrs. Lewis. Is, um, everything okay?"

"Nooo, Jinx." Mrs. Lewis was really sobbing now. "It's not. Not at all."

"Er, right," said Jinx, imagining the worst and suddenly feeling a bit sick. "Is Jennifer, um, all right?"

"She's in the hospital." The floodgates really opened at this point, and all Jinx could hear for the next couple of minutes was heavy breathing interspersed with huge sniffs.

"Mrs. Lewis, I am *so* sorry, I really am." Jinx was appalled. "Can I ask what happened? And Mrs. Lewis, if there is *anything* I can do, please tell me and I'll do it."

"That is so kind of you, Jinx." Mrs. Lewis finally found her voice. "But you see—gulp—the thing is—gulp—I had to—gulp—have her sectioned.

"She's not allowed any visitors," she went on, "and I haven't even spoken to her on the phone—for *weeks*." The sobbing started again in earnest, and Jinx, who had been truly shocked into silence, couldn't think of anything to say.

"Er, if you don't mind me asking, Mrs. Lewis," Jinx faltered, just before hanging up, not wanting to upset her further but desperate to know, "what was wrong with her that you had to do that?"

"She was surviving on an apple a day. A single apple! I'd always made sure she ate healthily, but over the summer she fell to 85 pounds, and her father insisted I do something about it. I blame that bloody boyfriend. I always told her he was no good. Why she couldn't go out with one of those lovely Bedales boys, I'll never understand. Anyway, he dumped her and she simply stopped"—Mrs. Lewis was clearly about to become incoherent again—"*eating.*"

Jinx's frustrated thoughts about how she might get in touch with Jennifer were interrupted when Stella held up the *Daily Mail* she was reading, pointing out the center-spread feature entitled "Girls Out of Control," accompanied by a huge color picture of two gorgeous-looking girls slumped on a step outside a nightclub. "Aren't lowlifes just gross?" she drawled, smoothing an eyebrow, clearly pleased with herself. "Look at the state of that. Makes me so pleased to be me.

"I don't have *any* friends who didn't go to private school," she continued proudly, "and looking at this, I'm glad I don't."

Jinx sat up instantly, knocking Chastity's half-finished cereal all over the floor, all thoughts of Liv's plan to let Stella hang herself forgotten. "You are so *fucking* stupid," she exclaimed. "Weren't you just telling us—in long, bloody boring detail, I might add—about how pissed you got all half-term with your stupid Chelsea friends?

"How is that *any* different to a load of girls going out in"— she snatched the paper and scanned the picture caption— "Newcastle and doing *exactly the same thing*?

"Just because," Jinx continued, her voice getting louder and louder, ignoring Liberty's stunned expression, "*you* might go out and drink champagne cocktails wearing Gucci dresses, it doesn't make you any better than them. In fact, I know who I'd rather hang out with, and it sure as hell isn't you."

Jinx jumped up and flounced out the room before Stella

had a chance to say anything, closely followed by an admiring Chastity. Chastity winked at an incoming Fanny Ho, noticing only in passing that her hair seemed to be a lot shorter than it had been last night when they'd been watching—for about the zillionth time—*Dirty Dancing*, their number-one favorite film. Those Chinese girls were so trendy, they seemed to change their hair as often as they brushed their teeth.

16

After a lunch break spent in their rooms, desperately dashing off the rest of the incredibly long French composition The Dick had assigned them, Liberty, arm in arm with Stella, yelled at Jinx and Chastity to wait up as they minced down the main school corridor toward double French with The Dick. First- and second-years flattened themselves against the corkboards filled to bursting with tennis and lacrosse fixtures, team lists, and drama society events as the sixth-formers approached.

Amongst Stagmount's many claims to fame was the dubious honor of having the longest corridor in any building in Britain. To the casual observer, the mud-stained brown carpet, curved ceiling, and myriad framed A-level artworks belied nothing more unusual than a walkway to maths. To the girls, however, the corridor was the site on which feuds and crushes were made and broken. Queen bees of all ages and their cliques reigned supreme and side by side, careful not to tread on the patch of anyone older than them.

Jinx and the rest paid no attention to the younger girls. Not out of spite, you understand: they simply didn't register their existence. They'd been in awe of the sixth-formers when they'd been in the lower school, and it was the natural order of things that the lower years would now be in awe of them.

Stella and Liberty, to Jinx's increasing but silent chagrin, were arguing about what they were going to do that weekend. "I'm bored to bloody tears with this provincial little town," Stella was saying, one of her customary sneers playing about her glossy lips as Liberty rushed to keep up with her.

Liberty wanted to stay in school and go out in Brighton on Saturday night with the rest of their gang. Stella wanted Liberty to go raving at Megatripolis at Heaven in London with her old Bedales mates. Jinx was frowning, half listening to Chastity wittering on about how much she hated her mother's new boyfriend, who'd taken them to Cannes for half-term, and half listening to Stella.

"Oh, stay, Lib, for fuck's sake," Jinx butted in. "I've hardly seen you recently, and we haven't all been out together for ages. It's not like you even know any of her Bedales lot anyway." Chastity's face fell as she realized Jinx hadn't listened to a word she'd been saying, and Stella pursed her lips together in excellent imitation of Renée Zellweger, who all the girls agreed had a face that looked exactly like an asshole.

Jinx was ripe for a fight after her outburst that morning and was just rearranging her features into her nastiest scowl when Lulu Cooper, Mimi Tate, and Chloe Thompson flagged them down, keen to check out what Stella was wearing today. The whole school was still stuck on eyeing her up every morning. Jinx found it more than a little irritating. These three were on their way from morning chapel to the same French class as the others, and talk quickly turned to the ridiculous amounts of homework The Dick had been setting and how much more they hated her than normal.

So, as they huffed and puffed their way up the steep, narrow, and winding staircase—clearly marked DOWN—to the languages department, which occupied the whole top floor, they were puzzled when an unusually silent, wild-haired Dick staggered past them, gripping tightly to the handrail that ran from top to bottom. Most of Stagmount's legends were all Greek to Stella, but she'd heard the folklore, so she also watched this highly unusual phenomenon with studied interest.

The girls always made sure to walk up the "down" stairs, and down the "up" ones, primarily, of course, to piss off The Dick. That she should walk past them going up the "down" and not have anything to say about it was a revelation, a proclamation that something was seriously rotten in the state of the French department.

Fascination turned to delight as they clocked a rivulet of blood running from somewhere above the ginger hairline, across her white and veiny forehead, down the side of her pasty face, disappearing, drip, drip, drip, into the open neck of her lilac shirt. Jinx snorted and nudged Chastity, whose jaw dropped faster than a porn star's knickers.

They stopped to stare, openly laughing and pointing in her glassy-eyed face by now, hardly believing their luck at finding The Dick so obviously caught short like this. Her faltering progress wavered as she tottered and seemed to miss a step. Liberty slowly reached out an appalled hand as if to steady her vacillating teacher, but drew back wide-eyed as The Dick regained her footing and continued her precarious, slow-motion descent.

"Hey," sniggered Chastity, sotto voce to Jinx as The Dick stumbled past them, "I guess French is off."

The girls whooped and hollered as they bounded up the few remaining steps and burst through the classroom door. Whatever had happened to The Dick, it was pretty clear that double French was off, and, best of all, they'd witnessed her agony firsthand. It didn't, of course, occur to them to go to her aid or fetch anyone for help. Why would it? They wouldn't piss on her if she were on fire. The Dick had tormented them for three years, and the only emotion they felt at her clear physical downfall was pure, unadulterated delight combined with exhilaration at the thought of the ultimate gossip they could save for the huge, and easily impressed audience in the canteen at supper that evening.

Lulu, the geekiest girl in the school, who wore glasses with lenses as thick as the bottom of a bottle of Grolsch lager, was the first to notice that one of the grand venetian blinds had come loose from its fixings and crashed to the floor.

As she stood, struck dumb, pointing a wavering hand toward the wreckage, the girls sent their desks flying in their haste to investigate the scene around and beneath the huge window, which looked out upon sea, sky, and blinding autumnal sun. The blind's partner was pulled down against the domineering light.

"Shit," sniggered a delighted Chloe. "It must have collapsed right on her head as she tried to pull it down." The girls collapsed themselves as they pictured the scene. Even quiet Lulu clutched her stomach and had to sit down, tears rolling down her chubby cheeks, the hilarity steaming up her thick glasses.

Jinx and Chastity clutched each other, both laughing so hard they fell over. They lay where they landed, atop the white shards of cracked plaster and silver screws that had fallen from on high, a mishmash of flailing limbs, rocking and sobbing so hard they thought they might never stop.

At least twenty minutes passed, in which no discernible sentences emanated from the shaking girls. As soon as one managed to collect herself enough to spit out an "oh, imagine the . . ." or an "if only we'd seen . . . ," it would cue a fresh fit of cackling, snorting, and snuffling.

Chloe managed to extricate herself from the flailing heap and was crawling doorward, with the charming warning that "I might actually piss myself," when Mr. Keyes's manly outline filled the doorframe. As the girls pulled themselves into standing positions and sought their seats, weak with hilarity, he surveyed the scene. A wry smile crossed the medieval history teacher's face as he simultaneously clocked the damage to the venetian blind while positioning himself behind the lectern at the front of the class.

"Girls," he said, his ear-to-ear grin somewhat inappropriate given the circumstances, "I am sure you have by now realized that Mrs. Dickinson will not be taking your class today. She has suffered . . ." Here he paused, presumably to lend his words some much needed gravitas. ". . . an accident, and is being taken to the Royal Sussex County Hospital as we speak. Mrs. Bennett is taking her personally. It seems that one of the—ha, ha—blinds fell onto her head as she was attempting to pull it closed."

The class closed its eyes as one, struggling to maintain some semblance of composure.

"So," he concluded, wanting to get back to the very rare and dusty Norman manuscript that contained some fascinating new insights into the character of Edric the Wild he'd been examining through a magnifying glass in his study, "the sensible—ha, ha—thing would seem to be that you return to your studies forthwith and continue with your private revision." Mr. Keyes beamed his wide smile around the room like a helicopter searchlight—he thought Susan Dickinson an extraordinarily tedious woman—winked cheerily, and began to back out of the open door.

A whole free afternoon! All thoughts of their rift forgotten, Jinx, Liberty, Stella, and Chastity tripped as fast as they could down the "up" stairs, past the bursar coming up almost as fast, who ignored them as he furiously pushed buttons on his calculator, desperately trying to work out exactly how much the damage would cost to set right. They raced along the corridor in the direction of the old reference library, crashed through the huge wooden door next to the sanatorium, and emerged whooping and hollering into bright daylight above the stone steps leading to the tuck shop.

17

Ms. Gunn was lounging in her favorite overstuffed rose-patterned armchair, laughing out loud in disbelief as she read a report in the *Times Educational Supplement* about how physical punishments were bad for girls. Ha! She'd never read such a load of bloody old nonsense. Wasn't this supposed to be the newspaper of *record*?

Only that morning she'd laughed heartily as she packed five of her most evil fourth-years off to run around the grounds—which were vast—five times without stopping before breakfast. Since none would own up to the crime of stealing her beloved punishments book—a record of every punishment she'd ever dished out and to whom—she'd decided on one circuit for each of the cretins. They could whimper and protest their innocence as much as they liked, but she'd known it was one of them. Bound to be, always giggling and laughing about the place as if it were their God-given right to be happy.

"Yes," Ms. Gunn muttered under her breath to a cowering Myrtle, who was looking longingly out the window, "watching those breathless, tearstained girls crying as they ran in the freezing cold dawn from the window of my warm and cozy bedroom has definitely put me in a much better mood." She'd been beside herself with fury most of this term, she really had. She'd had to put up with being made to look ridiculous by Jinx Slater and Liberty Latiffe, being never quite fast enough to catch them at their antics—and they weren't even in her house anymore.

"It's enough to drive a woman to drink," she spat, once again in a sudden fury, as she took the hip flask filled with sloe gin from her pocket and took a long, unthinking slug.

She was still cross at her failure to catch *them* out: last week had been a particularly bad one as far as adding to her bad temper was concerned. She'd woken up unaccountably early on Wednesday morning, desperate for a wee. She wrapped herself up in her dressing gown and stumbled to the loo just opposite the front door of her flat without putting the lights on. Half-blind without the glasses she'd left on her bedside table, she sat in the dark and started to relieve herself, grunting with pleasure as the pressure on her bladder gradually released. "Much as I hate to admit it," she'd said, fondling the hand towel drying on the radiator next to her, drunkenly assuming it to be one of Myrtle's silky ears, "maybe that bloody interfering busybody Sister Minton is right and I *have* been drinking too much."

After a minute or so she started to feel a strange sensation about her nether regions. Still half-asleep, it was a few more moments before she realized her bottom area was becoming drenched in some kind of warm liquid. "Bloody hell! Have I forgotten to pull my pajama bottoms down?" she asked of the hand towel, feeling about her sturdy calves on the floor before grabbing hold of the waistband, all present and correct where it should be. "No, I haven't. What on *earth* is going on?"

Since they'd never once been used, she didn't trust her pelvic floor muscles to stop the gush of tepid, foul-smelling wee midflow, and so she'd had to sit it out in the awful knowledge that the bunched-up back of her favorite ruby red dressing gown was undoubtedly becoming soaked through, too.

Ms. Gunn was confused and—most unusually for her—scared. Had she some sort of terrible medical complaint she had no idea about? Never one for looking on the bright side, she quickly decided she was dying, and that this was the first sign of the probably incurable disease her bladder was harboring. "Even my body has turned against me," she mumbled to her inanimate audience in the dark, dramatically wiping a single tear from her ruddy cheek.

She finished, shuffled to the light switch with her trousers round what the girls called her cankles—her calves went straight to her feet, ending in an unsightly overspill with no discernible definition where her ankles should be—and turned the light on. It took a few seconds for her eyes to adjust to the contrast before she noticed the sagging piece of wet cling film wrapped around the bowl underneath the loo seat.

Her relief in the knowledge she wasn't about to kick the bucket was swiftly replaced with furious rage that she'd been the victim of such a disgusting prank. And it had clearly been meant for her—she was the only person who used this bathroom. As the inevitable migraine began to throb around inside her head, she'd attempted to jump up and down with fury, forgetting that her sopping wet trousers were still down around her ankles.

In the manner of a carthorse hobbled for the night by its gypsy owners, she'd swayed, tried to steady herself by grabbing hold of the top of the radiator-cum–towel rail, and fallen crashing to the floor, landing in a cooling pool of her own putrid piss.

And then, as if desperate to add insult to injury, the stainless-steel towel rail had started creaking ominously before deserting its fixings and landing on top of her with an almost jubilant thud. "Oh, oh, oh," Ms. Gunn gulped, crying for real now. She hefted it off her, propped it against the wall, grabbed her hand towel, and gave the soaked floor a very cursory mopping, sobbing all the while, before she stumbled back to the sanctuary of her bedroom and her bottle of Talisker.

Unable to get back to sleep after drinking down half the bottle while cleaning herself up using a kitchen tea towel—which she returned to its drawer without rinsing—she'd lain in bed dreaming up the worst punishments she could think of before thumping down the stairs to breakfast with a face like thunder, intent on putting the fear of almighty God into her houseful of reprobates.

The only thing she could feel good about was that no one had seen her shame. Not even Myrtle, she belatedly realized, when the dog jumped out of her basket and poked a warm nose into her hand. "It's true what they say about dogs and man," Gunn had whispered tenderly to the shocked whippet, who'd never before known a kind word from her ill-tempered mistress. "You're my only friend."

Belinda Brown and Mary Hammerhead never had to put up with this sort of caper in their houses, she was sure. She could think of no reason on earth why her girls felt the need to behave so shockingly badly.

She'd stood up and screamed and shouted at her Wollstonecraft girls with such intensity at breakfast, practically purple in the face, that one of the dinner ladies had come in and asked if everything was all right and whether the housemistress was aware that everything she was saying could probably be heard all the way down at the marina. How Gunn had screamed at that! Even the bloody kitchen staff thought they could cheek her with impunity.

Not one of the little bitches had owned up, of course, so she'd gated the entire house for three weeks straight and banned them all from visiting the ice cream shop for the rest of term. Some of the parents had complained, as per usual, but she'd refused to return any of their phone calls, and most of them were too wary of igniting a deeper rage to complain further. And those who did could rest assured their daughters would wish they hadn't.

Anyway, nicely recovered by now, she was enjoying the sea breeze whispering through the window, calmly flicking through the pages of her *Times*, and thinking that this week was going really rather well so far. One concerned parent had rightly decided that bribery was the only option if her daughter was to be allowed out to attend her sister's wedding, and sent her a huge Harrods hamper full of delicious treats.

Another parent had a holiday request coming up and had couriered in a magnum of vintage Taittinger champagne. Gunn was planning—if she could keep her fat hands off it in the meantime—to invite that lovely Susan Dickinson to share it with her one night next week. She thought about how much she admired Susan and smiled to herself once more.

This pleasant reverie was destroyed by whoops and yells coming from the ice cream shop. Dashing to the window to check that none of her girls had the bare-faced audacity to ignore the housewide ban she'd placed them under, Gunn was appalled to see Jinx, Liberty, and that silly blond Chastity Something-or-other jumping about and screaming, clearly delighted by some evil deed.

"Look, Myrtle," she crowed, "we know they all smoke— maybe this time we'll catch them in the act!" It wasn't a bad enough offense enough for a suspension, but they'd get fined and it would be fun to see them squirm all the same. She just *knew* they did it—their moronic glazed eyes and constant stupid giggling at nothing gave them away—but she'd sadly never caught them at it.

She reached for the trench coat she'd flung across the sofa and was gratified to see her punishments book underneath it. Of course! She'd been reading through it in here last week. Feeling very pleased with herself indeed, she called Myrtle and rammed her ridiculous Nancy Drew glasses on top of her head.

Liberty insisted on treating the others to cheese-and-onion crisps and Diet Cokes in honor of their wondrous good fortune and The Dick's demise. Clutching their bounty, they raced down the closely mown green lawn and past the hockey pitches to the cricket pavilion just in front of the fence that separated the school from the road and, beyond, the sea.

They flung themselves onto a patch of slightly longer grass seaside of the pavilion and out of view of the main building. They lay on their jumpers and stretched luxuriously like cats in the fresh air.

Jinx reached into the side pocket of her book bag and pulled out a big bag of weed, a ripped and torn packet of long silver Rizlas—the only papers she would use—and a half-smoked Marlboro Light. She took a long swig of her Diet Coke and stuffed a handful of crisps into her mouth.

Stella was still droning on about Megatripolis to Liberty, who squinted at her from behind the slender hand she'd thrown up to shield her face from the sunlight. Chastity giggled as she rolled over toward Jinx.

"I cannot fucking believe The Dick. Whoever said pride comes before a fall was sooo right." Chastity sighed with extreme pleasure, rolled her head from side to side against the grass, and emitted a truly majestic snort.

Jinx nodded acquiescence but couldn't speak, as she was pulling one side of a Rizla tight between her lips at the same time that she was twirling the mixture of tobacco and weed into a tightly rolled slim cone with two careful hands.

"Hey, Lib." Chastity sat up, giggling: she was obviously quite stoned. "Do you remember that time you and Jinx put all Gunn's stuff outside?" She roared with laughter at the memory. Jinx and Liberty had been suspended for two days during the summer term of their third year for taking all of Ms. Gunn's furniture out of her flat and setting it up in exactly the same position on the lawn outside her window. Unfortunately, it had rained in the night, and Gunn had insisted that heads must roll. Mrs. Bennett had had to agree with her but had telephoned Caroline Slater to explain about Amir Latiffe's incredibly short fuse regarding any breach of behavioral standards on the part of his daughter and asked if she might accommodate Liberty, too. Caroline had naturally told her daughter everything, so Jinx was well aware of the special circumstances that applied to Liberty.

"Yep," giggled Lib, shaking Jinx's arm, "and once again poor old Jinxy baby had to take the flack!"

Chastity roused herself to peer round the corner of the pavilion—they took turns to check every five minutes to make sure no teachers were heading their way—before quickly leaning down to stash the half-smoked spliff in the secret compartment at the bottom of her backpack.

It was ridiculous, actually, that being caught smoking weed was an offense that called for instant expulsion, yet being blind drunk on alcopops outside the supermarket at the marina got the offender nothing more than a lightly smacked wrist.

"Gunn, two o'clock," giggled Chastity. They all laughed. Even in her short time at Stagmount, Stella had become used to the junior housemistress's ubiquitous evil omnipresence.

The girls whipped out their notepads, pens, and French textbooks, and pretended to be busily revising. By the time Ms. Gunn, huffing and puffing as if she'd just finished the London marathon, pounced from around the corner, they looked the very picture of innocence.

"What are you all doing here?" she snarled, furious not to catch them up to anything untoward. "Don't you have any lessons to go to?"

"No, Miss," said Jinx, affecting surprise at the sight of her old housemistress.

"A blind fell on Mrs. Dickinson's head and she's been rushed to hospital," Liberty added, spluttering as she turned a laugh into a cough, earning her a deeply suspicious stare from Gunn.

"What?" Gunn looked appalled. "What are you talking about? I spoke to her at morning break time and she was fine. If this is one of your silly jokes, Slater, it's not funny in the slightest. And stop laughing, Latiffe!"

"She's telling the truth." Chastity smirked. "Poor Mrs. Dickinson was in a very bad way. Mrs. Bennett's taken her to the Royal Sussex."

Gunn glared around at the girls, torn between deciding whether this was an elaborate ploy to get rid of her and punish them accordingly, or to race back up to the school to find out what had happened to Susan.

Susan won. Ms. Gunn spun round without saying a word and began her arduous progress up the gently sloping pitches. The girls killed themselves laughing at the unlikely friendship—who'd have thought *either* of the old dragons had any friends, let alone each other—before contentedly sparking up their spliff for the second time.

Chastity was bidding Paul, her handyman boyfriend, a fond farewell when Jinx burst into her room later that night.

"Shit. Sorry, guys," said Jinx, completely ignoring their snogging, clearly not planning on leaving any time soon. "How're you doing anyway, Paul? Not seen you for ages."

She really did like him a lot. At first Chastity had only started seeing him to piss her mum off, but she'd fallen for him big-time and they'd been going out for seven months.

"Fine, ta, Jinx." Paul smiled at her before turning to hug Chastity goodbye. "I've got to run—I'll leave you two to it."

He sprang out the window, blew Chastity a kiss, and waved before disappearing into the night.

Jinx kicked off her shoes, lay facedown on Chastity's bright pink bed, and moaned. "Shall we get a pizza in, Chas?" she mumbled into the pillow. Ordering in takeaways was one of their favorite sixth-form privileges. "Stella is doing my *head* in."

"I know, she's . . ." Chastity paused, rummaging about in her desk drawer before triumphantly pulling out a Domino's menu and her mobile phone. ". . . a bit of a weird one. Do you think she's actually, like, retarded or something? I can't work her out at all—I just know I don't like her. Where have she and Liberty gone?"

"I don't know." Jinx turned over and crossed her arms behind her head, frowning. "I can't help but feel a bit . . . left out, you know.

"Which is stupid," she continued, "because it's not like I want to go out with them anyway. It's just bloody Liberty. I wish she could see what a freaky little bitch Stella is, but she's just, like, totally obsessed with her."

Chastity ordered an extra-large Pepperoni Passion for delivery and pulled a bottle of very expensive pinot noir out of her cupboard.

"It's not," said Jinx, sighing heavily, "that I'm jealous or anything: it's just that I really can't stand Stella—she's so *fake*— and so the last thing I want to be doing is hanging out with her. There's something really poisonous about her; I just can't put my finger on it.

"Anyway," she continued, the frown fast becoming a scowl, "because Lib *does* like her, I'm not seeing anything of her at all. And," she added, her forehead wrinkling with the strain as her expression became blacker and blacker, "I can't help but feel that the more they hang out, the more likely it is that something's going to go terribly wrong for Lib. I've got an incredibly bad feeling about that friendship, and no matter how hard I try, I just can't shake it. But it's a catch 22, because if I *do* say anything to Lib, she'll just assume I'm jealous." Jinx sighed loudly and thumped the pillow in frustration.

"You know what you need," Chastity said, expertly uncorking the wine and pouring it into two of the ludicrously expensive Waterford crystal glasses she'd nicked from her mum's house. "A return to the band!"

They both sniggered, remembering their third-year attempts to put together the best air-guitar band in the world. Jinx, Chastity, Liberty, and a girl called Jessica—Chastity's best friend, who'd been expelled near the beginning of last term when a routine inspection had turned up a large bag of Ecstasy pills in her knicker drawer—had been the founding members of Fat Girls are Harder to Kidnap.

When Jessica left, they'd felt it appropriate to disband in honor of her memory, and they were also all a tiny bit bored of jumping about to Bon Jovi when they much preferred house music, not that they would have admitted that to one another. But even thinking about its name—the best band name in the world *ever*, according to Jinx, who'd thought it up—was enough to send them into paroxysms of glee.

Jinx sipped her delicious wine and thought about how inconsolable Chastity had been after Jess had been taken, kicking and screaming, to meet her lawyer dad at the police station in town. Jinx and Liberty had done their best, but not being in the same house had made it tricky.

Chastity started seeing Paul soon after, and he'd certainly filled the hole better than they ever could; and, knowing Chastity, in more ways than one probably. It seemed a lifetime ago.

"Chas," Jinx said, "I'm so pleased we're finally living in the same house."

"Me too," replied a clearly delighted Chastity with a big grin across her face. "The sixth form's great, even with Stella Fox in it." At the mention of Stella, Jinx's face fell, but then her phone bleeped. It was a text from her brother George inviting her and any friends she wanted to a party that weekend. She replied an almost instantaneous big YES PLEASE and fell asleep with a huge grin on her face for the first time since Stella had arrived.

Jinx screamed with delight and nearly fell out the first-floor common-room window she was leaning precariously out of when she saw George and Damian pulling up the drive in their battered VW Golf. It was only two weeks since she'd seen them both during half-term, but it felt like ages.

The boys' great pal Jamie lived in a palatial regency apartment on Brighton's seafront and was having a huge birthday house party. Jinx had naturally invited Liberty and Chastity. Unfortunately, Liberty had insisted that Stella come, too.

Jinx didn't want Stella to come at all, but she didn't want to put Liberty's back up and was even less desirous of being thought a big bitch in the manger and so had reluctantly agreed.

She just wished she could put her finger on exactly what her problem with Stella was. Apart from her gang, no one else seemed to see anything wrong with her—quite the opposite, in fact—but she made Jinx's skin crawl.

Jinx sprinted down the stairs, rushed out the door, and skidded to a halt beside the car's closed passenger door before wrenching it open and throwing herself onto Damian's lap. After the unfortunate incident with the lamppost when he'd been ogling a builder's bum, George never let him drive.

"Easy, tiger," he squealed in his usual high camp fashion as Jinx threw her arms around his neck. "I'm wearing linen trousers and they are gonna be so creased if you carry on wriggling about like that." He kissed the top of Jinx's curly head and winked at George.

"God," Jinx said, turning to throw her arms around George, "I have missed you guys *so* much."

They looked at each other, concerned. They were used to Jinx being thrilled to see them and to her enthusiastic greetings, but not at all to seeing her verging on needy like this.

"Is everything okay, darling?" asked Damian, a slightly worried look passing across his handsome face. "You seem a bit—I dunno—vulnerable. And that is so not the Jinx we know and love."

"Yes," said George, reaching over and squeezing her shoulder. "Anything your big brothers should know about? Not in trouble or something are you?"

"Oh God, nothing's wrong," said Jinx, suddenly horrified to feel she might be on the brink of tears. "I'm just so happy to see you, that's all. I don't know what's wrong with me at the moment. I just feel really emotional all the time—maybe it's PMS or something." Jinx had never once suffered even the slightest cramp. She smiled at them and surreptitiously scrubbed the corner of her eye with a somewhat dirty sleeve.

"Boys!" she exclaimed, worried by their concerned faces. "I'm fine, I promise. I'm so happy you're here, and I'm so looking forward to Jamie's party. I know you know that Liberty's coming, and I really hope you don't mind, but I've invited Chastity Max-Ward too—you know her, we were in *The Crucible* together last year. And a new girl called Stella Fox. Her and Lib are really quite friendly." Jinx sniffed involuntarily.

"Ah," Damian said, smiling his "wry" smile that he'd spent hours perfecting in the mirror while studying philosophy at Manchester, "is that what's wrong? Liberty's got a new friend and the apple cart feels all upset?"

"Humpf," snorted Jinx, both miffed and pleased that her brother had figured out the problem without her having to bring it up herself. "I don't know what's wrong with me, I really don't, but I'm finding this term really quite difficult, friendswise. Chastity's fine, as always. I'm really pleased to be in the same house as her, finally. We've talked about how great it was going to be since the freaking first year, and it is." Jinx paused reflexively and shook her head. "And Liberty's fine, too, except she loves Stella—everyone seems to, apart from Chas, Liv, and Charlie—and I really don't. In fact, if you want the honest truth, she makes me want to *puke*. And I don't want you guys to think I'm jealous—because I'm not, really I'm not."

Jinx stopped and ground her heels into the gravel as she spoke.

"It's nothing tangible I can put my finger on. . . . I just get a really bad *vibe* off her. And I know it sounds stupid and suspicious and jealous and all the rest of it, but it's how I feel and I can't help it. I guess if I'm really honest, I'm worried about what might happen to Lib. I know that might sound stupid, too, but you know what her bloody dad's like."

Damian and George had no time to reply as Liberty wrenched open the driver door and flung her arms around George's neck.

"George, Gaymian!" she squealed. "I'm so pleased to see you guys—how are you? How was the drive? What time are we going out?"

"One, two, three, *breathe*, Liberty, *breathe*," giggled Damian, who really did love Jinx's best friend. He looked her up and down and smiled.

"You look fabulous as ever, darling," he said in his gayest voice that he always reserved for matters of fashion. "Don't tell me, don't tell me." He frowned, putting one hand on his hip and pointing at her with the other. "*Dior?*"

"*Gaymian!*" she squealed, jumping up and down in the gravel. "You *know* it is, 'cos it says it on the front, doesn't it?" She laughed, fingering the hem of Stella's J'ADORE DIOR top.

"Oh, silly me, silly me," he continued, waggling his fingers at her. "I didn't notice that. I was looking at the unmistakable stitching—it's got 'Christian' written all over it."

George unfolded his long limbs and extricated himself from the front seat. He picked Liberty up and swung her round, cueing yet more high-pitched screams of delight.

He dumped her back down, patted her on the head, and began unloading a huge hamper from where it had been wedged in the backseat.

"What's that?" asked Jinx, eyeing it delightedly, for she was pretty sure she knew exactly what it was. Caroline Slater made up the best "Red Cross" parcels, and regularly despatched them to her offspring throughout the year wherever they might be. She was brilliant at knowing exactly when they were most needed, too. Jinx would have bet one hundred pounds that she knew what was in it without opening the lid. A sack of tangerines, all the clothes she'd left in a dirty heap on her wardrobe floor washed and ironed, a couple of bottles of Dad's nicest red wine, a massive bar of Cadbury's chocolate, and new shampoo and conditioner.

"It's for you from Mum," said George. "She says it's got to last you at least two weeks, which, since you're coming home then anyway, shouldn't be too hard."

Jinx, feeling her eyes fill with yet more inexplicable tears and not wanting anyone to notice, grabbed Damian's hand and pulled him along the path leading to Tanner House's front door.

George, carrying Jinx's massive hamper in one hand as if it weighed no more than a bag of sugar, followed behind with Liberty, who was still chattering excitedly about the night ahead.

Damian squeezed Jinx's hand and rested a reassuring arm around her shoulder. She gripped his hand back and mumbled an almost inaudible "thanks," resolving to pull herself together *tout suite*, as The Dick would say.

21

As they pulled up outside the very grand block of white flats on Marine Parade, Jinx felt a lot happier. She was sitting on Damian's lap in the front seat, next to George, who was driving. Liberty, Stella, and Chastity were in the back, singing along to Queen's "Don't Stop Me Now."

She loved her brothers so much. Whatever was going down, they always made her feel invincible and looked after. Also, no matter what she did or said, or how much they liked her friends, they would always take her side when it came down to it, no matter what and no questions asked. That's what brothers are for.

Jamie, George's pal from school and now the richest art student in Brighton, was a great guy and an extremely genial host. He had a huge trust fund and had bought this incredible apartment outright in his first week at college. He'd always felt slightly shady about his vast wealth, and so rented rooms out for practically nothing to his crusty sculptor friends and was constantly hosting champagne parties for the rest of his scruffy student chums.

Jinx really liked him, always had. Since the beginning of the summer holidays, in fact, she'd begun to feel distinctly hot under the collar at the very thought of him. So she was beyond delighted when he wrapped her in a huge hug and whispered, "Hey, you look hot stuff tonight, Jinxy," in her ear before ushering their gang up the stairs.

Chastity was dead impressed. "Gosh, thanks so much for inviting me Jinx," she said. "I really, *really* appreciate it. And I love your brothers—you're so lucky to have such a great family."

"I know," said Jinx, feeling a sudden pang as she thought about Chastity's disastrous mum and missing-presumed-dead dad. "And I'm really glad you're here. You'll love Jamie, and I know George and Damian like you loads already."

The boys disappeared into the kitchen and Jinx did a little dance at the top of the stairs. Much happier now, she was determined to have a great evening.

"Right, then, ladies," she smiled, mock curtseying, "let's have some fun. Basically, the only rule is, we leave when George and Damian do. No one leaves on their own or my mum will kill me, and then them, and then they'll never be allowed to take me out again. Then I'd have to kill you, and then my life would basically be over. *Capiche?*"

Liberty nodded, well used to Mrs. Slater's incredibly easy-to-keep rules, as did Chastity, who would have jumped off a cliff if Jinx had asked her to, so delighted was she to be out in town with such gorgeous older guys. Stella smirked. Although Jinx felt like punching Stella in the face, she smiled sweetly, spun round, and led the way into Jamie's capacious living room, where a hot Indian DJ was spinning house tunes from an impressive-looking pair of silver decks.

A very fit surfer dude wearing Diesel jeans and a faded green T-shirt with a silver dragon on the front was standing behind a shiny Art Deco drinks cabinet. He shook his silver cocktail shaker ostentatiously above his head and yelled at them to come over and grab a drink.

They didn't need asking twice. Clutching pint glasses filled to the brim with cachaça, lime quarters, mint, and crushed ice, the girls settled themselves down on some giant, sari-covered cushions artfully arranged in front of the double-glazed doors leading to the decked roof terrace complete with hot tub.

"Wow," said Chastity, her eyes on stalks, even though the Knightsbridge apartment she called home had been interior designed to within an inch of its life and contained every gadget known to man. "This place is *awesome.*"

"I know," Jinx said, smug as hell, and with one eye on where Jamie was standing talking to George in the corridor. "And check out all these cute boys!"

Stella slowly and purposefully crossed and recrossed her legs on the floor in front of her, flashing more than an eyeful of the yellow lace French knickers she was wearing underneath her extremely small distressed-denim miniskirt. Jinx ground her teeth and wondered, not for the first time, why Stella's clothes never seemed capable of covering her up for long.

Chastity was chatting to Paul on her mobile, telling him to get his ass down here pronto, and Stella had sashayed off to find the loo. Jinx threw herself onto the recently vacated leather beanbag next to Liberty, pulled out a ready-rolled reefer, and waved it in front of her face. "Share it, Lib?" she asked, nodding toward the roof terrace and winking.

It was freezing outside, but they snuggled up on a double rocking chair piled high with mohair blankets overlooking the seafront. They were sitting high enough up and far enough back to not see the road at all. Bloody Jamie—but at least he was sharing the wealth. It was like being out at sea up here.

They sat in companionable silence, inhaling, inhaling, and passing on until Liberty began convulsing with laughter. Jinx looked sideways at her friend and couldn't help creasing up herself.

The more Liberty laughed, the more Jinx laughed. Tears rolled down their cheeks and Liberty started to panic—as she always did—that she couldn't breathe. Jinx knew exactly what was going through her friend's mind. The redder in the face she went, the more uncontrollable Jinx became, until they were lying on top of each other in the by-now furiously rocking chair, screaming and squealing.

As they straightened themselves out, Jinx felt a zillion times happier. It wasn't just the weed, either. Liberty wrapped her arms around her and they sat like that, not speaking, for ages.

Chastity poked her head round the door, teetered as if she was going to say something, but then made as if to beat a hasty and silent retreat before Jinx shouted out to her to come and join them. "Come on, Chas," Liberty agreed, patting the space between them. "Come and sit down here!"

"Sorry, guys," Chastity said. "I didn't mean to get in the way or anything. I was just looking around for you, but if you're having a talk or whatever, tell me and I'll leave you be for a while."

"Shut up, Chas," said Liberty, amused. "We're just smoking a spliff, for Christ's sake. I feel like I've not seen Jinx a lot recently, or you—and I don't know why. But anyway, we're all here now, so let's enjoy ourselves. By the way," she continued slyly, one amused eye on Jinx, "have you noticed how a certain host can't keep his eyes off Ms. Slater here?"

"Shut up, Lib!" Jinx's face flamed fire-engine red as she cast desperately around for something, anything, to change the subject. Trust Liberty to hit the nail on the head like this for the first time in her life at exactly the wrong freaking moment. Jamie was her older brother's best friend, for God's sake! George was so protective of her, and she knew he'd think Jamie was too old for her.

It wasn't like she wanted to *go out* with him or anything— she just liked him, that was all. But George would go mad, she was sure of it. And now was clearly not the time to think about it, let alone discuss him with this lot, who were bound to take the piss. "How's the party, Chas?" she eventually and rather lamely asked.

"Brilliant. Paul popped down but he had to go and hear one of his mates play in a band down the road. Stella's snogging some guy in the hallway, and George and Damian are doing keg stands in the living room."

Jinx smiled gratefully at Chastity and pulled a second spliff from the inside pocket of her furry hooded parka. She passed it to Chastity to light—God, she *was* in a good mood tonight—and squeezed Liberty's hand. She tipped her head back against the extremely comfortable cushions behind her and gazed at the millions of stars lighting up the cold, dark night, thinking that really, whenever things looked bad, they always got better soon enough.

They didn't see Stella again until it was time to leave. She'd holed herself up in one of the two bathrooms with one of Jamie's dreadlocked artist friends. George got Chastity to describe him and laughed. "That's Rupert," he said. "He's an absolute *prick*." George was so rarely rude about anyone, the girls listened up and begged him to tell them why.

"Yeah," he continued. "He was going out with this great girl at school—we all got on really well with her. She even used to come to Southampton matches with us." George sounded incredulous. This was major praise—all the men in Jinx's family were manic about football and *fanatical* about Southampton.

At the mention of his beloved team, George bowed his

head and clasped his hands together in a highly pretentious moment's silence. All the Slater boys did it—even if you mentioned going shopping or to the cinema in the bloody place— and it was so incredibly irritating, Jinx punched him really hard at the top of his arm as punishment.

"Ouch!" he yelled. "That was a proper dead arm. Well done, Jinxy! Anyway," he went on, rotating his painful shoulder, "he totally fucked her over and we all thought it was a shitty thing to do."

"But what *exactly* did he do, George?" queried Jinx, raising her fist as a warning. "And if you don't tell us right now, I'm doing your other arm."

"The usual," sighed George, shaking his head sadly. "Fucked around all over town and eventually gave her a really nasty bout of syphilis. She was gutted."

"God," said Liberty, wide-eyed, "I didn't know you could even *get* that in the twenty-first century. I thought it was what Henry the Eighth and people had when they lived in, like, the Middle Ages and stuff."

"Ha," whispered Jinx in an undertone to Chastity as she banged slightly too aggressively on the bathroom door. "Imagine if he's given it to Stella—a particularly virulent strain! That would make my freaking day!"

They were still giggling as a somewhat disheveled Stella swanned out of the bathroom, closely followed by an admiring Rupert. "Don't call me, I'll call you," she said patronizingly over her shoulder, looking very pleased with herself as she carelessly shoved the crumpled piece of paper he'd given her with his number on it into her back pocket. As the others said their goodbyes and grabbed their coats ready for the waiting ride back with Jinx's brothers outside, Liberty stared admiringly at Stella. She was so busy looking at Stella that she didn't notice Jamie enveloping Jinx in an even huger goodbye hug behind the half-open front door, or the way Jinx blushed an even deeper red than before as he did so.

They slipped back into school, pretty wrecked, but through the front door this time, since dear old Mr. Morris—also a massive Southampton fan, who'd grown up in the area and was very taken with the Slater boys—had fully sanctioned their outing, even going so far as to tell them airily he couldn't care less what time they returned. In fact, he was so smitten, he'd waited up to see them in. "Gaymian, is it?" he enquired, throwing an arm around Damian's shoulder, clearly thrilled to have some male company for once. "That's an unusual name. Sit down boys, sit down. I'll make us a cup of tea."

George and Damian looked horrified at the thought of not being able to get away until the small hours, so Jinx apologized to Mr. Morris but said their mother would kill them if they were late. "Really, sir," said Jinx, "she'd go mad. She worries about them having car crashes. And she'd probably blame you." Mr. Morris prized a quiet life above all else and so quickly ushered the boys through the front door. When the girls had shouted their noisy goodbyes, they spotted Fanny Ho sitting on the sofa in the cozy hall area.

She was wearing her favorite Hello Kitty pajamas underneath a long pale gray woolen wraparound cardigan with pink Ugg boots. She waved shyly at the girls, asked them if they'd had a good time, and said she was going to bed.

Jinx, Liberty, and Stella collapsed onto the sofas while Chastity dashed off to her room to get them all a nightcap. Her closet was better stocked than your average bar.

Just after Chastity had gone Fanny reappeared. She was now wearing an I HEART NY T-shirt with black velvet tracksuit bottoms above bare feet.

"Bloody hell, Fanny," slurred an admiring Liberty, "you really *do* have more clothes than me. I've not seen you in the same outfit twice this term!"

"Ha ha, thanks, Lib!" said Fanny, more loquacious than she'd been a minute ago. "Has anyone seen my new Hong Kong *Vogue*?"

"Yep." Jinx pointed at the coffee table. "It's right there—you had it a second ago. You really are doing too much maths, Fan."

"You're right, Jinx." Fanny looked amused. "It's exhausting. Those, um, mechanics are keeping me up all night. I'm planning an extra-long lie in tomorrow. Can't wait! Night, girls." She grabbed her magazine and waved at them before heading back to her room.

"You know, guys," slurred Jinx thoughtfully, "there's something weird about Fanny this term. She seems . . . I don't know . . . different, I guess."

Stella raised an eyebrow and turned her back on Jinx. She

clearly didn't give a shit about Fanny or any changes Jinx may or may not have perceived in her since last term.

"Christ," Liberty said, still thinking about Fanny's apparently limitless wardrobe. "Anyone fancy shopping tomorrow? I refuse to be beaten in the clothes stakes by her."

"I will." Stella jumped in before Jinx could say anything. "There's an amazing new shop called Simultane in the Lanes. I read about it in *Marie Claire* last month. Fancy it, Lib?"

Liberty nodded and offered up her hand for a high five. "You coming, Jin?" she asked.

"Thanks, Lib, but I've got a pile of work to get through, and if I don't do it tomorrow, I never will." She smiled at them as she scooped up her bag and got up. "You two have fun."

Jinx lay in bed and wondered if she was being stupid. Okay, Stella was fucking irritating, but there was nothing concrete that Jinx could definitively pin the finger of hatred on. But before she could think about it any further she was asleep, dreaming about Fanny Ho sailing across the sea to Hong Kong in a giant wardrobe, using a Missoni dress as a sail.

Jinx woke up and stretched, feeling remarkably clearheaded despite the previous evening's excesses. She yawned as she reached over to push the switch on her pink Sony radio. REM's "Losing my Religion" was playing, and she suddenly felt like going to Sunday chapel service.

Unless exempt on religious grounds they were all expected to attend the daily service, but Jinx, who'd taken every opportunity to get up Gunn's nose, had usually not bothered. Now she rarely went in the week, since she mostly had to use the time to dash off a piece of homework—she always worked best right on deadline. On Sundays, however, chapel was optional. She looked at her watch, realized she had thirty minutes before kickoff, and decided to go.

She jumped out of bed and contemplated the piles of

clothes strewn across the floor. At the same time that she made a mental note to spend the afternoon cleaning up her tip of a room, she reached for the Sunday-best uniform hanging right at the back of the wardrobe. This consisted of a navy blue blazer with green trim, a pleated navy skirt, and a white shirt with a green-and-blue striped tie.

Every lower-school girl had to wear this uniform every day, but in the sixth form they could wear what they liked unless attending chapel on a Sunday, speech days—where they wheeled in some tedious old girl to bore them rigid discussing her glittering career, and all the parents wore sunglasses inside so no one could see them catching a surreptitious forty winks—school photos, and prize giving.

Jinx didn't mind the uniform at all. Navy looked great against her blond hair and lightly tanned skin, and it was actually a relief not to have to think about coordinating separates. Juicy tracksuit or jeans? Jumper or hoodie? Trainers or Uggs? Getting dressed in the sixth form took at least ten minutes longer than it had in the fourth and fifth. Today, though, she was out of her room and up the drive with fifteen minutes to spare.

She walked through the cloisters filled with rosebushes and past the ornamental koi pond and marveled, as she always did, at what a stunning place the chapel was. She stopped for a second, thinking about the rumor that one of the largest fish—donated by a Russian billionaire, delighted with his daughter's exam results, and which had sadly died a terrible death after it had a hole pecked in its back by a visiting heron—

had cost over a hundred thousand pounds. The pond was now covered with a stiff netting made of wire mesh. Not so stunning now, that was for sure.

Mrs. Stanwell, Stagmount's popular religion teacher, who was in charge of all church matters, stood at the top of the wide gray stone steps at the entrance and handed out sheets containing the order of service.

"Jinx Slater, how *lovely* to see you." Mrs. Stanwell was a very feminine woman who adored Jinx almost as much as she despised The Dick and Gunn. She was also highly impressed by the Chanel suits and Jimmy Choo shoes Caroline Slater sported at parents' evenings and sports days.

"How's life in the *sixth*?" Mrs. Stanwell just loved to gossip with the girls and spoke mostly in italics. "Isn't Mr. Morris an absolute *darling*?"

Jinx was about to reply in the affirmative when a suddenly skittish Mrs. Stanwell cut her off to greet the Reverend Martin McCloud, who was taking the service. "Reverend, you look *divine* in that suit. How *are* you?"

Jinx smiled at McCloud and waved at Mrs. S as she strolled past the vestry doorway into the cool arched nave. It was so big it could seat the entire school, all the staff, and at least three hundred parents.

It was really more of a church than a chapel, but today only the front four rows were filled. Jinx recognized the girls there as mostly juniors from Wollstonecraft. She smirked to herself, sending a silent prayer heavenward for Tanner House and Mr.

Morris. Forcing her youngest girls to attend the Sunday service en masse was obviously one of Gunn's new punishments.

Gunn herself was glowering down at the poor girls from her customary vantage point to the left of the organ. Jinx gave her wave and a jaunty grin. An enraged Gunn stared at Jinx, appalled, before glaring fixedly in front of her.

Jinx found a seat at the end of a free pew near the rear and leaned back to gaze at the absolutely stunning stained-glass window behind the pulpit. She'd painted a huge copy of it for an art project in the summer term of her fourth year and had loved spending hours at a time on her own in the cool chapel. A blinding shaft of light shone through the window, illuminating the order of service in her hand, and she glanced down at it.

SANITY AND SUBVERSION, she read at the top. THE THEOLOGY AND POLITICS OF LAUGHTER. Brilliant. She'd always thought church *should* be more fun. She smirked over the top of her sheet at the still-glowering Gunn. And they wondered why people didn't seem more interested.

Everyone stood up as one when the organ started pumping out its introductory notes and McCloud strode down the central aisle followed by a team of robed choristers holding candles.

He clambered up the steps to the pulpit and smiled genially around the room. He loved doing the Stagmount Sunday service, as he loved to see so many pretty girls staring up at him so appreciatively.

"Hello, girls!" His booming voice rang out around the

chapel. He loved saying that.

"Firstly, Mrs. Bennett has asked me to remind you of the fete being held at the beginning of next term." He winked jovially.

"Your parents have all been sent a letter, but please do remind them, because if no one turns up, it will surely be— boom boom—a 'fete' worse than death." They all laughed delightedly. He puffed his chest out—there was little danger of any member of *his* congregation dropping off when he was in full flow.

"To me," he said, beaming at the girls in front of him, "laughter is a form of prayer. A way of opening ourselves to life and God, a way of expressing the inexpressible delight we feel at being alive.

"Many people," he continued, a slightly more serious expression on his face now, "think of church as being a place for the pious and holy veneration of God. They think that in church you must be serious and respectful and even regretful. They will try to tell you that you must never reveal a sense of humor about religion or see any funny side of God."

Jinx leant back in her seat, folded her arms, and thought about what he was saying. She thought about the cultures of guilt, shame, and penitence that seemed intrinsic to so many modern religions and about how the world would surely be a nicer, better, and safer place if more people had a good old giggle about things rather than get so offended by them. She thought about Liberty's dad.

As the congregation processed to the front to take communion, Jinx sat and stared in amazement at how far Ms. Gunn's vast ass spread out over either side of her thighs as she knelt down in front of McCloud.

As the last of the procession took to their seats, Jinx gasped in delight as she clocked McCloud swigging down the rest of the communion wine in a huge gulp. She emitted an involuntary giggle and clasped her hand over her mouth, just managing to keep down a bout of hysterical laughter.

"Waste not want not," she hummed under her breath, grinning widely at a glaring Gunn, who was lumbering past on her way back to her seat.

After a lusty rendition of "Immortal Invisible," she shook Reverend McCloud's hand and thanked him for the service before filing out of the cloisters, strolling through the mainschool front door and into an icy breeze coming off the sea. The wind picked up as she walked back to Tanner House, and twice she nearly lost the scarf from around her neck.

At the same time that she shoved the house door open with her hip, the heavens opened. Jinx pressed her face against the glass and watched huge raindrops lashing down the other side. She thanked her lucky stars she'd said no to the shopping trip, grabbed her favorite You and Style magazines from the huge pile of communal Sunday papers on the coffee table in the hallway, shoved them under her arm without a single thought for anyone else who might want to read them, and decided to tackle her disgrace of a bedroom.

Jinx stuffed twenty-pence pieces into the soft-drink vending machine just outside the common room door and looked at her watch. A silver Tag Heuer that her dad had given her for her sixteenth birthday, it was one of her most favorite and precious things. She wasn't too fussed about designer clothes or flashy handbags, but the one item she'd never be seen dead with was a cheap watch.

She also loved it because she'd wanted one for such a long time, and her dad had chosen it himself. It wasn't the exact one she'd thought she wanted, the one she'd pointed out to her mum—it was better. And since everyone knows it's rare for dads to get matters of fashion right, she loved it all the more because of that.

It was twelve o'clock. Jinx leant down to grab her Diet Coke before it got trapped in the temperamental tray at the bottom.

She flipped back the ring pull and took a long, reflexive swig of the stuff she called brain fuel. Forget fish oil: DC was the business. She realized she had at least another six hours or so before Stella and Liberty got back from Brighton. She pushed in three more twenties and a backup can released itself with a loud bang.

Muttering an apology to Lulu, whose room was also next door to the common room and who was—given the anguished moans she let out every time the noisy machine was used—obviously trying to have a lie-in, Jinx turned left instead of right and started up the small flight of stairs that led to the third floor.

She rarely ventured up here, as most of her friends lived on the first and second floors, and she much preferred seeing people in Chastity's room anyway, as Chas always had the best booze in her cupboard.

She walked down the dimly lit corridor peering at the names on the doors. Gosh, Chloe lived up here too—Jinx had no idea. As she approached the bathroom at the end, she saw Stella's name badge stuck to the fourth door on the right and looked around before pushing it open.

Not that anyone would question her. And anyway, if anyone *did* ask what she was doing in there she could say she was returning something . . . or borrowing something . . . or leaving Stella a note. Anything, really. There was very little stealing at Stagmount in general, and there'd been none whatsoever in her year since they'd caught Tiffany Bigsworth with her hand—

literally—in Liberty's knicker drawer at the end of the first year.

Liberty's dad was fond of giving her large wads of cash with which to pay her school fees and keep herself in shoes and pizzas at the beginning of term, and once she'd paid her visit to the bursar, Liberty just used to stuff the rest of it in the back of her jumbled-up pants drawer.

Liberty never had any idea how much money she had and certainly never bothered to count it, but even she realized something was up when the cupboard was bare after only ten days. And they weren't even allowed out unaccompanied past the marina in the first year, and there are only so many bottles of shampoo and packets of Tampax a girl can buy in the supermarket at the Marina, after all.

They all thought it odd but assumed that scatty Liberty had somehow mislaid the cash . . . until her replacement wad also disappeared. Amir Latiffe agreed to replace it once more but said—and in fairness, one could hardly blame the man—that this was the third and final time he'd bail her out. Terrified at the prospect of no more shopping trips, the girls had set about masterminding the catching of their thief.

They'd tried hanging surreptitiously around outside the room, but since they all had lessons at the same time in the first year and precious little free time in between, their spying had come to nothing. It had been Liv who'd finally come up with the master plan. They agreed to mark a cross on a fifty-pound note and leave it right at the top of Liberty's cash pile. When—as expected—the wad went missing again, the girls had sent Daisy to see their housemistress.

Since Ms. Gunn fancied herself as some kind of girl detective anyway, and sneaky Daisy was easily her favorite pupil, the old goat had immediately galvanized herself into action. Calling all of their year to wait in Wollstonecraft's drawing room, Gunn had set a crack team of her older favorites to systematically search the first-year rooms and bags and gone through all of the notes they'd unearthed, checking them for Liv's distinctive red cross.

She'd finally found the offending fifty hidden in Tiffany Bigsworth's makeup bag, and a lot of other fifties scattered amongst her possessions. Tiffany had left the same day, and no one had missed so much as a pound coin since.

As Jinx quietly pushed Stella's door open, she decided that although she knew snoopers normally only find out bad things about themselves, there was no law against it, and anyway, she needed to familiarize herself with her enemy.

In fact, the only thing she was beginning to feel weird about was that she'd been on her own pretty much all day. Even if she wanted to, she normally never had a bloody *chance* to feel lonely at Stagmount—there was always someone around. Apart from today, of course, which, she reluctantly admitted to herself, was probably why she was feeling the loss of Liberty so acutely.

Jinx stood in the dim light in Stella's doorway and looked around. She pushed the door closed behind her and switched on the light. Unlike Jinx's, and in fact pretty much everyone else's, Stella's room was very neat.

Her bed was perfectly made with crisp white sheets, and there was not a makeup brush out of place on her chest of drawers. Next to the crystal lamp on her bedside table was a large silver photo frame. Jinx assumed it was Stella's mother inside and moved closer to bend down and peer at the picture. She snorted as she realized the black-and-white photograph was a blowup of a stunning-looking Stella. It had obviously been taken professionally and was admittedly gorgeous, but really—what kind of person has a photo of just *themselves* by their bed, however attractive?

Smiling to herself, Jinx turned round to inspect the photos Blu-Tacked to the corkboard by the bed. Her smile grew wider as she realized they all showed Stella, invariably looking fantastic, and that pictures where she'd obviously been standing next to someone else had been covered with ones of just her. It was like Stella Fox's wall of freaking fame in here.

She turned round to face the opposing wall and laughed as she clocked all the designer carrier bags hanging from pins around the wardrobe. Chanel, D&G, Emporio Armani, Moschino—they were all there, plus many more. Jinx imagined Stella staring at the wall in a trance. It was set up like a shrine to high-end capitalism.

Liberty had all that stuff, too, but Jinx had never seen her hang the bloody bags on the wall. And in marked contrast to all the other boarding school rooms she'd ever been in, there was not one note from a friend, not one photograph of a dog or cat, and nothing in here to suggest the girl had any friends or family whatsoever.

Although Stella was obviously far more in love with herself than even Jinx had thought possible, there was nothing incriminating in here. Jinx wasn't sure what she thought she would have found anyway—she'd just fancied a snoop. She switched off the light and left. She couldn't put her finger on exactly what was bothering her as she walked back down the corridor toward her own room, but she was feeling very uncharacteristically uneasy about something.

24

Jinx flopped onto her bed and looked round her own room. The only neat thing in here was the huge American flag she had hanging over her bed. She was obsessed with America, and hated, hated, *hated* people who said Americans were stupid. Jinx genuinely believed that all the best living English writers were American. Philip Roth or Martin Amis? John Updike or Tony Parsons? She knew who *she'd* choose. And what about their incredible movies, their fantastic music? She sighed, took a final gulp of Diet Coke, and thought that maybe she'd clear up her room tomorrow.

As she reached over to stick her current favorite Killers into her CD player, she smiled and picked up the rather dusty photo of the Slater family in its dirty silver frame that sat next to her bed alongside the Polaroid of her and Liberty.

She plumped her pillow behind her head, crossed her legs, and studied the photograph. It had been taken at Martin and Caroline's twenty-fifth wedding anniversary party last summer, and all the Slaters were grinning like mad. In fact, Jinx herself, although she was wearing a stunning outfit, had her eyes shut—it was a recent development that she couldn't seem to stop herself from blinking whenever a flash went off, and as a consequence, there were precious few photos of her with her eyes open.

She didn't care. All the others looked gorgeous, and it had been such a happy day and a wonderful party that she loved the photo more than any other. It even had their beloved boxer dog, Flash, in it, lying at Damian's feet with his trademark big slobbery grin all over his beautiful squashy face. It had been such a hot day, too, she thought, looking miserably out the window at the wild sea and massive raindrops still lashing down. This terrible weather was enough to drive a girl to drink.

She wondered whether it might be time to pay Chastity and her well-stocked wardrobe next door a little visit. As she was deciding between red wine and more Coke, her mobile phone started playing its slightly tinny rendition of *The Great Escape*'s theme tune. Jinx replaced the photo on her nightstand and grabbed the phone from where she'd chucked it on the floor, scrutinizing the screen. She didn't recognize the number, and blushed scarlet as the unbidden thought that it might be Jamie popped into her head.

"Hello," she said brightly, just in case. She sat up and

automatically reached for her second Diet Coke.

"Jennifer!" she half squealed when she recognized the voice on the other end, surprise causing her to sit up straighter and spill sticky Coke all over her white pillowcase. She righted the can, stuck the phone between her ear and shoulder, and absentmindedly brushed at the drops with her free hand. "How are you? I thought you were . . ." She paused. How the hell were you supposed to ask someone you hadn't spoken to in about three years whether they were calling you from the nut house?

"Hi, Jinx," said Jennifer, "I'm fine, you know."

Well, *no*, Jinx didn't know, but Jennifer *sounded* pretty normal—especially for someone who'd only very recently been let out of a mental institute, anyway.

"Mum said you rang the other day about wanting me to go to your brother's party or something. I cannot tell you . . ." Jennifer paused to laugh in a rather self-consciously bitter fashion, ". . . how much I would have loved to be at one of your Slater parties rather than stuck in Clouds with that bunch of freaks."

"Ahem." Jinx coughed, unsure of how to proceed from here. Christ, she could barely stand dealing with people who had *colds*, let alone a certified mentalist.

"Don't worry, Jinx." Jennifer let out another bitter laugh. "I'm totally fine—it's my mum who's gone totally stark fucking raving mad. Just because I broke up with Todd and lost a few pounds she convinced Dad I was a looner and had me banged up in that Berkshire hellhole before I had time to realize what was going on."

"God, Jen." Jinx was appalled, but not sure what she thought about the whole thing. After all, would a clinic like that even *accept* a girl as a patient if she weren't clearly an anorexic? It surely wasn't the kind of thing you could hide . . . was it?

"I'm really sorry," she continued, trying to push any hint of skepticism out of her voice—Jinx had known Mrs. Lewis for a long time and had always thought she was a Froot Loop and capable of pretty much anything. "How awful for you."

"Yah." Jennifer laughed again, a lot less resentfully this time. "But it wasn't all bad. There were a few lead singers and a gorgeous Hugo Boss model—Jorge. He and I managed to keep each other entertained!"

"But what about your mum? . . ." Jinx tailed off, wondering whether the amnesty on never ever slagging off any of your friends' parents or siblings no matter what they'd done could be broken, given the unprecedented evilness of Mrs. Lewis's actions this time.

"Oh, fuck her," Jennifer spat out. "You know what she's like. So fucking bored she's always tried to live her life through me. I think she *wanted* an anorexic daughter. They're all the rage amongst stay-at-home, home-counties mums who claim it's the worst thing in the world but are secretly delighted about having girls who can fit into the latest Missoni bikini and look like they might be model-spotted at Victoria Station."

"Right," Jinx agreed, to keep the peace and because she thought Jennifer was indeed beginning to sound a bit mad, but she was shocked. True, she'd never liked Mrs. Lewis much, but she would no more speak about her own mum like this than she would take any of her brothers' friends sides against them. It just wasn't done.

"Anyway, Jinx," Jennifer carried on, "I'm at home for the next week—supposedly 'recovering' but in reality bored out of my fucking mind—and Dad's driving me back to school next Sunday. I'd love to see you. . . . It's been ages. Are you around over the weekend?"

"Yes, I am." Jinx was delighted. In the shock of hearing Jennifer's story and the venom she'd reserved for her mother, Jinx had clean forgotten the reason she'd tried to get in touch with Jennifer in the first place. Yes! She was finally going to find out about Stella. "I'm back on Friday, although probably quite late. Do you want to come round on Saturday—about lunchtime? You can spend the day at my place if you fancy it— sounds like you might need a break."

"Brilliant." Jennifer paused and Jinx could hear a muffled banging from Jennifer's end of the line and then a loud "*Just fuck off, will you? I'm on the fucking phone!*" Then: "See you then, yah. Must go—looks like the bloody woman's set up a vigil outside my bedroom door."

Just as she was about to say goodbye, Jinx realized the line had gone dead. Gosh, Jennifer did sound different. Jinx didn't remember her ever sounding so harsh or brusque.

She lay back on her bed and made a mental note to ask her mum to give them some kind of small salad for lunch on Saturday. Jinx still wasn't entirely convinced that Jennifer's mum could have had her daughter sectioned in an institute if there really was no problem, and she didn't fancy making Jennifer uncomfortable if Caroline laid on one of her usually massive meals.

Christ, thought Jinx as someone tapped quietly at her door. Most of her friends never bothered to knock, nor did she. *What now*?

A faintly grimacing Fanny Ho slipped through the door and sat delicately down on top of the pile of clothes on Jinx's desk chair.

"Hi, Fanny." Jinx grinned at her and gestured around the room. "Sorry about the mess. I'm supposed to be having a cleaning binge today, but things keep conspiring to put me off. How's tricks?"

"Fine." Fanny smiled, although Jinx thought she looked a bit put out. "I'm just wondering if you've got any Vaseline I can borrow?"

"Vaseline?" Jinx looked confused and thought she detected a hint of a squirm as Fanny made her request, but jumped off her bed and started rummaging through the wicker basket she kept full to bursting with every beauty product known to man, woman, and beast beneath her window.

"Got a cold sore or something? Tell you what," she said, chucking the pot at her, but not looking too closely at Fanny's face as she shuddered involuntarily—she really couldn't *bear* any suggestion of less than perfect health, and she *certainly* didn't even want to look at a total gross-out cold sore. "You can keep it and get me a new one!"

"Thanks, Jinx," Fanny sounded positively relieved and then smirked. "I'll definitely get you a new one. You're right—you probably won't want this pot back once I've finished with it."

Jinx half glanced up at Fanny's face as she thanked her—*very* profusely for such a small favor—and left the room, but she couldn't see any sign of a cold sore. Fanny's face *did* seem thinner, though, and why would she now never go anywhere without a baseball cap squashed down over her forehead? A*h, well, it could be because of the cold sore,* she supposed before finally deciding to give the cleaning up as a bad job and seek out Chastity for a nice glass of wine and a spot of MTV D*ance.*

Ms. Gunn sat behind the desk in Wollstonecraft House's study, her bloated face almost as red as the pen she was holding in her hand and using to slash thick red lines through much of the first year's history essays stacked up in front of her. She was furious that she'd been asked to mark it due to the junior-history mistress Theodora Thomas's taking a week off to attend a conference in Albuquerque on the teaching of the First World War.

Albuquerque? Bah! She'd never even been on so much as an away day to Bognor bloody Regis, let alone anywhere overseas.

Today was no different. She'd lugged the groaning pile of prep around with her for most of the week, but in between doling out detentions, supervising thousands of lines—I *must not tell lies, especially to Ms. Gunn; I must not tell lies, especially to Ms. Gunn—*

and stuffing her face with the contents of a large tin of sugared pineapple confiscated from a fifth-year for no reason whatsoever other than that she could, she'd simply not seemed to find the time to get round to it.

She slashed a line right across the first page of one poor girl's paper from top to bottom so vigorously that the pen nib tore straight through to the page underneath. Gunn growled and looked out the window at the rain lashing down outside: it was so heavy she couldn't even see the sea beyond, let alone the games pitches where she'd sent five fuming fourth-years to pick up litter as penance for giggling after lights-out.

Ms. Gunn really was furious about the weather. Normally she didn't give two hoots whether it rained or shone; in fact, she often preferred the former since it meant she could hole up inside, shoving vast quantities of food into herself with impunity and much fewer demands on her precious time. But today she felt bitterly about it, as if even God himself was against her—and she could hardly put him in detention, could she, much as she might have liked to.

During one of her unnervingly solicitous phone calls asking after Susan Dickinson's slowly returning health, Ms. Gunn had tentatively suggested to her friend that the two of them might enjoy a health-giving ramble on Devil's Dyke—ooo, she just *loved* it up there—with Myrtle that afternoon. Since Ms. Gunn was not in the habit of issuing invitations, largely because she had no friends, she'd been delighted when Mrs. Dickinson had accepted and had been looking forward to it for the last two days.

Gunn growled furiously again at her misfortune and turned back to her marking. She gave each paper only the most cursory glance before running riot across it with her red pen and was gratified to see that the "marked" pile to her left was growing steadily higher than the "unmarked" one in front of her. As she slashed, she consoled herself with the thought that at least Susan was due to return to teaching at Stagmount next week.

Gunn's small smile turned quickly back into her customary screwed-up frown as she recalled Jinx Slater giving her that cheeky wave in chapel. Really, who did that devil child think she was? Cheeking a senior mistress like that was unforgivable, especially in front of the whole school. Gunn felt a familiar prickling in her palms as she thought about how dearly she would like to bend that particular reprobate over her knee and give her the kind of beating she'd never forget.

Thinking of Jinx always made her furious, and fury always made her hungry, so Gunn swept the pile of prep papers to one side and reached for the secret sweet tin she always kept fully stocked with confiscated goods underneath her desk. She fished about in it and grabbed a king-size Mars bar, ripped it open, and gnawed off more than half with her first bite, filling her big mouth fit to burst with sticky chocolate and caramel.

At that very moment, deeply unfortunately for both of them, Christina Walker's debonair barrister father, Tony, chose to stroll into the study, hand outstretched in greeting only to hesitate just inside the doorframe. He blanched slightly and lowered his hand, evidently disgusted by the sight that greeted him.

"Ah, hello, Ms. Gunn," he said, unable to remove the last hint of disdain from his handsome features despite his poker-face courtroom training. "How are you?

"Good, good. Now . . ." He paused to smooth one of what looked like his suspiciously dyed eyebrows. ". . . Christina begged me not to say anything to you, but really I felt I had no alternative under the circumstances."

Gunn was still chewing masterfully and attempting to gesticulate an apology for her inability to speak, but it would have been obvious even to a blind man that it was no single solitary toffee stopping up that fat mouth, just as she was clearly no loveable grandma.

"As you know, Christina has been off sick for a week with a nasty cold." He coughed slightly.

"As I was driving her back to Stagmount this afternoon, she started crying and told me she thought she needed another week at home. Now, her mother and I are reasonable people and we trust our daughter implicitly but it was obvious to us that while she might be fully recovered physically, there was something upsetting her *psychologically*."

Gunn attempted to make a concerned face, but it came out as more of a grimace.

"Eventually," Mr. Walker continued manfully, trying to look anywhere but at Gunn's by-now-puce face that was dripping with sweat, "she admitted to me that there *was* something bothering her. And it was not—as we had assumed—a problem with her classmates, but rather a problem with *you*, Ms. Gunn.

"Yes, she told me that she and four of her pals had been made to get up at the crack of dawn and run around the grounds as punishment for a crime she assures me none of them had committed.

"And furthermore"—Christina's father was getting into his stride now, wagging an authoritative finger at the despicable Gunn in front of him, delighted the old goat was clearly not going to be able to interrupt him having his say as she always had in the past—"she said that none of them were allowed to wear jumpers or overcoats and that it was a particularly freezing cold morning.

"In fact, Ms. Gunn, I would not be at all surprised if this"—he shuddered theatrically, rocked on his heels, and stared fixedly at a point somewhere above the housemistress's head—"so-called punishment was the root cause of my daughter's illness."

Gunn's bloodshot eyes were bulging out even further than normal, and she was waving her arms about her head as she finally forced the last gulp of the sticky, masticated mess from her mouth down her throat.

"Mr. Walker," she gasped, such exertion having made her voice a mere shadow of its formerly booming self, "that is absolute nonsense!

"Yes." She was getting back into her stride remarkably quickly for one who had literally been rendered mute a few seconds before. "I *did* send Christina and some others out on an early morning run, and, my good man, I can assure you the punishment was well deserved."

"But—" Poor old Tony was cut off before he could even begin to respond properly.

"Christina and her friends thought it amusing to steal—and yes, thank you, Mr. Walker, I know full well you are a man of the law, *steal!*—my punishments book."

Gunn stood up to make her point and, thanks to the rather short pair of sailing shorts she was sporting underneath her demure navy crewneck sweater, Tony was treated to the horrific sight of her huge mottled calves, fatty knees, and grotesquely bunioned feet as she emerged from behind her desk.

"Thank you Mr. Walker, I think that's covered everything." Gunn slowly and deliberately turned her small eyes toward the paper on top of her pile. Mr. Walker, feeling as if he was back at Eton for the first time in twenty-five years, stood in front of her for a second before realizing that he had been dismissed without so much as a by your leave.

Ms. Gunn thoughtfully nibbled on the remaining end of her king-size treat. She nursed grudges like they were patients in intensive care.

She chortled with glee as she made her decision and a corresponding note in her punishments book to get one of her pet house prefects to conduct a full and thorough search of all Christina Walker's personal effects. The girl was bound to have a few illicit cigarettes or bottles of alcopops hidden somewhere in her room, and when Gunn found them—*To hell with it*, she thought as she slapped her huge thigh. If there wasn't anything incriminating in there, she'd plant it herself!—the little sneak would have far worse than an early morning run to deal with. That would teach the spoilt little brat to get Daddy to come in and try and have a go at her housemistress.

Licking her fat lips with pleasure at the thought of this imminent outwitting of yet another one of her juniors, Ms. Gunn gathered up the rest of the history essays, called for Myrtle, and began her torturous ascent up the wide, red-carpeted staircase to the sanctuary of her little flat and an early evening snooze.

26

Jinx was in the middle of a deep and dreamless sleep when she was suddenly awoken by a loud tapping at her window. She checked her watch, saw that it was half past five in the morning, and groaned as she extricated herself from underneath her huge goose-down duvet and pulled the curtain aside.

Liberty stood outside, swaying and stumbling. Although she was wearing what Jinx recognized as her smartest indigo Miss Sixty jeans stuffed into brown-and-white patterned cowboy boots with her new cream French Connection cardigan over a Moschino Cheap and Chic bright pink T-shirt, she was covered in splotches of mud and, by the state of her hair, looked as if she really had been dragged through a hedge backward.

Jinx flung open the window and saw that it wasn't only rain

pouring down her friend's face—Liberty was also sobbing uncontrollably.

"Fucking hell, Lib, what's wrong, sweetheart? Don't move, darling, just hold on a tick. . . ." Liberty leant against the wall outside as Jinx jumped off her bed and ran to get the miniature screwdriver kit she kept locked in her tuck box.

Liberty was still crying as Jinx unscrewed the safety bolts, threw the window wide open, and jumped out to give her pal a leg up.

By the time Jinx had scrambled back in and slammed the window shut behind her, Liberty had wrenched off her filthy cowboy boots and was curled up on Jinx's bed sniffing huge involuntary gulps every thirty seconds and looking extremely woebegone. There were muddy stains on Jinx's navy blue duvet cover and clumps of wet grass sticking to the fluffy white rug that covered the floor—Caroline Slater had been right: white anything for Jinx was always an ill-advised choice—but neither of the girls paid the mess any attention.

Jinx pulled her curtains closed, squatted down in front of Liberty, and used her thumbs to wipe the tearstained mud tracks from her best friend's face before pulling her into a huge bear hug. Liberty started bawling even harder, and Jinx rubbed her back and stroked her hair, knowing she wouldn't be able to get a decent word out of her until she was all cried out.

They sat like that for ages, Jinx rocking Liberty gently until her sniffs became more infrequent and her great gulping breaths returned to something resembling normality.

"Right, then." Jinx was getting a really bad cramp in her thigh, feeling more exhausted than she could ever remember, and simply had to change position. "Let's have it, Latiffe. What's happened?"

"You know I went shopping with Stella. . . ." Liberty paused for a solitary sniff. Jinx nodded encouragingly at her to continue. She'd just *known* it was something to do with that bitch. "Well, we were having a really good day. You know, shopping and stuff, and then we decided to go and have some drinks in that blue bar on the seafront.

"Everything was fine. In fact . . ." Liberty stopped again and gave Jinx a watery smile, ". . . we were talking about you." Jinx arched a skeptical eyebrow but didn't say anything.

"Yeah, she was asking me about you, and I was telling her how great you are and how long we've been friends and all about your family and that amazing time we went skiing in Canada. You know, just chatting about stuff."

"And?" Jinx prodded her gently as Liberty paused to stare into space. "Then what happened?"

"Well, we'd had a couple of bottles of wine and were about to leave to come back to school when these two blokes who'd been sitting near us in the bar came over and offered to buy us each another drink." Liberty sniffed again and looked on the verge of more tears but managed to pull herself together and carried on. "It was getting late and I didn't really fancy it, but Stella insisted—she was really, like, *adamant* about it—so I phoned Mimi and asked her to sign us back in the register. I knew Mr. Morris wouldn't check, and I thought we'd only be an hour or two late anyway so it wouldn't matter even if he did.

"When I realized it was way over curfew, like past midnight or something, I stood up and said we should go, but Stella said she was staying. . . ." A few more hot tears escaped Liberty's eyes and started falling down her flushed cheeks, but Jinx carried on stroking her back and she continued. "I said I was going to the loo and that when I finished I was going back to school even if she wasn't.

"She laughed at me and told me to stop being such a baby, said that Mr. Morris was so old and stupid he wouldn't notice anything amiss and that I should just lighten up. I didn't want to say anything in front of the boys, so I just said we'd talk about it when I came back.

"Jinx! I knew you'd blame her." Liberty had belatedly registered the look of black hatred on Jinx's face and was quick to defend Stella. "It wasn't her fault. You've never liked her, and I don't want you to use this as an excuse to hate her even more. Let me finish, okay?"

Jinx nodded her assent while privately wondering whether it would be possible to hire some kind of hit man to inflict maximum damage and pain but stop short of actual murder. She quickly decided against it. She wanted to take care of this one herself. She was also surprised to find herself in exact agreement with Amir Latiffe for once in her life. "Anyway, when I got back to our table, Stella and one of the guys had disappeared, and the other one—I can't even remember his *name*, for God's sake—was holding my bag. He said they'd gone to another bar and that he'd help me get a cab. I was really tired and, you know, drunk and grateful so I went outside with him."

Liberty clearly *couldn't* be trusted to handle herself around any guy desperate to get into her knickers.

Jinx's face was white with fury and she felt an incredible urge to leap off the bed right then and there, run down the corridor and up the stairs to Stella's room, and kung-fu kick the door down before grabbing hold of the back of Stella's stupid side ponytail and smashing her face repeatedly into the wall of photographs by her bed until it resembled nothing more than a messy pulp of blood and shattered bone. "And then what?" she asked, through gritted teeth, clenching her fists by her sides.

"So we're walking past the pier and we can't see any cabs. He says we should walk further up toward the school and wouldn't it be nice to walk along the beach. . . ." Liberty was crying for real again now.

"And?" Jinx looked relatively calm, but she felt that if she opened her mouth again actual steam might come out in a hot, fiery spurt like the breath of a dragon. She clenched her fists until her nails dug into her palms so hard they started to hurt. She couldn't remember ever having been this cross.

"Well . . ." Liberty shuddered. "As we got down onto the beach, he grabbed me and tried to k-k-kiss me, so I pushed him away and said I wasn't interested and that I just wanted to get back to sc-sc-school and that I needed a taxi.

"He didn't look bad or anything, and I thought he was so

nice helping me with my bag and the cab and everything, so I turned to walk up toward the road and h-h-h-he *pushed* me." Liberty stopped and looked at Jinx through her puffy red bloodshot eyes—she was clearly still very upset.

"And?" Jinx asked again, her usually warm voice colder than ice.

"And I fell over and he leaned over me and sp-sp-spat on me, called me a 'frigid Paki bitch,' grabbed my bag, and ran off."

"He grabbed your bag?" Jinx's mind was whirling.

"Yes," Liberty wailed. "He ran off with it. Jinx, it was my Mulberry *Roxanne!*"

"For Christ's sake, Lib, don't worry about that!" Even though she was appalled at this story, Jinx still found time to wonder about Liberty and her bloody ridiculous priorities. "So how did you get back?"

"Well . . ." Liberty hung her head, looking more miserable than she had since she'd climbed in Jinx's window. "I had *nothing* on me. No phone, no wallet, no change, nothing. I didn't know what to do."

"Most people would consider that a good time to go to the police," Jinx mumbled sarcastically.

Liberty threw Jinx a sharp look as she heard what the latter was muttering under her breath and shook her head. "Shut up, Jin—I could hardly call the fucking *police*, could I? How would I explain not being at school at two o'clock in the fucking morning when they brought me back here? What if they phoned my *dad*?

"Anyway, so I started walking back along the sea road and then cut across the miniature golf course thinking no one would see me if I slipped in the back way we always use. Everything was fine—apart from my feet, which are absolutely killing me—until I saw two guys walking in the opposite direction and got the fear that *they* might be muggers and rapists, too.

"I threw myself behind a bush so they wouldn't see me, only to land full-on in a ditch—right on my ass. After all this rain, it was *filled* with filthy mud." Liberty shuddered again before continuing. She was so fastidious, she wouldn't go on a country walk in even the lightest drizzle. The thought of her splashing about in a dark, waterlogged ditch was enough to raise a smile from Jinx—who couldn't stop thinking how awful it was that Liberty preferred to take her chances with a rapist than phone her dad, admit she was in trouble, and ask for help—but it didn't last long.

"We've got to *do* something." Jinx was apoplectic again, bouncing up and down, her tiredness long forgotten. "That bloke should be locked up. This is Stella's fault. I am going to actually *kill* her. I'm going to fucking murder her." Jinx stood up in a rage and punched the wall. "And I'm going to do it right now."

"Jinx!" Even through her gasping sobs, Liberty managed to insert a note of menace into her tone. "How many times do I have to tell you it's *not* Stella's fault—she wasn't to know what would happen. If anything, it's *my* fault for deciding to leave when we were all having such a great time."

"Why can't you see it, Liberty?" Jinx was raging now, and

nothing was going to stop her saying her piece. "You could have been raped tonight, or beaten up or . . . worse. I don't care how many handbags she's got, or *boyfriends*. Just what does she have to do to make you realize she doesn't give two shits about you or anyone else?"

Liberty sat up in protest, muttering under her breath about "not understanding" and "overprotectiveness" and "we were just having fun," but Jinx had whirled out the door and was halfway up the stairs before Liberty had even had time to flop back down on the pillows.

Stella was nowhere to be seen. When Jinx got back to her own room she found Chastity—who'd been rudely awoken by the furious punch to the wall she and Jinx shared—also lying on her bed, getting the full story from a much happier-looking Liberty.

"Fucking hell, Lib." Chastity was incredulous. "I can't *believe* she just upped and left you like that—with some bloke you'd never even fucking met before. Anything could have happened to you. . . ." Chastity tailed off as Jinx gave an almost imperceptible shake of her head.

"Anyway, Lib, I'm so glad you're okay. You two must be exhausted. You've not got anything until double French at eleven. Are you—do you want me to sign you out in the morning so you can sleep until class?"

"Yes, please!" Jinx was delighted by the thought of a nice lie-in. "Thanks, Chas, you're a star. And trust me—Stella fucking Fox is going to wish she was anywhere but here when I've finished with her."

Chastity returned to her bed, and Jinx and Liberty cuddled underneath Jinx's king-size duvet. Jinx was just drifting off to sleep when Liberty mumbled something under her breath.

"Jinx," she asked again, louder this time, "why do you think he called me a Paki?"

"I don't know, darling," Jinx replied, stroking Liberty's arm, a beam of white-hot fury rushing from her heart straight to her head. "I don't know."

27

Jinx checked Stella's room again as soon as she woke up, but she'd obviously not been back at all. Her white bed was as perfectly made as it had been the night before, and her matching towel was dry.

It was fifteen minutes before she and Liberty were due at dreaded double French, so Jinx rushed downstairs and into the kitchen/dining room where the lower sixth made and ate their own breakfast.

She walked in to find Liv and Charlie sitting on a table, swinging their legs in unison and wearing matching horrified expressions as Liberty repeated her tale of the night before while haphazardly spreading four slices of wholewheat toast with butter and Marmite.

"You never do the bloody corners properly." Jinx grabbed

one off her and chewed off a huge bite all the same. "Hi, guys. So, what do you think about fucking Stella's latest, then?"

"Fucking appalling. You know . . ." Liv shook her head and pulled out a packet of Camel Lights, tapping one on the table before lighting it up and leaning backward to blow a long, thoughtful plume of smoke out the open window behind her. ". . . . I can't help but think all this might have something to do with *you*, Jinx."

"What are you talking about?" Jinx was confused. "I don't like her. I've never liked her and she knows it. And she's certainly not going to be any friend of mine after treating Liberty like that. In fact, she's going to wish she was dead when I'm finished with her."

"That's my point!" Liv tried to flick her ash out the window but missed, and it landed on the inside sill. "I think she's jealous of you. Maybe she wanted to be friends with you when she got here but realized you and Lib were joined at the hip and decided to muscle in. I think she's very manipulative—an arch-manipulator, in fact."

Liberty's eyes were flicking between Liv and Jinx as if they were tennis players batting their words back and forth in a rally. "I don't understand," she said. "Stella is *always* asking me about Jinx, and anyway, we'd had a really good day yesterday. It's not like she could have known anything bad would happen to me last night. She was just pissed! And come on—it's not like *we've* not done stupid things before."

Charlie snorted loudly before jumping down off the table,

saying she had to get to orchestra practice. Jinx looked at her watch, grabbed a piece of toast with one hand and Liberty with the other, and followed Charlie out the door. Liv ran her cigarette end under the tap, chucked it out the window where it joined a fetid pile of damp half-smoked fags, waved them off, and turned back to studying the pages of chemical equations she'd spread out on the table in front of her.

"Jinx . . ." Unusually for her, Liberty looked cross as they marched quickly up the drive. "Stella will be in French, I'm sure of it. And I don't want you having a go at her. I know I was upset last night, and she probably shouldn't have dumped me like that, but she *is* my friend, and I don't want any rows."

Jinx mumbled a noncommittal response but rolled her eyes over Liberty's head at Charlie as they swung through the main door, said their goodbyes, and waved Charlie off to orchestra practice in the chapel.

As Jinx and Liberty raced up the "down" staircase to double French, they caught an unmistakable whiff of terrible body odor mingled with Parma Violets coming from the classroom. Damn it, The Dick was obviously back. Jinx wondered if this day could possibly get any worse as she and Liberty pushed through the door.

"Jinx Slater, Liberty Latiffe." The Dick stood in front of the class, looking—as much as she could, with her practically albino skin, bright ginger hair, and horribly contrasting flushed cheeks, anyway—the picture of health. "How very kind of you to grace this class with your presence. I want both of you in my office at lunchtime, writing me a three-page essay on why promptness is the essence of good manners."

Jinx glowered at her as she threw herself into her seat, but didn't say anything—she knew full well that if she did, she'd likely find herself writing pointless essays in The Dick's cramped and airless office every bloody lunchtime this week. She craned her neck and looked round the room; Stella was nowhere to be seen.

"So . . ." The Dick turned round and tapped the board behind her with her thin silver meter rule. "As you will see here, the forms of the present subjunctive are similar to the present indicative forms. In many cases they are indistinguishable. . . ."

As The Dick droned on and on, Jinx doodled in her notebook, thinking about what Liv had said that morning. She decided it was absolute nonsense that Stella was using Liberty to get at *her*. Christ, she'd barely spoken a whole sentence to the girl since the hockey-ball incident, didn't know anything about her, and didn't bloody want to, either. And even if Stella hadn't *intended* anything bad to happen to Liberty, it was sheer fucking lunacy to leave her on her own with some unknown bloke in the middle of the night. And regardless of anything Liberty had to say about it, Jinx was going to tell her that, too.

"So, Jinx . . ." The Dick always licked her bloodless lips before she pounced on an unsuspecting victim. "If the stem of the verb remains the same, what would the subjunctive ending—"

At that moment, Stella slipped through the door, thankfully throwing The Dick and her impossible question off course.

Wearing a dark gray pencil skirt and a pristine white T-shirt with muted makeup and flat shoes she looked the picture of innocence—not at all, in fact, like someone who'd been up all night drinking bourbon, smoking dope, and shagging a Brighton grunger in his dirty squat.

Jinx felt a grudging admiration at what was obviously an Olympic gold feat of endurance combined with excellent make-up skills. She felt it even more when Stella informed The Dick—in freaking French, for God's sake—that she'd been unavoidably detained at a doctor's appointment, apologized prettily for her lateness, and was rewarded with the closest The Dick could come to a warm smile.

Stella smiled sweetly right back at her and took her seat at the back of the room. Jinx glared at her but couldn't say anything from her seat in the front row right opposite The Dick's desk. She'd been caught in the act of writing a note to Liberty—*in the first year, for fuck's sake*—and had been made to sit here ever since, so The Dick could "keep an eye" on her. Make her life a misery, more like.

The bell signaling the end of their first lesson rang, but since they were trapped here for yet another forty-five minutes, none of the class packed anything away. The Dick was the only teacher who didn't let them have a little break in between the double to stretch their legs and have a chat, so they all sat there in bored and resentful silence as she plowed on.

"Right." The Dick clapped her hands together, giving the class a disgusting and entirely unnecessary view of her yellow sweat-stained armpits. "That's the present subjunctive dealt with. There will be a pop quiz on the subject next week, and I now want you all to take your seats at the language lab."

A general sighing sound rang out around the room as the girls scraped back their chairs and stood up. They hated the bloody language lab. Desks with radio equipment and head-phones made up three sides of a square at the very back of the room, and The Dick patrolled behind them as they listened to whatever turgid piece of French literature she'd decided to bore them rigid with that day before asking them to recall stupid details about it in one of her beloved pop quizzes.

"Come on, we haven't got all day. Stop dawdling, Mimi! Hurry up, Chloe!" She really was the most irritating woman—patronizing and rude, supercilious and haughty. None of them could bear her. They'd had such a lovely time with Mademoiselle Dupont, the junior French mistress who hated The Dick as much as they did, and had been subbing their lessons while the latter recovered from the bump to her head.

She twiddled the knob on the main control panel and their ears were filled with André Gide's *La Symphonie Pastorale*—even read by Gérard Depardieu, this was a strong contender for probably the most boring book in the whole bloody world.

Jinx looked up as The Dick lingered behind her before moving along the row. *God*, she thought catching a nasty whiff, the woman really did *stink*. Jinx was still looking after her and thinking this when she saw little Lulu Cooper, who couldn't hear a thing due to the heavy-duty headphones encasing her small ears, absentmindedly lean back in her chair to stretch out her legs and pull her hair back into a ponytail.

The Dick was craning her neck to peer over the backs of the girls in the opposite row at the exact same time as Lulu's chair thrust back out of line with the others. Jinx's eyes widened and she held her breath.

Bingo! The unseeing Dick walked straight into Lulu's chair and flailed wildly as she caught one of her legs in it and lost her footing. Jinx had jumped up and was clasping her hands in front of her. Her prayers were answered.

The Dick floundered and flapped to save herself, but the only thing at hand was the corner of the small square table that sat in the middle of the three-sided square and held the bulky control panel. She grabbed hold of it as she fell forward and— oh, happy day!—it fell with her, before crashing down on top of her, pinning her to the ground. Adding final insult to injury, the hefty control panel skidded along the top before landing squarely, and with a delicious cracking thud, right on the back of her head.

As Jinx screamed with delight the others ripped off their headphones and jumped up to see the wonderful spectacle of a yet-again disabled Dick, all of them delighted beyond belief at having borne witness to her second bang on the head. None moved a muscle to help her, of course. They laughed and pointed and exclaimed until it became apparent she was not moving.

"Shit, guys—have I killed her?" Although she'd laughed

joyously alongside the rest, true geek Lulu was now white and shaking.

"No! Don't be ridiculous." Chloe, the future medic, was taking charge. "Look." She nudged The Dick's prone form with the pointy toe of her sensible black sling-back. "She's definitely still breathing. She's probably just unconscious—worst luck. Well, I'm not fucking touching the sweaty hag. I'll go and get Mademoiselle, she can call Mister Sinton."

Chloe practically skipped out the door as Jinx turned to Lulu. "Well done, Lu." She winked. "She looks totally fucked! I think you've just got rid of her for the entire rest of term—we owe you big-time!"

They were all whooping and laughing, giving three cheers for Lulu, when Jinx noticed Liberty race over to where Stella was standing, a wide smile plastered across her face. "Stella!" Liberty said, somewhat breathlessly as she raced to her side, obviously still—despite everything—deeply impressed by what she evidently saw as Stella's amazing maturity, sophistication, and worldliness, especially compared to the rest of them. "What happened to *you*, then? Come on, 'fess up—I want to hear *all* about last night!" Stella smiled—rather evilly, Jinx thought—before the two of them fell into a very cozy-looking huddle in the corner. Liberty was giggling and laughing at something Stella was telling her, and Jinx was beyond furious when she heard what it was.

"If you had a boyfriend, last night wouldn't have happened," Stella was saying as she reapplied her trademark pale pink lipstick in a gold-backed hand mirror. "You *so* need to get yourself one. You're definitely pretty enough."

"Actually," Jinx yelled as she walked over, "what she needs is a friend who won't dump her on her own in the middle of the fucking night in fucking town. Someone"—her voice was getting louder and louder—"who won't leave her alone with a bloke neither of you knows who steals her fucking bag, pushes her over, and tries to shag her on the beach!

"You really are a terrible fucking bitch, Stella Fox." Jinx was right up close to Stella, had shoved her against the wall, and was jabbing a furious finger in her face. "Why you can't crawl back underneath whatever stone you crawled out from under, I just don't know."

"Jinx"—Liberty looked really cross as she narrowed her eyes and glared at Jinx, grabbing her arm—"shut the fuck up! I told you earlier, what that bloke did is *not* Stella's fault. How was she supposed to know what he'd do? I'm a big girl, and I can take care of myself."

"Well, I think you proved last night that you *can't*, in fact, look after yourself. Just leave it, will you, Liberty? I'm talking to Stella."

Stella, a smirk playing about her pink lips, looked positively unconcerned as she leaned against the wall and— supremely casually—examined her nails.

This drove Jinx mad. She was screaming right in Stella's face about friendship, responsibility, and basic good manners, *yeah*, and punching the wall beside her when Ms. Gunn shuffled her bulk through the door.

"Jinx Slater!" Gunn was puce and sweating. She always found struggling up those devilishly steep stairs a terrible strain. "What the hell are you playing at? I could hear your voice down at the main foyer!"

Gunn gasped and went white beneath her sheen of sweat as she looked around the room and spotted The Dick's prone form in the middle of the floor, half buried beneath the table.

"Susan," she wailed, pushing Jinx out the way and stumbling toward her friend as the horrified girls melted away to the other end of the room. "Susan, please!"

She bent down and took Susan's clammy white hand in her own huge paw, desperately feeling for a pulse—since she was groping her friend's elbow, however, it was unlikely she'd find one. "Please don't die!"

"You lot!" she screamed over her shoulder at the girls, her eyes almost popping out her head as they swivelled round desperately seeking the guilty party. "What the *hell* is going on in here? Who did this? W*ho did this?*"

A trembling Lulu, tears shining bright in her eyes, was about to step forward and claim responsibility when Mister Sinton bustled into the room wearing her starched white nurse's outfit. She'd been changing out of her bathing suit when Mademoiselle Dupont had phoned, and there was a solitary pink roller still affixed to the back of her head.

"Right, then." Mister S was equally horrified by the sight that greeted her but assessed the situation with one glance, and her obvious capability, despite her usual over-enthusiasm with the aspirin, acted as a balm to the onlookers. "Give me some space. *Space*, please, Ms. Gunn! Chloe and Mimi, I want you two—gently, mind you—to come here and lift the table off Mrs. Dickinson."

"That's it, girls." Mister S was an oasis of calm. "Well done." She leant over The Dick and hefted her into the recovery position before examining the nasty bump on the back of her ginger head.

"Right, girls, there's nothing to worry about here. Mrs. Dickinson . . ." She paused to glare at Gunn, who was snuffling in the corner in the most pathetic fashion, ". . . has taken a direct hit to the head and passed out, poor thing. The ambulance will be here soon and, apart from a nasty headache when she wakes up, she'll be absolutely fine, I promise."

"Damn it," muttered Chloe almost inaudibly to Mimi, who put her hand over her mouth to preempt any hysterical giggles.

"Girls," Mister S continued, beaming round at the girls— the nurse loved them all indiscriminately, as if they were her own daughters, little treasures, each and every one—"treat the rest of this lesson as break time. Off you go."

Once the girls had left, Sister Minton turned to Gunn, who was still snuffling and wringing her hands in the corner. "And as for you, Patricia . . ." An unprecedented steely look lit her usually warm eyes. "I was appalled to find you screaming on the floor like that. You—a housemistress, of all people—should have taken charge of the situation." Mister Minton glared at Gunn.

Gunn, the inevitable dull headache beginning to throb in

her temples, took one last, lingering look at the horizontal Dick on the floor, hung her head, and shuffled out the door, hoping to reach the sanctuary of her flat before the inevitable migraine properly managed to take hold.

"I will," she resolved as she went, "have my revenge. I must."

The lower sixth were having a standoff in the Tanner House kitchen. Stella had disappeared to God knows where after the precipitous end of double French, and Liberty had refused to speak to Jinx all the way back. Trailing behind and whispering about the row, Lulu, Mimi, and Chloe had bumped into Chastity on her way back from a piano lesson, and she'd filled them in on the events of the previous evening. Liv was still seated in front of her homework at one of the long tables but had pushed her papers aside and was joining in with gusto.

"Come *on*, Liberty," she was yelling. "Don't get it twisted! You've got to admit Stella should never have just dumped you like that—Jinx is totally right!"

"I don't care what you think." In direct proportion to her mood, Liberty's hair was becoming wilder by the second. "And

it's none of your business, anyway. Or *yours*, for that matter."
She spun round to point at Jinx. "I can do whatever I fucking like
and with whom I like. And I don't like any of *you* lot at the
moment, so why don't you all just piss off and leave me alone."

"Come on, Lib." Lulu was fiddling with a pencil and quaking more than when she thought she'd murdered The Dick, but
she never failed to step in and play the peacemaker. "They don't
mean it—they're just worried about you."

"Yes we fucking *do* mean it." Jinx was pacing as she always
did when in the middle of a massive disagreement. "Your problem, Latiffe, is that you're just too fucking *stupid* to realize what
she's like. She doesn't give a shit about you, and you're so
moronic you haven't noticed."

"Well!" An obviously stung Liberty had stopped stock-still
in front of the open door. "If that's what you really think, then
fuck you, Jinx Slater. FUCK YOU!"

She slammed the door so hard behind her as she flounced
out the kitchen that the framed house photograph of them all
on the wall next to the oven came off its fixings, fell to the
ground, and smashed.

The ensuing heavy silence was broken when Daisy
Finnegan, her mouth so pursed she looked like she'd been
sucking on a lemon all morning, gingerly stuck her head
through the door. "Some of us are trying to work," she intoned,
glaring round at them with the most infuriatingly self-satisfied
expression plastered across her smug face. "If you can't be
civilized, could you at least *please* keep the noise down in here."

"FUCK OFF, YOU CREEP!" they yelled in unison, until the head girl spun on her silly Garfield slipper and slammed the door once more. The corkboard appeared to teeter on its fixing but remained stuck to the wall.

"Shit." Jinx sank into a chair and put her head in her hands. "I shouldn't have said she was stupid. When I'm cross I just want to hurt the other person by saying the worst, most below-the-belt thing I can think of."

"Oh, come off it, Jinx." Chloe was kneeling on the floor and picking up tiny shards of glass. "It's not that bad, is it? I can think of worse things to be called."

"It's what her dad always says to her, Chlo." Liv also had her head in her hands. "Whenever they have a row he says she's stupid and that her marks prove it and that he might as well stop paying for her to be at Stagmount and bring her home to Saudi."

"Yep." Jinx nodded. "And then she has to back down. Every single fucking time, in case he decides to do it. Christ, I am a fucking idiot."

It was a small and subdued group that trudged up to the sports hall to get changed for tennis with Strumpet and Gosh that afternoon. Stella was still nowhere to be seen, and Liberty had barricaded herself in her room after asking Mr. Morris to write her a note excusing her from games due to terrible period pains.

Jinx went to bed that night feeling awful about Liberty. She'd stuck a note under her door apologizing profusely and promising never to say another word to or about Stella but had been resolutely ignored.

The next day Jinx's black mood was not at all helped when Mrs. Carpenter handed her a note from Jo, Mrs. Bennett's secretary, in tutor group. It requested that she attend a meeting with the headmistress at 4:15 P.M. that afternoon. Jo had missed off the X she usually put at the end of her signature.

Liberty was sitting next to her in her usual seat at the back but pointedly looked the other way when Jinx sat down. She'd gathered her stuff together and hurried off to her art lesson so quickly at the end of tutor group that Jinx had no time to try and apologize again. Jinx totally ignored Stella—wouldn't even look at her—but was irritated beyond belief when she raced off giggling and arm in arm with Liberty. Although she was convinced it was largely put on for her benefit, she pretended she hadn't noticed.

There was no moussaka—one of the few things the kitchen staff made that Jinx actually liked—left in the canteen at lunchtime. She spilled Diet Coke all over a nearly finished English essay and had to start again from scratch, and she smashed her favorite fountain pen—a sixteenth-birthday present from her favorite godmother—when she trod on it on the floor of the reference library.

By the time Jinx was standing next to Jo's desk waiting to see Mrs. Bennett, she felt like sobbing with rage and frustration. And since Jo was on the phone the entire time she waited there, Jinx couldn't even ask her for a hint as to what the head wanted.

When Mrs. Bennett opened the door and ushered Jinx into her office, it was with none of her usual bonhomie and good humor—actually, she looked pretty cross about something.

And it wasn't long before Jinx realized she was the target.

"Sit down, Jane." Jinx winced. Mrs. Bennett hadn't called her Jane since she'd conned Daisy Finnegan into drinking a pint of urine—admittedly not her finest hour—at their third-year Christmas party and been suspended for the first three days of the Easter term.

"Right." Mrs. Bennett did that pyramid thing with her fingers and leant forward in her chair, fixing Jinx with a pair of gimlet eyes. "I'd like you to explain to me exactly what went on in your French lesson with Mrs. Dickinson yesterday."

Oh, Christ, thought Jinx. *She thinks I had something to do with The Dick's injury. I could get expelled for that, and it wasn't even my fault.*

"Mrs. Bennett," Jinx said earnestly, leaning forward herself, "I promise you—I *swear*, on my mother's life!—it was an accident. Mrs. Dickinson caught her foot in a chair leg and—"

"Oh for God's sake, Jinx!" Mrs. Bennett exclaimed impatiently. "I'm not suggesting you or anyone in your class *attacked* Mrs. Dickinson. No, no. I know you had nothing to do with that. What I want to get to the bottom of . . ." She paused to push her Prada spectacles up her nose. ". . . is why you felt it necessary to shove Stella Fox up against the wall and scream abuse at her. Members of staff tell me they could hear you screaming in the most unedifying manner from the main-school foyer."

"Oh." Jinx gulped. Fucking Gunn, this had to have come

from her—but at least she wasn't being accused of attempted murder. "Well . . ." Her voice petered out as she realized she could hardly tell Mrs. Bennett the real reason without totally dropping Liberty in it by revealing she'd been out in town so late at night—and, worse, drinking with strange boys way after she was supposed to be tucked up in bed. Jinx stared out the window, but the weather was so bad she couldn't see any sign of the sea beyond the games pitches.

"The thing is . . ." She was racking her brains to think of a decent excuse, but nothing was coming to her. "Well . . ."

"Yes?" Mrs. Bennett was getting crosser and crosser. "I'm waiting, and I don't have all day, you know."

"Look, Mrs. Bennett." She was going to have to wing it and hope for the best, but she knew whatever she said was bound to sound pathetic under the circumstances. "I'm sorry, I really am. Stella and I had an argument the previous evening and I was trying to sort it out—"

"You call that sorting it out? I'm very surprised at you, Jinx, I really am. Especially as I personally asked you to *look after* Stella this term." Jinx squirmed in her seat and cursed the bad fortune that had brought Stella to Stagmount.

"What was the argument about? Well?" Mrs. Bennett's glasses had slid back down her nose, and she was peering over the half-moons at Jinx, clearly waiting for a reasonable response to her question.

"I, um, I'm sorry, but I'd really rather not say, Mrs. Bennett." Jinx flushed a deep red as she said this.

"I'm very disappointed in you, Jinx, I really am." Jinx couldn't look her headmistress in the eye.

"Very well." Mrs. Bennett made a note on the pad in front of her and turned to the computer screen of her desktop. Jinx bleakly decided she'd choose hot fury anytime over this cold disenchantment.

"You give me no choice but to suspend you for a day. Today's Tuesday. I think this Friday works best—you *are* supposed to be studying for your A-levels, after all, and I see no reason to interrupt the working week anymore than it already has been. I'll phone your mother this evening and tell her to expect you at home on Thursday night. This will be on your file . . . Jane."

Jinx gulped. She was gutted that Mrs. Bennett was taking this so seriously but pleased she wasn't going to be gated for the weekend—she was desperate to go home, and this would give her a nice long weekend. She rearranged her features into a suitably despondent expression and said sorry again.

"I'm sorry it's come to this, Jinx, I really am." Mrs. Bennett stood up to open the door. "But I cannot be seen to condone brawling and bullying—especially during a lesson—and if you can't give me a straight answer or any kind of explanation, then I have to assume there was no root cause for it." She paused. "And of course, even if there was a rational reason for your fury, there is never any excuse for violence."

"Right." Jinx hung her head. "I do understand. You're only doing your job, and I am sorry."

Jinx walked back to Tanner House through the pouring rain and lost her scarf to a particularly strong gust of wind. She couldn't even be bothered to chase after it as she normally did, so she walked through the door looking like a drowned rat. She put the gold DO NOT DISTURB sign she'd stolen from a lovely hotel when skiing in Canada on her door, got into bed, pulled the duvet over her head, and didn't leave her room until the next morning.

The rain did not stop for the rest of the week, and despite Jinx's best efforts, Liberty did not say a word to her. The only good result was that Jinx did more homework over the next two days than she could remember ever having done—but this was a very poor trade-off as far as she was concerned.

It was with mixed feelings that Jinx packed her weekend bag—stuffed full of dirty washing that she knew Caroline would sort out for her—on Thursday afternoon. On the one hand, she was pleased to be going home straight after games. She needed a change of scene. On the other, Liberty was still not speaking to her. Jinx frowned and called a taxi to take her to Brighton station.

"Mum!" Jinx pressed her nose against the glass window at the end of Brockenhurst's railway bridge that looked over the parking lot, waved like a maniac, and sprinted down the steps, narrowly missing a collision with the ticket inspector standing officiously at the bottom.

She threw open the passenger door of Caroline Slater's E-class Mercedes, chucked her bag full of dirty laundry onto the backseat, and enveloped her mum in a huge hug.

"Sorry I got suspended again," she muttered into her mother's Miller Harris–scented neck, "but jeez, am I happy to be home!"

"Don't worry about it, darling. Daddy and I are thrilled to have you back—you know that. Let me have a look at you." Caroline held Jinx at arm's length and was less than thrilled when she saw how baggy her jeans were around the waist and noticed the mauve shadows under her eyes. "Dad and I have been talking about pizza all day—do you fancy Il Palio this evening? Is Liberty coming down too this weekend?" asked Caroline as they turned left out of the station road. "We haven't seen her for ages."

Jinx fiddled with the radio, narrowed her eyes, and mumbled a no before turning to stare out the window at the New Forest rushing by, and Caroline didn't press her daughter for a reason.

The next morning, Jinx lay in her own bed glaring at a shaft of winter sunlight that had pierced through her supposedly blackout curtains and was illuminating a framed photograph of her and Liberty sitting by the edge of the Slaters' pool, swinging their legs in the water with their backs to Caroline, the obsessive documenter of Slater life.

They were exactly the same height, wearing matching pink swimsuits, and tanned the same shade of deep brown. The only thing that told them apart was their hair—with Jinx's curly blond mop next to Liberty's long dark tresses, it could have been a picture-perfect postcard advertising the pleasures of the English pastoral idyll.

Jinx groaned as she rolled over. She'd absolutely stuffed herself with cheesy garlic bread, tomato-and-mozzarella salad, and a massive ham-and-mushroom pizza, before shoveling in a huge bowl of strawberry ice cream in the restaurant last night, and she felt distinctly, uncomfortably bloated.

Thank God the is-she-or-isn't-she-anorexic Jennifer was coming for lunch today, a day earlier than originally planned. Jinx could pretend she was on a diet, too, in solidarity. As she lay in bed, Jinx could hear the ponies snorting and thundering around the paddocks outside, and decided to go for a ride. Liberty hated riding—and horses, actually—so Jinx normally got up criminally early or didn't bother at all when she was staying for the weekend.

Always one for looking on the bright side, she decided being able to get out in the forest in daylight hours would be a major positive if she and Liberty actually weren't going to be friends anymore.

Neither of the boys were at home. Jinx wandered outside and stood in the courtyard giving Gaymian's old hunter, Pepsi—or Pansy, as they all started calling her when Damian came out—a very cursory brushing. She breathed in the familiar smell of hay, damp horsehair, and saddle soap and felt a zillion times better.

Cantering along a track in one of the forest enclosures, Jinx laughed out loud for the first time since The Dick took a gastly spill under the table. Pansy kicked her heels and snorted through her flared nostrils at the forest ponies they passed, enjoying being out for the first time in a month, too.

Mud-splattered and tired but happy, Jinx turned down the road to home, slouching back in the saddle, her reins long against Pansy's sweaty neck. She was humming Leo Sayer's revamped "Thunder in My Heart" under her breath when Pansy leapt sideways and practically landed in the ditch. Jinx lost both her stirrups and nearly fell off.

"Fucking stupid idiot!" she shouted as she regained her seat and gathered up her reins, turning round to glare at the car that had tooted its horn so loudly behind her, startling the horse practically into the ditch. "Don't you know *anything* about horses?"

Jinx peered into the half-open blacked-out window of the silver Range Rover Vogue as it crept past her, exaggeratedly slowly, and was appalled to see Mrs. Lewis at the wheel. "Hello, Jinx," smarmed Jennifer's mum as she stuck a slim wrist out the window and waved, jangling her many gold bracelets and causing Pansy to shy away from her again. "Sorry about that! Didn't realize the old nag had so much life in her."

Jinx stared at her openmouthed—how dare she insult Pansy like that—and was about to respond with something very rude about morons in blingtastic Chelsea tractors driving her off the road when she heard screaming from the passenger side. "*Fucking hell, Mum, what's wrong with you? Not content with nearly killing me, you could have killed her, too!*"

"Er, hi Jen." Jinx bent down and waved at her prep-school pal through the half-open window. "Everything okay?"

Jennifer lifted her hand and gave a desultory waggle of her fingers as Mrs. Lewis revved the engine—nearly sending Pansy flying into the ditch once more—and made a sharp left turn into the Slater's drive, spraying gravel behind her in the kind of impressive arc the boy racers from down the road spent hours trying to master.

By the time Jinx had hosed Pansy's legs down, dumped her filthy saddle and bridle in a very untidy heap on the table in the tack room, put the horse back in her box with a fragrant hay net, and raced around the back of the house to the kitchen door, Jennifer was lounging on one of the overstuffed sofas, clutching a mug of steaming tea and chatting to Caroline Slater.

"Jinx!" Jennifer *was* a lot thinner than she had been at prep school, but then, so was Jinx. In fact, they'd all been positively chubby back then—a combination of puppy fat and the excellent cook they'd had at school who'd not only dished up huge meals but also homemade cakes and biscuits twice a day.

Jennifer looked great in skinny black jeans tucked into black biker boots, and her green T-shirt made her violet eyes sparkle. She jumped up and gave Jinx a very pretentious air kiss on each cheek. "How great to see you! I am so sorry about my fucking—oops, sorry, Mrs. Slater—mother trying to run you off the road like that."

Caroline Slater raised her eyebrows but winked at Jinx as she made her excuses and disappeared out the back door in the direction of the stables, where she'd no doubt shake her head over the mess Jinx had left in the yard but clear it up all the same.

"Yah," Jennifer continued through great puffs of the Marlboro Red she'd lit up as soon as Caroline had left. "Fucking woman's been doing my head in ever since I got back from Clouds. What a fucking name. Clouds! Not much chance of any silver linings in there, either." She paused to pat Flash the boxer's brown head and dropped ash all over his brindled back.

Jinx giggled nervously before jumping up to get them an ashtray and a couple of wineglasses. She'd need a bloody drink to get through this, she thought as she rummaged in the fridge for the remains of the Chablis they'd started on as soon as they got back from the restaurant the night before.

"So, Jen." Jinx smiled triumphantly as she brandished the bottle in front of her and put another one in the freezer compartment to speed-cool. "How are you? I mean—I know you've been in . . . um . . . Clouds and everything, but you look great. Really great, in fact . . ." Jinx paused.

How the hell was she supposed to know what kind of events led to someone being sectioned; it must be a case of cause and effect, right? She definitely didn't want to say the wrong thing, so she decided it would be best to take her lead from Jennifer.

"I know, I *know*." Jennifer smirked and started tapping her right foot incessantly against the flagstone floor. "I'm not an anorexic or a bulimic or any of it. Look at me—I *do* look great and I know it! It's that bloody woman. She just couldn't stand it when I started going out with Todd. Actually, that's not quite right. I'll tell you what the fucking witch couldn't stand about Todd—the fact that he's not going to university and works at Tesco in Bournemouth."

Jennifer sighed and lit another fag from the end of the one she'd just finished, never once ceasing the tapping. "She is *such* a fucking snob. All she wanted was for me to end up married to one of the Bedales boys. Christ, you should have seen her at sports day, running round and sucking up to them all—I nearly died of embarrassment every time she got out of the bloody car. She's like my fucking *pimp* or something. Anyway, she couldn't stand Todd, and when she found me crying after we'd had a stupid row—it was only about where we were going clubbing that weekend for Christ's sake—she convinced Dad I was going mad and decided to have me locked up. She hoped it would make me 'come to my senses,' as she put it. But I know how her twisted mind works—she knows those places are full of celebrities, and she hoped I'd hook up with one of them and forget the 'shop worker,' as she called him."

"But . . ." Jinx paused again to take a thoughtful sip of her wine, still not convinced that Jennifer was quite right in the head.

"Yah, I told you about Jorge on the phone, didn't I!" Jennifer's tapping intensified, and another load of ash landed a few millimeters from the end of Flash's squashy nose. The dog sighed, stretched, and ambled off, pushing his head against the swing door that led into the dining room, no doubt planning a happy day spent shedding hair all over Caroline's best upholstery. "Gorgeous, just *gorgeous*. He's a Hugo Boss model, you know." Trying hard to maintain a straight face, Jinx nodded.

"Of course," Jennifer sighed wistfully, "we couldn't really talk to each other, what with the language barrier and everything."

"Right." Jinx was relieved the conversation was at last moving onto if not familiar, then at least accessible territory. "But I bet the sex was worth it?"

"Yah." Jennifer stubbed her cigarette out and reached for

the bottle of wine on the low table in front of them. "It was." She sighed again and gulped half the huge glass down in one. "But I still miss Todd. In fact, I hope you don't mind, Jinx, but he's picking me up from here in a couple of hours. I told Mum I was staying the night with you. She'd probably have us both killed if she knew we were still seeing each other."

"That's fine, totally fine." Jinx was also relieved she wouldn't have to entertain Jennifer all day and all night—she wasn't sure she could stand it. "Don't worry about a thing. If she calls here, I'll tell her you're in the shower or something. So, Jen, how *is* school? I've not seen you for ages."

"Yah." Jennifer laughed rather harshly. "Three years, to be exact. I thought you'd gone off me. So does Josephine, actually."

"No, not at all," Jinx lied through her teeth, desperate to get Stella's backstory. "You know what it's like when we're all so far apart." She waved her free hand expansively to illustrate the great distance between Stagmount and Bedales. "Geographically, I mean, of course," she added hastily, not that Jennifer was likely to pick up any implicit metaphorical slur.

"Yah. Know what you mean." Jennifer finished her wine and lit her third cigarette. "It's school, you know, but it's fine. There are some nice people there, but the fucking lessons aren't all that. They're all the same, though, aren't they?"

"Yeah." Jinx nodded. She certainly couldn't be bothered to get into a chat about the relative merits of Stagmount versus Bedales.

"In fact," Jinx added, keen to get the business of Stella

done and dusted before Todd turned up to whisk Jennifer off to God knows where, "we got one of your old girls at the beginning of this term."

"Yah?" Jennifer looked curious as she ripped off the foil covering on Caroline's second-to-last bottle of her favorite wine. "Which one?"

"Stella Fox," Jinx said neutrally, waiting to see Jennifer's reaction.

"Stella Fox? Hmmm . . ." Jinx could hardly believe that Jennifer didn't immediately know who she was talking about. Maybe Jennifer really *was* a raving lunatic.

"Oh, I know!" Jennifer smiled and poured more wine. "Bloody boring, we all thought. Well . . ." she leaned forward conspiratorially. "Until she left, of course."

"What do you mean, 'until she left'?" Jinx was having trouble maintaining her composure but didn't want to influence Jennifer's train of thought. *Boring*? Stella? Whatever she was, she certainly wasn't boring. Not in the conventional sense, definitely.

"None of us paid her much attention, you know. She was one of those girls who never had anything to say and just faded into the background all the time. She stayed there, basically."

Jennifer noted Jinx's shocked face and started ticking off reasons on her fingers. "She wasn't on any of the teams, she never had a boyfriend, and she didn't come to any of our parties or anything—well, if you want the *strict* truth, she probably wasn't invited to any. But you know what I mean."

"In fact"—Jennifer mock yawned as if to emphasize how very

little impact Stella had made on her—"I barely knew her name until the beginning of this term. And I'd forgotten about all the commotion, what with being involuntarily *sectioned* and all."

"So . . ." Jinx quickly butted in, as she desperately didn't want Jennifer to segue off into another rant about her mother and how unfairly she'd been treated. "What happened?"

"Well . . ." Jennifer lowered her voice slightly. "It was really weird. Like the mouse that roared."

Jinx stroked one of the cats—she didn't know which one it was; some of the stables ones looked *very* alike—and thought deeply. Roaring, yes—but a mouse? This did not sound like the Stella she knew *at all*.

"Yah." Jennifer smirked, obviously enjoying Jinx's confusion. "It was *très* bizarre. Basically, Stella had auditioned for the lead part in the school play at the end of last term. Some Chekhov bollocks or something. Anyway, none of us knew why she'd even bothered auditioning—I mean, it was *obvious* that Frances Levy was going to get it. She's had the lead in every production probably since she was born *and* she's just been accepted at the Royal Academy of Dramatic Arts summer school, the youngest person ever, I think. And none of us had ever seen Stella act in anything—she's probably crap at it."

Jinx grimaced. She was beginning to think quite the opposite but held her breath. "We didn't see the audition," Jennifer continued, "as our drama teacher, Mr. McGregor, holds them all individually in his office. He's always done it like that. Or he *did*, anyway."

"McGregor always makes his mind up over the summer holidays and posts the cast list on the drama board on the first day of the Christmas term. Frances, naturally, got the lead—playing a sister or something? I can't remember exactly what the part was, but it looked bloody boring, if you ask me—and Stella was down to be in a couple of crowd scenes.

"Which actually"—Jennifer sat up and fumbled in her navy corduroy slouch bag for her lighter—"was pretty fucking good when you consider she's never been in a school production before and never shown any interest in the theater department. And she's got no friends—and everyone knows it's the popular people that do drama.

"I mean even I"—Jennifer nearly burnt a hole in the front of her T-shirt as she jabbed the cigarette at herself—"for example, wouldn't bother trying out for the school play, even though I'm totally one of the most popular girls in the school. They get agents and stuff down from London to come and see it. It's a big deal, and they only want people who can act in it—in fact, they always use the same people every year."

"So Stella tried out and didn't get in," Jinx said, looking confused. "So what? I don't understand what the big deal is."

"Well . . ." Jennifer stubbed out her cigarette and swung her feet onto the table. "None of us understood it either, but a couple of people said they saw her storm off crying after she saw the list. Anyway, the next thing you know, McGregor mysteriously disappears, and all our parents get a letter saying he's been suspended from teaching pending an inquiry into his conduct."

"So"—Jinx couldn't get her head round this at all—"what's that got to do with Stella?"

"Come on, Jinx." Jennifer was practically frothing at the mouth, positively delighted at having such a captive audience. "Isn't it obvious? She *accused* him of sexually harassing her, because she was so cross about not getting the part she wanted! It was a total lie to pay him back."

"But . . ." Much as she wanted to believe it, Jinx was wondering how they knew for definite that it was Stella who'd made the accusation, and also how they knew the accusations were false.

"I know exactly what you're going to ask," Jennifer interrupted, "and I'm going to tell you how we know. Firstly, if you'd met McGregor you'd totally *know* that he would *never* do anything like that. He's been teaching at the school forever, and there's never been a hint of anything like that—he's just a nice old man, for Christ's sake. All the drama students loved him.

"Secondly," she continued, waving her hand to shush Jinx, "and more importantly, Frances Levy's mum knows Stella's parents. Mrs. Fox told her all about it at a dinner party a few weeks ago. She said that Stella had phoned home in a right state in the first week of term, saying she'd gone to see McGregor about the play and he'd put his arm round her and tried to snog her in his office. Which is *absolute crap*. Honestly, if you knew McGregor you'd know it was total bullshit—or wishful thinking, probably, as far as she was concerned.

"Anyway"—Jennifer was on a roll—"obviously, Stella's dad

gets straight onto the head and demands he call the police. He *had* to, I guess. And the next thing you know Stella's left, too. Not"—she yawned again—"that we'd have noticed. It was only when Frances told us the reason that we connected the two things. Frances was well cross—she *loved* McGregor and hated Stella. She used to have to see her sometimes in the holidays and said Stella was always hanging around, trying to chat to her and stuff and pretend they were friends. Frances says she always used to ignore her."

"Right." Jinx thoughtfully slurped her wine as she processed this astonishing news. "That's really, really weird."

"Why? What's she like now then?" Jennifer was abruptly cut off as Flash came storming through the swing door, knocking over the stool on which the Slater family's vast pile of magazines and newspapers sat, and stood, barking and growling, by the back door.

"Daft thing," Jinx murmured affectionately as she caressed his head and opened the door for him to get out. He raced off round the corner by the utility rooms, where he was joined by Missy, the Slaters' ancient chocolate Labrador, and Trojan and Bella, George's Yorkshire terriers.

They all headed to the front of the house in a pack, barking furiously the whole time. "Wonder what's wrong with them?" Jinx mused. "*Shit!*" she exclaimed as realization hit and she jumped up and raced off in hot pursuit of her dogs, leaving a very confused Jennifer lolling half drunk on the sofa.

30

"Aaaaargh!" A lovely looking blond boy, at least six-foot tall with a gorgeous hint of a tan and piercing blue eyes, was leaping about the drive as the four dogs circled around him, jumping about and barking. "What the fuck is this? Get these fuckers off me! Help, *Help!*"

"Ha!" Jinx *wanted* to help, but the sight of the dogs pretending to be so fierce and guard the house was too much for her. They were pathologically friendly, that was all, especially Flash. Every time Jinx tried to call him off, she couldn't help herself from singing, "Dada, he saved every one of us," from the *Flash Gordon* theme tune. She was bent double, laughing hysterically and crying weakly for Jennifer.

Eventually, after much leaping and anguished screaming on Todd's part—especially when Flash bent low and pretended to pounce in the boy's terrified face before twisting away at the last minute—Jinx managed to get a grip on herself and call the dogs off. At the same time, Jennifer threw open the front door and launched herself into the boy's arms.

"Did I hear you scream, babe?" she enquired brightly of him when she'd finished snogging his face practically *off*.

"No, love." He grinned weakly at Jinx. "Just shouting your name, that was all—couldn't see the doorbell anywhere." Jennifer looked at the huge ring-pull bell hanging smack-bang in the middle of the wall next to the front door but didn't mention it as she introduced her boyfriend.

"We've just met." Todd smiled. "Jinx was introducing me to her lovely dogs."

"But you don't like dogs, do you, babe?" Jennifer said, puzzled. "You didn't even like it when Mum's pug tried to sit next to you on the sofa, did you?"

"He loves Flash, just *loves* him." Jinx was leaning against the low wall at the front of the house, gripping Flash's gold-star-studded red leather Harrods collar, weak with laughter. "From the first moment he saw him, I should imagine. It was like love at first sight, wasn't it, Todd?"

Jinx was waving Jennifer and Todd off when a familiar battered Golf pulled into the driveway, tooting its horn as it spun round in a handbrake turn in front of the house, spraying even more gravel behind it than Mrs. Lewis had achieved with her Range Rover Vogue. The dogs started barking again, in delight this time, and jumping up at the driver's door, scrabbling on the paintwork with their sharp nails, and drooling all over the window.

"George!" Caroline Slater had dashed over from the stables when she heard the telltale tooting. "How many times have I told you *not* to do that in front of the house. I am *forever* picking bits of gravel out of the dogs' water bowl and the hanging baskets. Come here!" She enveloped him in a huge hug and laughed delightedly as he picked her up and swung her round, patting his back in a futile attempt to make him stop. "George! Put me down!"

"All right, Ma, keep your wig on." George winked at Jinx as he carefully lowered his mother to the ground, slammed the car door shut, and slung his arm round Jinx's shoulder. "This is a surprise, Jinx—you've not been suspended again, have you?"

"Um, basically," she muttered into his shoulder. "Yes, I have. But not for anything too serious this time. I only got a day."

"Ha! I knew it. Actually, I *did* know it. I spoke to Dad this morning and he told me. Seemed pretty pleased with it all, in fact—you've got more lives than a bloody cat, young lady. I was locked in my room for the entire week when I got caught shagging Claudia McCartney. Nearly killed myself climbing down the fucking drainpipe every night. Pub later?"

"No!" Caroline was picking gravel out of the dogs' bowl and flinging it futilely into the new deep grooves on the drive. "I want you both here tonight. We've not seen you for ages, George, and we've only just got Jinx back. We're having a family dinner, and I don't want any arguments—it's nonnegotiable!"

After dumping a huge mound of dirty washing in the utility room, George was delightedly picking bits of crumbly feta cheese out of the delicious Greek salad Caroline had made for Jinx and Jennifer, which had remained untouched in the fridge, and teasing Caroline. "Come on, Mum, *nothing's* nonnegotiable. Dad always tells us that—can't we just nip out for a couple of pints before dinner? I've not seen my sister properly since Jamie's party, and that was weeks ago! And she spent half the night snogging Matthew Wicks in the broom cupboard, so it wasn't like we really *talked* to each other."

"I freaking well did *not!*" Jinx, also well used to George's little jokes, threw a dishcloth at him from where she was lying top-to-toe with Flash on the sofa. "You're nothing but a dirty liar."

"George." Although she was pretending to be stern, Caroline was smiling—she loved nothing more than being teased by her boys. "If I have to tell you again, it'll be bed with no dinner for you. And as for you"—she turned to point at Jinx, picked up the cloth, and threw it back to her—"you can bloody well go and clean Pansy's tack. You left it in a disgusting state."

Jinx, moaning loudly about slave drivers and child labor, shuffled off wearing a pair of wellies at least three sizes too big for her because she couldn't be bothered to get her own from the front of the house, leaving George and Caroline to put on the first of his five loads of washing.

The Slaters ate steak and chips, drank three bottles of lovely red, and spent the rest of the weekend sleeping in, reading the papers, making little jokes at one another's expense, walking the dogs, and admiring Caroline's new rose garden.

A couple of times George, who had somehow realized that his little sister was more than a bit smitten with his best friend, tried to tease Jinx about Jamie, but—very disappointingly for him—she didn't rise to the bait once, so he gave up. Jinx was vaguely surprised at her own lack of curiosity but didn't dwell on it. The only person she had room in her brain for right now was Liberty. She was so worried about Stella's evil intentions toward her best friend, she simply couldn't muster up a single iota of interest in anyone else, even the beyond-gorgeous Jamie.

Jinx didn't say a word to any of them about what Jennifer had told her about Stella, nor did she discuss her falling-out with Liberty, but when Martin dropped her back to school on Sunday night, she was feeling a lot better. She obviously had to make a plan but, refreshed after her weekend at home, for the first time she thought everything might turn out okay.

31

Jinx dumped her bag in her room and grabbed the bottle of vanilla-flavored Absolut vodka she'd lifted from the drinks cabinet at home. She went and stuck her head round Liberty's door, planning a grand apology followed by a big drinking session. The lights were blazing and her window was flung wide open—as per usual. But Liberty wasn't in.

Jinx ripped a pink heart-shaped Post-it note off the pad on the desk, scrawled a hello, and stuck it in the middle of the mirror. She left the bottle on Liberty's desk as a peace offering. Where the bloody hell was she? Since the girls in the year above them had made a Sunday tradition of getting absolutely wrecked all day in a pub in the marina, Mr. Morris now wanted all the lower sixth to be back in Tanner House by nine-thirty on Sunday nights.

Jinx flicked the light off, shut the door, and wandered into the common room. Fanny Ho was the only occupant. She was sitting cross-legged on a beanbag on the floor, wearing a pair of sharply tailored men's pajamas, eating a huge bowl of stinking greasy noodles with the special bone-china chopsticks she took to every meal, and watching News 24.

"Fucking hell, Fanny, those reek!" Jinx flopped down on the other beanbag, kicked off her shoes, smiled at Fanny, and did a double take. Christ—she'd changed her hair *again*. The glossy locks poking out from underneath the ubiquitous wide peaked hat were at least six inches longer than they had been last week. "Good hair, though. How did you do it?"

"Thanks, Jinx." Fanny looked very pleased about something underneath her hat, and Jinx somehow doubted it was related to the turgid analysis of the budget playing across the screen in front of them. "I go to that Chinese place in the North Laines. The woman put a few extensions in."

"Wow." Jinx was peering at the side of Fanny's head. "She must be awesome—I can't see *any* of the joins."

"Yeah, she's very good. Do you want some of these? I've got loads here." Fanny was still smirking as she proffered the bowl in Jinx's direction, and Jinx had to stop herself from retching as she caught a disgusting whiff of something way too fishy and saw what looked suspiciously like chunks of eel floating about in the gray liquid at the bottom.

"No, thanks, Fan. You couldn't pay me to eat that." Jinx—who was not ordinarily a fussy eater—had gone a bit green and had to look away. "Have you seen Liberty anywhere? Did she spend the weekend here?"

"Nah, haven't seen her all weekend." Fanny—the little freak—was giving the television a longing look, obviously desperate not to miss out on any more of the budget talk. She loved stuff like that. Jinx thought it was downright weird. "Actually, I'm sure I saw her going off in a taxi with Stella on Friday. They had their weekend bags with them."

"Right." Jinx scowled and stood up. Her desire to make peace was rapidly dissipating. "Thanks. See you later."

Jinx kicked the bin on her way out and decided to bloody well take that vodka back. She'd share it with Chastity instead.

"Jinx! How was home?" Chastity was lying on her bed with a green clay face mask plastered from her hairline to the base of her neck, wearing her flowery dressing gown, and listening to her Dido CD when Jinx walked in. Jinx *hated* Dido.

"Cool, thanks, Chas." Jinx pulled Chastity's chair out from under her desk, turned it round, and sat back-to-front on it with her arms resting along the top of the back before reaching over to turn the volume on the CD player right down. "What did you get up to?"

"Mum came down on Friday night with Ian, her not-so-new boyfriend. I think this one's going to last." Chastity grimaced as best she could. "He says he wants to buy a flat in Brighton, so they spent the night and looked at loads all day Saturday. I had dinner with them at the Hotel Du Vin—he's *all right*, I suppose, and at least he really seems to love Mum. And I guess if he does get the flat, I'll probably get a key, which will be good for all of us. Anyway, I told Morris I was staying with them, and them that I was coming back to school, and spent Saturday and Sunday with Paul. It was brilliant, but I'm missing him madly already! What about you?"

"Oh, I had a lovely time mostly stuffing my face and messing about with the dogs. Took Pansy out for a nice ride, and George came home late Friday, so we got quite pissed and just hung out, really. Let's hear it for being suspended!" Jinx grinned.

"By the way, Chas, have you seen Liberty anywhere? Fanny said she saw her going off somewhere with Stella on Friday."

"Yep." Chastity was scrubbing her face at the corner sink and sounded muffled. "She spent the weekend with Stella in London."

"Did she ask any of you lot?" Jinx asked, nibbling on the corner of a broken nail.

"No—totally NFI. Not that we would have wanted to go anyway. Lib's been a bit off with all of us since the row last week, but she did say they were going clubbing or something."

"Well, you know what the only decent response to NFI is?" Jinx said, grinning broadly. "FGA!"

"What's that?" Chastity looked confused.

"Fucking Go Anyway. Ha! Now *that* would have pissed the stupid bitch off. Not that you'd have wanted to spend the weekend with her."

Jinx desperately wanted to tell Chastity what she'd learnt from Jennifer, but she had decided in the car on the way back that it was best to wait until she'd got her, Liv, and Charlie all in the same place, as she'd have to swear them to secrecy, and that could only be done when they were all together. Instead, she proudly brandished the vanilla vodka. She opened Chastity's mini-fridge and discovered a bottle of tonic and a lime.

"Chastity Max-Ward," she said, dead impressed. "Ten out of ten. I don't know anyone our age who takes drinking as seriously as you. *Limes*, for fuck's sake! You're brilliant."

"Thanks, Jinx." Chastity bent low in a mock bow before jumping back onto her bed and chucking one of her squashy cushions at Jinx. "I obviously take after my mum. I'm getting an ice machine for Christmas. So are they not back yet, then? I know Morris is cool and everything, but he's really keen on his Sunday-night rule. The only time I've seen him really lose it this term was when Chloe and Melissa rolled in absolutely steaming at eleven a couple of weeks ago."

"I don't think so. By rights I shouldn't even give a shit, particularly as Lib's being so pathetic and not speaking to me, but I can't help worrying about her going off with Stella. You know what she's like—not exactly the most streetwise, especially in fucking London. And look what happened last time the two of them went out—it was a fucking disaster. So it's not really Morris I'm concerned about—Stella doesn't give a shit about anyone except herself."

"Yeah." Chastity sighed. "And she sucks up to Lib like I've never seen. You should have seen them on Friday—we were all nearly *puking*. I think you were right the other day, you know:

Liberty *is* a bit stupid. In the nicest possible way," she added hastily when Jinx scowled.

"Of course she is, but that's part of her charm, isn't it? It makes her more fun somehow . . . the poor daft cretin. What you see is what you get. Well, I'm not fucking phoning her. You do it, Chas—go on, just see where she is and point out to her in words of not more than one syllable that she'll definitely be in loads of trouble if she doesn't hop it back here quick smart."

Chastity was dialing the number when they heard a commotion in the corridor outside. Jinx stuck her head round the door and looked over to the hall area. Sure enough, Liberty and Stella were standing in the foyer being berated by Mr. Morris, who was wearing his pajamas and looking incredibly cross. She motioned for Chastity, and the two of them lay on the floor with the door open a crack so they could see what was going on without being seen.

Stella was wearing a very short denim miniskirt, black-patterned fashion tights and platform shoes. A pale pink peasant blouse was visible underneath her tailored H&M beige trench coat, and she had a Mulberry weekend bag slung over her shoulder. Liberty was wearing jeans tucked into Stella's Chloé boots and had her long hair tied in a side ponytail like Stella's. Both of them were wearing full makeup, and they looked at least twenty-five.

"What time do you call this?" Mr. Morris was tapping his watch and glaring at the pair.

"It's—" Stella attempted to get a word in, but Morris cut

her off.

"No, Stella, don't interrupt me. That was a rhetorical question. I don't want any of your excuses."

Stella folded her arms and gave him a very frosty look.

"Christ, she's rude," Jinx whispered in Chastity's ear. "Just look at the face on her! He's only doing his bloody job." There was an unwritten rule that the girls didn't cheek any of the nicest teachers, especially those—like Mr. Morris—who really made life very easy for them.

"You all know you've got to be back at nine-thirty on Sunday nights," he continued. "If Mrs. Bennett had decided to do one of her unscheduled walkabouts tonight, it would have been me that got it in the neck."

While Stella stood there scowling and refusing to look him in the eye, Liberty at least tried to make amends. "We're sorry, sir, we really are. We should have phoned when we realized our train was going to be massively delayed, but both our phones had run out of batteries, and the pay phone at the station had been vandalized." She smiled beseechingly at him from underneath her manically fluttering black eyelashes.

"A likely story," sniggered Chastity under her breath. "Look at her! Do they think he's stupid or what?"

"Apology noted, Liberty. Thank you. And what about you?" Mr. Morris turned to look at Stella. "Have you got anything to say for yourself, or are you just cross at having been caught?"

Stella mumbled something that Jinx and Chastity couldn't hear from their prone vantage point down the corridor, but whatever it was, it was in a decidedly sarcastic tone.

"Right." Mr. Morris did not look pleased at all. "If that's the way you want to play it, you can both be gated all this week. That means no trips into Brighton whatsoever, and I want you to report back here to me at six o'clock on the dot every night this week."

Stella looked furious as she hefted her bag further onto her shoulder and swept through the swing doors in the direction of the stairs leading to her corridor. She turned to give Mr. Morris a very black look and disappeared off without saying another word.

Liberty apologized again and then started making excuses for Stella. "She didn't mean it, sir, I promise. We're both just really tired and the train was an absolute nightmare. Does she really have to—"

"Thank you, Liberty. I appreciate the sentiment, but there is absolutely no way I'll be spoken to like that. The punishment stands."

He locked Tanner House's front door, said an unusually terse good night to Liberty, and headed through the front door of his staff flat, adjacent to the foyer on the ground floor.

Jinx and Chastity quickly rolled out the way of their own door and quietly closed it as Liberty headed their way. They lay on the floor giggling about Stella's punishment. "She fucking deserved that, the rude bitch," Jinx said delightedly. "Good old Brian!"

"Yeah," Chastity added, equally mirthfully. "And it means we can go out every night this week if we want and leave her behind. And tired, my *arse*—that was an 'I've been up all night chowing down E's' face if ever I've seen one."

They gave each other high fives and poured another vodka and tonic in celebration.

Since Stella and Liberty had been gated for the week, Jinx knew she wouldn't have to worry about what the two of them were getting up to—or *into*, in Liberty's case. She was delighted they'd inadvertently given her more time to think things over, and she took a long swig of her V&T.

"I'd like to make a toast," she said, raising her glass high above her head and winking at Chastity, "to Mr. Morris."

32

While Jinx and Chastity drank their vodka and cackled like witches imagining the many and varied punishments *they* would dearly like to dish out to Stella, Ms. Gunn was knocking back the whisky alone in her flat.

Gunn fingered the globe that sat next to her sofa, twirling it round on its axis with her fat forefinger stuck on Japan. She put the whisky tumbler to her lips and tilted her huge head back. A solitary piece of fast-melting ice was all it contained, so she reached for the bottle by her feet.

Gunn growled as she realized the liter bottle was empty. She'd only bought it that morning, and she'd only been up here drinking for about two hours. Things were bad, very bad indeed. She vented her rage on Myrtle, who'd scuttled away to hide in the kitchen when Gunn had growled so viciously, screaming after her that she was nothing but a bloody deadweight, and why should Gunn be expected to feed and water her when she gave nothing in return, and why in hell didn't she put herself to some kind of *use* around the place. Which was a bit rich, considering that Myrtle was a dog.

Gunn stomped into the kitchen, causing a quivering Myrtle to dash back into the sitting room. She thumped and banged and rooted around, becoming progressively redder in the face as she sought something, anything, to drink. Eventually she unearthed an ancient bottle of ouzo from the bucket filled with cleaning products underneath her sink. A Greek girl's parents had given it to her for Christmas years ago, and she remembered now that she'd stashed it down there in case of a real emergency, which this clearly was.

Gunn normally hated ouzo, but she was so desperate she'd have drunk methylated spirits without a second thought if she'd been able to find any tonight. In fact, she thought bitterly as she ripped the top off the ouzo and caught a whiff of it, she'd probably prefer a nice icy meths to this terrible aniseed crap, but she had to make do.

Gunn drank a full glass in one gulp before placing it on the table next to her and stretching herself out full length on the sofa. She put her arms behind her head, crossed her legs, closed her eyes, and sighed deeply.

What a funk I'm in, she thought. *What a terrible bloody funk.* And it was the worst kind it could possibly be, and, for all her normal grievances, fits, and general bad temper, it was one that she'd never experienced before.

Gunn sighed again before opening one eye and glaring at the phone on her desk. She'd been staring at it pretty much all day, willing it to ring. Every so often, mindful of her mother's favorite cliché, "a watched pot never boils," she'd trundled downstairs to harangue the juniors, glare evilly at the parents dropping their daughters back to school, or glance through her beloved punishments book.

She'd not managed to stay away for more than ten minutes, though, before hefting herself back up the stairs and hopefully crashing through the door, only to be faced with the desolate sight of no red blinking light indicating a message. She'd even unplugged it a few times to check that it was still working. It was. For the first time in recent memory there was no option for Gunn but to face the unpalatable truth: there was no message.

Gunn lay there in the near dark, desperately willing her to call, sweating despite the cold breeze blowing in through the open window. She'd always believed her awful migraines to be the absolute apex of pain, but the painful thoughts running through her mind tonight hurt much worse, and deeper some- how. She was slowly facing up to a lot of things she'd never allowed herself to think about before.

She gulped down another full glass of ouzo, finding she was quite enjoying the sickly taste of it now she'd guzzled her way through half the bottle. She decided she'd have one more glass before bed and stumbled into the kitchen in need of more ice, her huge bulk swaying slightly from side to side.

As she reentered the sitting room, the phone rang. Gunn stood stock-still in the doorway for a couple of seconds, then dropped her drink on the floor in her haste to reach the instrument, not appearing to notice the smashed glass, sticky ouzo, and melting ice all over the rug. She shuddered, cleared her throat, and swallowed nervously a couple of times before picking it up.

"Susan?" she asked in an unprecedentedly girlish and hopeful voice. "Is that you?" Her face lit up in a beatific smile that not a single one of the girls in her house, her colleagues, or anyone else who came into contact with her had ever seen, and she settled down on the sofa clutching the handset as if it were the most precious, delicate thing in the world.

Jinx scowled at Liberty and Stella as they walked into Mrs. Carpenter's room the next day, arm in arm. Liberty hadn't mentioned a word about the note she'd left in her room, had pointedly ignored her in the bathroom that morning, and was obviously still in a raging mood about the fact she'd had a go at Stella the week before.

Stella and Liberty sat down on either side of her, but she didn't look at either of them. Instead, Jinx took her mobile phone out of her bag and started composing a joint text message to Liv, Charlie, and Chastity, saying she had news about Stella and suggesting they all go out for dinner that evening.

She was damned if she was going to show any weakness in the face of Liberty's ridiculous obduracy and Stella's smug delight. In fact, she'd have dearly loved to turn round and push

Stella off her chair—that would wipe the smug smile off the bitch's face. She would have done it, too, if she didn't think Mrs. Bennett might actually expel her this time.

Liv swaggered in with wet hair with minutes to spare, having clearly just jumped out of the shower. She was holding her phone and walked straight up to Jinx. "Hey, Jin, you're on for tonight," she said, before throwing a pointed sideways evil glance in Stella's direction. "Charlie's got a doctor's appointment this morning, but she says she's up for it, too—we can't wait to hear your news."

Liberty wasn't quick enough to stop a spark of interest from playing about her face, but Stella, unconcernedly reapplying her pink lipstick in her gold hand mirror, didn't appear to have heard them.

Mrs. Carpenter walked in beaming, clearly in one of her extra-good moods. She trilled her customary "good morning, girls" in an unusually high-pitched voice and placed her steaming mug of coffee on the desk in front of her before sitting down in her ergonomic chair and looking round the room.

"Ah, Jinx," she practically sang. "Good to have you back." Her eyes moved along the back row and came to rest on Liv. Immediately, her face turned sour and the class braced itself for one of her manic mood swings.

"Olivia Taylor." The singsong nursery-school voice was gone, replaced with a harsh bark. "How *dare* you come into my classroom with wet hair?"

All the girls in the class suddenly seemed to take great

interest in the books and pencil cases spread out on the desks in front of them, not wanting to attract attention to themselves or look at Liv in case she pulled one of her funny faces and made them laugh.

"You know how I feel about personal grooming." Mrs. Carpenter was obsessed with the girls' appearances and, in fairness to her, regularly gave them lectures about professionalism in the workplace.

Charlie had once made the mistake of cheekily pointing out that Stagmount was not, in fact, an office, and Mrs. C had gone into such a marvelous rant about the fact that they were nearing the end of their school careers and she was merely preparing them for their inevitable existence in the real world that none of them had dared turn up underdressed or without brushed and dry hair ever again.

Out of the corner of her eye, Jinx caught Stella nodding as if she was in full agreement with their tutor, and felt a burning desire to stick the sharp end of her compass into the girl's denim-clad thigh.

Just as Mrs. Carpenter was winding up a fabulous soliloquy that Shakespeare himself would have been proud of and would no doubt end in lines or a gating or litter picking around the grounds, there was a knock at the door. A tiny first-year stood there, shaking and clutching a piece of paper in her hand. Mrs. Carpenter's mood changed as fast as the wind.

"Come *in*, sweetheart," she trilled in the same singsong voice she'd been using earlier. "There's nothing to be afraid of here. These big girls don't bite, you know. Ha, ha, ha. What have you got there, darling?"

The first-year was blushing like anything as she handed over the note from her own form teacher; she practically fell over in her haste to back out the open door she'd kept a foot stuck in to aid her speedy getaway.

"*Sweet* little things, aren't they, with their tiny ties all done up wrong? Like little Smurfs, aren't they? Before I forget, can one of you run a new packet of chalk in to next door? Thanks, Chloe. Now, where was I?" Mrs. C had clearly forgotten all about Liv and the issue of the wet hair and was back in a great mood.

Jinx ripped the corner off a page in her prep diary, scribbled something on it, and chucked it over Stella's desk to Liv. Liv stifled a giggle as she read, *The benefits of bipolar: discuss*, and Mrs. Carpenter began banging on about the marvelous weekend she'd just spent hill walking.

34

Liv, Charlie, Chastity, and Jinx sat in a booth downstairs at the Dragon Palace, their favorite Chinese restaurant in town. It was so expensive they normally only went there with their parents, but Chastity's mum's not-so-new boyfriend was so keen to get her on side he'd phoned earlier, and when she told him they were going out to eat, he'd told her to take the girls wherever they wanted and that he'd pick up the tab.

Jinx was by now champing at the bit to tell her story, but she knew of old that until the food was on the table in front of them, there was no point bringing up anything remotely unconnected with the menu—the world could be ending in five minutes and all this lot would worry about was whether their appetizers would arrive first.

"Result, Chas," mumbled Charlie through a mouthful of the

chunkiest and most delicious sesame prawn toast any of them had ever tasted. "This is the nicest meal I think I've ever had."

"Yep, cheers to Mr. Ian," sighed Liv, raising her glass of Sancerre rosé to the middle of the table. "Oops, I think we need another bottle. This is going to be extortionate, Chas—will he *really* not mind?"

"Nah." Chastity smiled, obviously very pleased with the situation. "He's rich. And he's desperate to get me on his side. Let's just say he's going about it the right way! He told me to take you wherever we wanted and said we should push the boat out. He's not bad at all, really—and Mum does really seem taken with him."

They finished their starters in record time and were already on their third bottle of wine. As the empty plates of prawn toast, salt-and-pepper ribs, and crispy fried wantons were taken away, the waitress—who'd asked them if they were really, really sure they wanted to order so much food—reverentially placed a whole duck with a basket full of pancakes and a dish swimming with plum sauce in front of them.

"Yesss!" They all fell upon it like fat people who hadn't eaten for a month. Jinx put down her fork, coughed importantly, and prepared to tell them what she knew. "Listen, everyone," Jinx said, desperate to get a word in.

"I swear, I will never understand anorexics," Liv said, taking absolutely no notice of Jinx whatsoever, as she carefully loaded up another pancake. "Apart from anything else, where do they get the bloody willpower from? If my life depended on it I don't think I could stop myself from eating for even, like, two days."

"I don't think I could do *one* day," Chas said, motioning for another bottle of wine. "And do they drink at all, or is booze too fattening?"

"*Anyway*!" Jinx said loudly, all this talk of anorexia forcefully reminding her of what she'd wanted to speak to them about in the first place and tapping her fork on the side of her plate to make them listen once and for all. "What I wanted—"

"I don't think they do," Liv said, once again paying no attention to anything that wasn't on the table in front of her, thoughtfully sipping her wine. "I mean, if you want to kill yourself, why not just slit your throat or something? It's so much quicker and easier than starving yourself for years and years until your organs fail one by one, leaving you a brain-dead paraplegic in a home waiting out the bitter end, surely?"

"Will you all just *shut up*?" Jinx yelled in a desperate bid for airtime.

"Sorry," she giggled as she registered the astonished expressions in front of her. "It's just I've got some really important news, and I'd like to tell you before it's time to go back to school." The girls sat back expectantly.

"I saw my old friend Jennifer over the weekend." She looked around meaningfully. "You know, the girl who goes to *Bedales*." The others leaned in close, and Jinx told the whole story right through.

She didn't leave anything out, and the girls gaped at her as she talked. Liv was the first to interrupt.

"Okay," she said, picking crispy bits off a duck leg and dunking them in the remains of the sauce, "that is an amazing story, and it does sound as if she totally made it up to get one over on that poor drama teacher man and the girl who got the main part, but what can we do with it? It's not like she's even mentioned anything about it to us, and Mrs. Bennett obviously believed her, or she wouldn't have let her start at Stagmount."

"Yeah, I was just thinking that." Charlie had her elbow on the table and was leaning her face on her hand, clearly in thoughtful mode. "But what about all the *lies* she's told us? The way she tells it, she was the most popular girl in the school—in all the teams, best friends with everyone, editor of that fucking stupid magazine, and all-round bloody genius."

They stopped talking as the waitress began laying out plates filled with sizzling fillet steak in pepper sauce, Singapore noodles, kung pao chicken, pak choi in oyster sauce, fried rice, boiled rice, prawn crackers, and garlic prawns. As there wasn't enough space on the table for their many dishes, she had to stick some of them on the table next door.

If they had been of a different mentality, the girls might have been embarrassed. As it was, they whooped and cheered and thanked her so profusely the chefs came out of the kitchen to see what the commotion was. They laughed and bowed as the girls gave them a standing ovation, and for a few minutes there was no talk as the girls shoveled food into their mouths. Ian would have been beside himself with delight at the number of times the girls clinked their glasses and drank to his good health.

"So," Jinx said, putting down her fork and leaning back in her seat. "Stella is obviously a lot more evil than your common or garden bitch, but what are we going to do about it?"

"You know, I'm not sure there's *anything* we can do," said Liv, surreptitiously undoing the top button of her extra-tight Joseph black cords under the table before breathing out with relief, "apart from sit on it until something comes up. She's clearly a total psycho, but she'd not stupid, and whatever the Bedales drama man thought about it, she's practically a world-class actress, too. We don't want to get burned."

"It's just so fucking frustrating," added Chastity. "And I'm worried about Lib. It's not like we can tell her any of this, because it'll look like sour grapes after everything that's happened."

"I know." Jinx was frowning. "The only person Stella cares about is Stella, and she knows how much we all love Lib—although I have to say I am *rapidly* going off her."

"No, you're not." Charlie smiled. "Come on, you're just cross that she's not talking to you at the moment, but she'll get over it. How many rows have we all had? Loads, that's what, and we're all still here."

"Yeah, you're right," Jinx sighed and looked at her watch. "Shit, guys, it's nine-thirty—we should call a cab."

"Yep," said Chastity waving for the bill. "We don't want to be late back, especially after last night."

They were joshing and laughing as they walked through the door of Tanner House at five to ten, shoving each other and giggling manically. They were absolutely stuffed to the brim with all the delicious food, and more than a little drunk. Chastity pushed Charlie, and Liv cannoned off the low wall to the side of the entrance path.

Jinx was walking ahead of them. When she stopped suddenly as if she'd been shot, they all piled into the back of her and shrieked loudly with more drunken hilarity.

"What are *you* doing here?" Jinx asked, staring in an appalled fashion at Ms. Gunn, who was sitting on the foyer sofa, her huge bulk filling the whole thing even though it was a two-seater. "Where's Mr. Morris?"

"Hello, Jane." Ms. Gunn's fat face was split in two by its most terrible smile. "Good evening, you others. I don't know your names yet, but I'm very sure we'll make each other's acquaintance. And that will probably be"—Gunn smirked evilly again, causing her jowls to shudder beneath where her chin would have been had she not been so fat—"sooner rather than later."

Liv stepped forward and held out her hand. "Olivia Taylor," she said brightly as a somewhat confused Ms. Gunn gingerly took Liv's beautifully French-manicured hand in her own huge paw. "Simply *delighted* to meet you. Ms. Gunn, isn't it?"

The others, who'd been holding their breath and wondering what the hell was going on, collapsed into a fresh fit of snorting, snuffling, crying laughter, totally unable to stop themselves. Gunn, belatedly realizing that Liv was being sarcastic, hefted herself off the sofa and raised herself to her full height.

"Well, well, well," she said. "If that's how you want to play it, there are going to be some changes around here, mark my words. Now go to bed, all of you. Immediately."

"But Mr. M—" Chastity was about to tell her that once they were back in the house, they were allowed to go to bed whenever they liked. It was a lower-sixth privilege, and Mr. Morris trusted them to look after themselves.

"I don't *care* what Mr. Morris has ever done or said." Gunn immediately went bright red in the face, a clear signal to all who knew her that she was about to start shouting at the top of her voice. Sure enough, the bellowing commenced. "I'M IN CHARGE NOW, AND YOU WILL ALL GO TO BED THIS MINUTE OR FACE THE CONSEQUENCES!"

The girls didn't need telling twice. They gave one another gloomy looks all round but trudged off to their respective rooms rather than spend another minute in the company of the terrible Gunn.

As they had next-door rooms Jinx and Chastity walked off together, in silence until they reached the safety of their corridor.

"What the fuck is going on, Chas?" Jinx was seriously put out. She'd counted down the days for three years to get away from Gunn and was horrified to find her nemesis dishing out punishments in her beloved Tanner House.

"Don't worry about it, Jin." Chastity was still giggling a bit about Liv and Gunn's subsequent outburst and had no idea how vindictive Gunn could be. "Morris has obviously been taken ill or something. She's not going to be here forever—

she's got Wollstonecraft to look after, anyway. He'll be back soon, I'm sure of it—he was fine when I saw him this morning."

Jinx said good night to Chastity and lay down on her bed, feeling very out of sorts indeed. She was freaked out even further when she heard the unmistakable thud of Gunn's huge footsteps patrolling the corridor outside at least three times in the night. It transported her back to her most miserable times in the junior school, when Gunn had seemed determined to destroy her spirit and everywhere she turned that fat face was staring malevolently at her. After tossing and turning for a bit, Jinx got up and rammed her desk chair underneath the door handle to ensure no unwanted visitors could get in to spy on her in the night, but even so, she didn't sleep well at all.

35

Jinx was even less amused when she woke up the next morning to the incessant sound of someone stomping around the house and vigorously ringing one of the loud school handbells. They never had a bell in Tanner—Morris trusted them to get themselves up and sorted out in the morning. They were seventeen, after all.

She groaned and swore and put her pillow over her head, but whoever was ringing that bell was determined that not one member of Tanner House could possibly avoid hearing it. Jinx had a pretty good idea who the bell ringer was, too.

She switched her bedside radio on, fiddled with the volume to try and drown out the sound, and looked at her watch. It was seven-fifteen! She lay back against her pillows and sighed deeply. None of them got up until at least an hour later than that normally, and they always stayed in bed longer if they could at all help it.

She was grinding her teeth in time with the bell when Chastity walked in and collapsed onto the end of her bed. Chastity looked as terrible as Jinx felt, her blond hair standing straight up and the remains of last night's mascara in black rings underneath her puffy eyes. "What the *fuck* is this?" she moaned, shielding her eyes with her hand. "It's that bloody Gunn woman, isn't it? What the hell is she playing at? This is like a bad thriller. Jinx, I'm *shattered*."

Jinx was just getting up—a long process that involved rolling the duvet, inch by torturous inch, down to the end of the bed—and listening to Chastity's moans of impotent rage, when Gunn's voice came into the bedroom loud and clear.

"Good morning, Tanner House," she shouted. "I repeat, good morning, Tanner House."

Jinx threw her duvet off, jumped out of bed, and turned to Chastity. "I don't bloody believe it," she said, aghast. "The fucking old witch is using a freaking *megaphone*."

"No way!" Chastity jumped up and opened the door a crack, peering out into the foyer before slamming it shut and leaning against it with an equally shocked expression on her face. "You're right. She's standing out there shouting orders like a sergeant fucking major."

"I want every girl down here, fully dressed and ready to go in five—I repeat—*five* minutes to sign the register."

"What register?" Chastity wailed as she raced out of Jinx's

room to get herself sorted. "We don't *have* a morning register! This is a nightmare."

As Chastity ran out, Liberty ran in: the shock of Gunn's arrival had obviously pushed the feud right out of her mind.

"Jinx! What's going on?" Liberty was wearing the boxer shorts she slept in, one sock, and her bright pink bra, and clutching her favorite Lancôme mascara wand in her hand. "What's *she* doing here? What's happened to Morris?"

"I don't know, Lib." Jinx was pulling on her tights with one hand at the same time that she was plucking a few stray hairs from underneath her eyebrows with the other. She was obsessed with her eyebrows, and nothing—not even a screaming Gunn—would make her appear in public if they looked ragged. "You'd better get dressed, sweetheart, or she'll do something terrible—you know how unpredictable she is, and she hates us anyway. I'll see you outside—we'll talk about it then."

"ONE MINUTE TO GO, GIRLS, I REPEAT, ONE MINUTE TO GO!" Gunn was obviously enjoying using the megaphone—not that she really needed it. There was a perky tone to her voice that Jinx had never heard her use in Wollstonecraft, or anywhere, come to think of it. The whole business was becoming more suspicious by the second, and she felt highly unsettled as she wandered into the foyer with a few seconds to spare and saw that Gunn—clutching her megaphone as if she were a five-year-old with a favorite new toy—was marshaling the lower sixth into a row along the path outside the front door. It had just started to rain, for Christ's sake.

Jinx joined the row next to Lulu Cooper and was delighted to find Charlie and Liv lining up behind her.

"I take it all back, J." Charlie's short brown hair was standing on end, and she was still wearing her pink-spotted pajama bottoms, which she'd tucked into a pair of very grimy Ugg boots. "She *is* fucking mad. We always thought all you Wollstonecraft lot were exaggerating when you told us stuff like this."

"So did we," whispered little Lulu, who looked positively terrified. "We thought you were terrible show-offs. What's this in aid of?"

"Who knows?" Jinx said grimly. "She's a power-hungry motherfucking psycho bitch from hell, and knowing her, this is probably only the start of it."

The sixty or so girls who made up the lower sixth were all standing in a ragged line outside in the spitting rain by now, in various states of undress and lots of sleepwear with big, fluffy, hooded parkas buttoned up over the top.

Gunn, who was striding back and forth in front of them, had obviously taken the army theme to heart. She was wearing a pair of steel–toe-capped DM boots that Jinx had certainly never seen before, and had wound a khaki scarf around her thick neck. In her right hand she was holding tight to the handle of one of the red-and-white megaphones the sports staff used at tournaments and school sports days. In her left she was gripping an official-looking clipboard on which a long list of names was being spotted with drizzle.

Despite the fact that she was standing only a few feet in front of them and that none of the girls was saying a word, having been shocked into silence by the weirdness of the morning, Gunn raised the megaphone to her thin lips.

"STAND UP STRAIGHT!" she yelled. "WHEN I CALL YOUR NAME, YOU WILL RAISE YOUR RIGHT HAND AND SAY, 'HERE.' YOU WILL NOT TALK, YOU WILL NOT LAUGH, AND YOU WILL NOT LOOK AT EACH OTHER. YOU LOT HAVE HAD IT TOO EASY FOR TOO LONG, AND I'M GOING TO SHAPE YOU UP WHETHER YOU LIKE IT OR NOT."

"Excuse me." Liv raised her hand. "I don't mean to be rude, but I really don't think it's necessary for you to speak to us through that thing. I mean, you *are* only standing a meter in front of us."

"Oh, you don't, don't you?" Ms. Gunn was standing right in front of Liv and using what Jinx immediately recognized as her fake-reasonable voice, easily the most dangerous. "Well, take it from me . . . Olivia Taylor, isn't it?" Gunn made a note on the top sheet of paper. "What you might think is necessary and what I think is necessary are two very different things. And since I am the one in charge here, I'll thank you to shut up and not interrupt me again."

Gunn turned away before spinning round and screaming into the loud-hailer right in Liv's face, "AND YOU'RE GATED FOR THE REST OF TERM. THAT SHOULD TEACH YOU NOT TO CHEEK ME AGAIN."

Most of the line recoiled in horror, and Lulu started crying.

But Liv stepped forward and opened her mouth to speak again.

"I'm sorry, Ms. Gunn, but that is the most ridiculous thing I've ever heard. I certainly won't be spoken to like that, and I shall be seeing Mrs. Bennett about this at the earliest available opportunity. You're absolutely mad."

Although none of them could decide whether Liv was being incredibly brave or very, very stupid, there were lots of nervous giggles and snorts of horrified laughter at this.

Gunn stood stock-still, as if she couldn't believe her ears. She probably couldn't, thought Jinx, who was dead impressed with Liv.

"Oh you will, will you?" Gunn's voice was even silkier than previously. "I want you in my office at the end of registration. NO ARGUMENTS."

"Fine," Liv said combatively, looking and sounding like she didn't give a shit. "See you there. Oh, and before I forget— where exactly *is* your office? I only know where our *housemaster's* room is." Liv folded her arms and cocked her head to one side expectantly, hoping to have wrong-footed Gunn with this mention of Mr. Morris.

"Oh, did I forget to mention?" Gunn said, smiling more wickedly than she had all morning before playing her trump card. "Mr. Morris won't be back this term—*if at all.* I'm in charge now."

The girls were shocked into silence, and Gunn finished taking the register, ticking off each name with a flourish before conducting what she informed them was the "daily dress inspection."

"You *could* have made a complaint," Jinx muttered into Liv's ear, "if only Mrs. Bennett hadn't dashed off to the States on yet another of her international recruitment drives."

"What?" said Liv, aghast.

"Yep," Jinx nodded sadly, "I saw her getting into a taxi this morning."

Charlie and about ten others were banned from taking trips into town all week for daring to still be in their pajamas, Liberty was given lines for wearing heels that were more than two inches high—"not appropriate for school, I'm sure you agree, Latiffe"—and Jinx was given three evening detentions for general untidiness. In fact, she looked exactly the same as most of the others, but Jinx knew that Gunn was delighted at being able to punish her again, and that this was a mere warm-up. This was just the beginning of what Jinx was sure would become an unbearable onslaught of punishments. She was freaked out.

The girls wandered off to chapel in a daze. Most of them hadn't been all term, and on the way there they joked that at least Mrs. Stanwell would be thrilled to see them. However, when they got there, the usually smiley Mrs. S had a very pinched look about her face, and puffy eyes, as if she'd been crying. What the bloody hell was going on?

36

Mrs. Carpenter was lovely to them in tutor group. She hated Ms. Gunn, too, and was very sympathetic to their plight but couldn't—or wouldn't—answer any of their questions as to how long they were likely to have to endure her.

Liberty was speaking to Jinx and the others again, but the only topic of conversation was what had happened to Morris. Stella wasn't at lunch.

In case he'd come down with a contagious flesh-eating disease that the rest of the teachers were trying to keep quiet, Charlie went to see the nurse and pretended she was suffering from terrible period pains. She surreptitiously checked all the cubicles while Mister S was off fetching her trusty jar of paracetamol but came back dejected, saying they were full of nothing but flu-y first-years.

Despite their best efforts, by the end of the day none of the girls knew anything about where Mr. Morris was, and if any of the teachers knew, they certainly weren't saying. The only thing they did know was that Miss Cusk, Gunn's timid deputy, was in temporary charge of Wollstonecraft House. They clung to that word, *temporary*, as if it were the last disco biscuit in the dance tent at a summer music festival.

By the end of the day, the old reference library was uncharacteristically packed with lower sixth-formers. They were pretending to revise but in reality were avoiding returning to Tanner House and the dreaded Gunn until the last possible minute. When Mrs. Bennett was appointed, she'd decreed that no Stagmount girl was allowed to study after seven o'clock at night, reasoning that they worked hard enough all day. Today— wishing they could stay in there all night—was the first time any of them had ever dissed this rule.

As they trudged down the drive in small groups, the girls discussed how they were going to get round Ms. Gunn. Jinx and the rest of the old Wollstonecraft girls strode ahead looking bootfaced—they knew there was *no* getting around The Gunn when she was in a full on strop like this. The best strategy was avoidance, pure and simple.

And there was not much chance of that, either. Most of Jinx's gang assembled themselves in the common room on the second floor, where the Sky system was set up, and settled down to watch *Laguna Beach*, their favorite show on MTV.

Anyway, they were about ten minutes in and loving every

second when dreadful Daisy Finnegan kicked open the door—a deeply uncharacteristic act in itself—and rushed in with the palest face they'd ever seen on her. Even though none of them liked Daisy, Ms. Gunn's shocking arrival had caused a definite sense of comradeship amongst the lower sixth, so they didn't shout at her to get out, as they normally would have done.

"What's wrong, Daisy?" Chastity pressed pause on their Sky plus, and they all turned round expectantly.

"You've not seen them have you?" she panted, leaning despondently against the wall and pointing a shaking finger toward the window. "Look out there."

The girls ran to the window and stared out, shocked into silence. On the path outside were cardboard boxes filled with bottles of booze of all descriptions, boxes and cartons of cigarettes, myriad Rizla papers, stacks of takeaway menus, and a solitary miniature fridge.

"Oh my God," Chastity screamed. "That's my fridge!"

"And our vodka," yelled Jinx, glimpsing the vanilla Absolut they'd nearly finished the other night.

"What's with the menus?" asked Liv, who was leaning so far out the window Charlie had taken the precaution of grabbing hold of the back of her thick woven leather belt.

"There's posters up all over the foyer," said Daisy, "saying she's done a room inspection and that she's chucking all this stuff out."

"Whaaat?" the girls yelled in unison, turning around and staring at Daisy openmouthed.

"Yep." Daisy's face was slowly regaining its original color. "This first lot is an amnesty, apparently. She's getting rid of this stuff but says that if she finds any more booze, fags, or—as she calls it—drug paraphernalia after this, the 'perpetrators' will be suspended or expelled, depending on the severity of the offense."

"But we're *allowed* to drink in Tanner. It's practically the whole point of making it into the sixth form." Chastity was apoplectic. "And Morris lets you lot smoke so long as you keep quiet about it. Everyone knows that!"

"It gets worse," Daisy interrupted. "You know I don't drink or smoke anyway, so I don't really care about her taking all this stuff but thanks to her finding all of it, we're all banned from town for the rest of term, we've got to be in our rooms by nine-thirty every night, there's to be no more ordering food in, and she's put up a cleaning list. I told her I had nothing to do with any of it and she," Daisy gulped, "told me to 'get stuffed.' I hate to say it, but I think you lot were right about her from the start."

"I am *not* cleaning this fucking house," Chastity raged. "What does she think our parents pay the fucking fees for? I'm phoning my mum right now. I'm going to have her sacked."

"Hold on, Chas." Jinx was pointing past the cardboard boxes lining the path at someone walking in their direction up the drive. "There's Stella. Where's she been all afternoon? I *bet* you she's got something to do with all this. Everywhere she goes, shit happens. In fact," she gasped and covered her hand with her mouth, "what if *she* got rid of Morris like she did that guy at Bedales?"

At the mention of Stella having something to do with Gunn's sudden instatement, a dark look of utter disbelief passed sharply across Liberty's face, and she scowled furiously at her erstwhile friends.

"You could be right, Jinx," Liv agreed. "I think it's time we had a serious word with Ms. Fox."

Liberty spun round. "What the *fuck* are you all talking about?" she yelled, stamping her foot and positively quivering with anger. "You've all gone fucking mad. Especially *you*." She turned to point at Jinx. "You've been jealous of her since the day she arrived. You just can't *stand* the fact that I've got a new friend, can you? Well I've fucking had enough of it. I'll be happy if I never see or speak to you again. That's it—we're finished."

Liberty ran out of the room, slamming the door behind her with such force that it jolted the Sky plus back into action. None of them paid any attention to *The Hills*, however. They were too busy looking at Jinx, whose face was fixed in the grimmest expression they'd ever seen on it.

Fanny Ho wandered in a few seconds later, looking very dapper in her lilac Paul Smith suit with newly short hair. "Hey, guys, what's with all the boxes outside?" she said. She'd just returned from a long day in London, where the University of Miami was holding pre-entry interviews, and was oblivious to Gunn's instatement. "What's going on?"

As they filled her in, she looked increasingly despondent. "Oh shit," Fanny whispered, her head in her hands. "Oh shit."

"Come on, Fan." Charlie put her arm round Fanny's shoulder.

"It's not *that* bad, is it? Anyway, you're probably the most model pupil here."

"Yeah," Liv added, "and I'm sure Gunn won't be here next term. She's got Wollstonecraft to run. It's only for a couple more weeks."

Fanny shook Charlie off, picked up her *Financial Times*, and left the room without saying a word. A very subdued Daisy followed her, while the others sighed and settled down in front of the telly again, although there was no more shouting at the screen, and it was an uncharacteristically quiet group who shut themselves in their rooms at nine-thirty as ordered. Jinx was the quietest of the lot. She'd been staring into space since Fanny's outburst and hadn't said a word since.

37

"LIV!" Jinx hissed, pulling the end of Liv's duvet in what was proving a futile attempt to wake her up. "Liv! Wake up, will you!"

Jinx looked around in the dark and spied a jumbo bottle of Evian on Liv's bedside table. She grabbed it, opened it, and spurted it all over Liv's face before quickly holding a pillow over her friend's mouth to muffle any screams. Liv's room was not far from Mr. Morris's flat, and Jinx knew Gunn's amazing super-sonic hearing of old.

"Jesus *Christ*, Jinx!" Liv gasped when Jinx lifted the pillow, her terrified eyes wide. "What the *fuck* are you doing? I thought I was being murdered. What do you want? This had better be good."

"Sorry, *sorry*! Keep your hair on." Jinx couldn't stop herself from giggling in the face of Liv's outrage. "I need to talk to you, and I don't want Gunn hearing anything. This is like being in the fucking first year again.

"I couldn't sleep, so I was smoking out the window just now, and I heard Stella on the phone in the common room. I'm *sure* she was talking to her mum about everything that's going on here, but making out like *we* were bullying *her*. I'm sure I heard my name, and that's the last thing I need—especially given I've only just got back from being suspended."

Liv was still half asleep, but she looked skeptical and muttered something about fucking mad paranoia into her pillow.

"I'm *sure*, Liv!" Jinx bounced up and down on the side of her bed in irritation. "She was talking about the row tonight, and I'm convinced I heard something about Mr. Morris and no one knowing yet."

"So what if it was?" Liv loved her sleep and clearly wanted to get back to it. "We'll find out soon enough if that's the case, and in the meantime, what can we do about it? It's not like we're going to get a confession out of her, is it? I don't think there's anything we can do except sit tight and sweat Gunn out for the rest of term."

"Liv," Jinx said seriously, "I'm disappointed in you. You used to be able to do anything, get rid of anyone."

"Okay," she continued as Liv pointedly rolled over and pulled her duvet up to her chin. "I'm going. But I'm going to do something about this, and if I have to do it alone, I will. I'm not going to sit back and be made a fool of, even if all of you are."

Jinx said good night and carefully opened the door to let

herself out. As she crept silently down the corridor leading to the foyer, she heard voices and threw herself behind a thick velvet curtain covering the long-disused tradesman's door a few meters to the left of the front door everyone now used.

As she stood in the dark holding her breath, she heard Gunn's unmistakable baritone and a lighter voice she immediately recognized but couldn't quite place. It was only when the latter giggled girlishly and said, "À *bientôt, ma cherie*," that it clicked. It was The Dick. She didn't even live on the school grounds, *and* she was supposed to be laid up at home with a serious head injury. What the fuck was she doing with Gunn in Tanner House at midnight?

Jinx waited until she heard the front door being locked and bolted and for Gunn's heavy footsteps to thud in the direction of her flat, followed by the unmistakable sound of her shutting her own door behind her before she came out from behind the curtain. She legged it back to her room and breathed a sigh of relief as she softly closed her own door and rammed the handy chair underneath the handle. She turned off the lights, planning to lie on her bed in the dark and analyze the evening's many events. However, barely had she shut her eyes before she slipped into a deep and dreamless sleep, only waking to the sound of that bloody handbell the next morning.

Gunn took the register and did her dress inspection again. Although there was a palpable sense of rage and injustice hanging in the air where the girls were lined up on the path outside, the events of the previous evening meant the lower sixth were taking her seriously now. Despite this, the old witch still managed to dish out a couple of punishment essays for inappropriate facial piercings and demand that the perpetrators remove them by the end of the day.

As they marched off en masse to chapel, Liberty grabbed Stella's arm to make her hang back, clearly not wanting to be anywhere near Jinx et al. Chastity was punching in each of her mother's many numbers on her top-of-the-range mobile phone, leaving urgent messages with cleaners and hotel staff all over the world trying to locate her. She was still spitting about the theft of her fridge and the ransacking of her booze closet, adamant that she was going to have Gunn fired. Jinx was grinning as she whispered to Liv and Charlie, telling them what normally happened to girls whose parents complained—normally their daughters found themselves in *all sorts* of extra trouble they hadn't anticipated. But Chastity *was* funny when she flew into one of her rages.

Jinx was in the middle of double art, sitting in the mezzanine drawing area above the studio proper and lining up all the pastel crayons in a circle in the order of the rainbow, when she decided she was bored and hungry. Lunch had been a monstrous bean pie, and Jinx hated beans. The kidney, the baked, the broad, the white—all of them, in fact, apart from the green, which any fool could see was not a bean but a vegetable. She was not a fussy eater at all, but the texture of beans was so abhorrent to her, she knew she'd vomit if one found its way into her mouth. So, having hardly eaten anything since breakfast and feeling peckish, she told Professor Crawford she needed the loo and excused herself in search of a few biscuits.

She was wandering down the corridor in the direction of the dining rooms, halfheartedly looking at the team lists and "interesting and/or relevant" articles cut from the broadsheets and pasted onto the notice boards each day by the various heads of departments, when she bumped into a harassed-looking man with ginger hair. Wearing khaki trousers, walking boots, and a navy blue jumper, he was carrying a bulging backpack that was so full he hadn't quite managed to zip it all the way up. Staring around in confusion, with beads of sweat sprouting on his top lip, he was obviously lost.

"Hi there," she said, approaching him and sticking out her hand. "Jinx Slater, lower sixth. Can I help at all?"

The Stagmount girls were always helpful to strangers and lost parents; it would have been more than their lives were worth if any of the staff caught them behaving otherwise. Mrs. Bennett was red hot on politeness and what she called common courtesy.

"Oh," he said, staring at Jinx, apparently rather taken aback that she'd spoken to him, and belatedly taking her hand in his decidedly clammy one. "Oh, yes, that would be fantastic. If you don't mind."

"Of course I don't mind." Jinx smiled, thinking how dearly she would like to wipe her hand on her jeans but forcing herself to resist the impulse. What a loser. If she minded, she wouldn't have bloody offered, would she? "Who are you here to see?"

"Mrs. Bennett. Your headmistress? I, uh . . ." He seemed dazed. "I'm, er, Brandon Brannington. From the *Guardian*? I'm here to interview her?"

"Right, Mr. Brannington, I'm walking that way myself." Jinx smiled again, suddenly recognizing his pale face and realizing that *this* must be the ridiculous journalist who'd crashed his car that day several weeks ago. She desperately wanted to tease him about it, but the man seemed so distinctly uneasy, she thought it only fair she control herself. And so much for all that stuff adults normally say about teenagers using up-speak—she knew *far* more of them that did it. It was nerves. Anyway, the only time some adults seemed to actually like teenagers was when they were lying dead in a secluded beauty spot somewhere and thus unable to mooch about wearing hoodies and looking threatening.

As they walked up the corridor—frustratingly slowly, so Brandon could admire the framed artwork and (or so Jinx thought, anyway) perv over the team photos pinned to the walls, Jinx noticed a tape recorder sticking out of his bag.

She had a sudden eureka moment standing there on the muddy brown carpet in the yellow hallway. "Mrs. Bennett loves journalists," she said conversationally, leaning against one of the walls he was admiring, in what she hoped was an alluring manner. "She's back from America and she'll probably keep you in her office for *ages*. There was a woman from the *Times* who missed five trains! She wrote about it in her piece."

She was gratified to see Brandon look slightly uncomfortable. "Yes," she continued, gazing into his eyes, "Mrs. B can natter on for absolute hours. She's got so much to say about really interesting stuff—you know, *political* stuff about education. It's *especially* interesting when she gets on to the government threat to remove private schools' charity status and things. She's really hot on that one and totally knows her stuff. I expect you do, too." Jinx smiled winningly at him. "Don't you?"

Brandon coughed, blushed, and mumbled something that could have been in the affirmative if only she'd heard what it was.

"Sorry," Jinx said. "I didn't quite catch that. Did you say you wanted to use the loo? Look," she continued, taking his arm and frog-marching him in the direction of the men's room, "it's right over here. Don't worry about a thing. I'll look after your bag and take you to her office when you're done."

Brandon looked a bit confused as he was practically shoved through the door, but toddled off inside obediently. Jinx breathed a sigh of relief as the door slammed shut behind him, and scanned the corridor both ways. Thankfully, it was deserted as it always was in the middle of lessons, and she delved into the bulging backpack, rooting around to try and find the tape recorder that seemed to have slipped to the bottom when he dropped it on the floor.

"Yesss!" She grabbed hold of the silver device—a Sony digital, no less—and shoved it deep into the back pocket of her jeans before tying her jumper around her waist in case Brandon was planning to scope out her ass again as she dropped him off. She'd definitely noticed him casting a few bottomward glances as they'd made their way up the corridor. He emerged a few seconds later and thanked her for her trouble. Poor deluded fool.

"No trouble *whatsoever*," she trilled as she deposited him by Jo's desk with a jaunty wink. "I do hope you have a pleasant interview. Byeee!"

Forgetting all about her desire for biscuits, Jinx skipped back down the corridor to double art, shocking a couple of first-years practically into tears when she grinned widely and waved at them as she passed. Professor Crawford didn't notice her slip back in and dash up the winding staircase to her desk. She put her head down and got sucked into her project without saying a word to anyone about her dealings with the journalist.

"Jinx. *Jinx!*" It was already teatime, and Chastity was staring at Jinx. "You've not listened to a bloody word I've said, have you?"

"God, sorry Chas." Jinx looked up from the Bakewell tart she was crumbling into tiny pieces on the plate in front of her. "I'm not ignoring you, I promise. I was, um, thinking about my English essay. What did you say?"

"Your *English* essay? Christ, you've changed! Don't worry about it—I still can't get hold of my freaking mother, that's all." They dumped their plates on top of the precarious dirty pile on the trolley and set off to the reference library that hadn't seen so much action in years.

Jinx had to stifle a giggle as they walked past Jo's desk and heard her bitching on the phone about incompetence, useless journalists and having to rearrange Mrs. Bennett's diary once again. "What happened to shorthand?" she squawked, tossing her red curls around self-importantly. "It was mandatory at secretarial college."

Stella and Liberty were sitting at a table on their own in an alcove at the back of the room: their heads were close together, and they were whispering about something. All day, whenever Liberty had seen any of them, she'd turned her back or walked in the opposite direction. Stella had strutted about with an infuriatingly smug smile on her face as if she owned the place.

Jinx sat on her bed painting her nails. There was nothing like the smell of acetate to concentrate the mind, and she often had her best thoughts while performing a mini-manicure. She gave her newly hot pink fingertips a quick blast under the hair-dryer and looked at her watch. It was eleven-thirty. She'd heard Liberty switch her stereo off an hour earlier and knew that the dance music only stopped when sleep was imminent. She peeked around her door—the rest of the house was dark and silent.

Jinx stood in front of her chest of drawers and looked in her mirror. She wasn't putting loads of makeup on, but whenever she knew she was having an important encounter, she liked to go into it looking at least decent. Like armor, she felt it gave her an edge. It was more psychological than anything else, but still—whatever helps.

She ran some extra-strength Frizz-Ease through her curly hair and spritzed her Chanel perfume generously all over herself. She smoothed the front of her baggy boy jeans and slipped on her black haviana flip-flops. Finally, she switched the slim silver tape recorder on for the umpteenth time to check that it was working. It was. She set it to record and slipped it deep into the front pocket of her baggy jeans. She wasn't planning to sit down at all, but even if she did, the jeans were so voluminous an observer wouldn't see it or, worst case, they'd assume it was a mobile phone.

Jinx flicked her light switch off and opened the door. She stepped into the corridor and allowed it to swing gently closed against her hand. She took a deep breath in the dark before tiptoeing silently to the stairs leading to Stella's room. She cast a longing look at the Diet Coke machine but told herself not to be so bloody ridiculous and carried on.

Jinx stood outside Stella's door and saw a sliver of light underneath it. Good. She'd hoped the bitch would be awake, since she couldn't stand the thought of having to wake her up. She didn't bother to knock as she pushed the door open and stood in the frame.

"What the hell do *you* want?" Stella asked, looking up from where she was sitting at her desk, typing something on her laptop. "I thought you weren't talking to me."

"Well, I am." Jinx edged into the room and shut the door behind her.

"In fact," she carried on, sneering massively, "I thought you hated me because your so-called best friend prefers *me* to you now."

"I don't hate you, Stella." Jinx moved into the room carefully. "It's true I don't *like* you very much, but I don't hate you."

"In fact," she continued, leaning against the wall as insouciantly as she could, "I feel *sorry* for you."

"What are you talking about?" Stella jerked her head up and stared at Jinx. "I don't need your sympathy. Far from it." She laughed maliciously. "Yes, I should imagine you're feeling pretty low right about now, Jinx Slater. Whereas I am totally happy with the way things are going."

"Yeah, I bet you are." Jinx took a step closer and bent down so she could look Stella directly in the eye. "I know all about you, Stella. I know how miserable you were at Bedales. I know that you didn't have any friends, weren't on any of the teams, and didn't get the main part in the school play. In fact," Jinx went on, delighted by the shock on Stella's face, pleased to have wrong-footed her so early on, "I know a lot of things about you I bet you wish I didn't."

Stella blinked, evidently taken aback. "So what?" she asked eventually. "It's not like you can do anything about it, is it? I've got you all exactly where I want you. I'm in charge now, and there's nothing you can do about it. Anyway, what do you want?" Stella gestured at her laptop. "I'm busy, and I certainly don't have the time or the inclination for a heart-to-heart with *you*."

"What about McGregor, Stella? I find it hard to imagine that even you could stoop so low as to falsely accuse someone—a married old man, for Christ's sake—of something like that."

"Shut up, Jinx," Stella spat, twisting round and slamming the lid of her laptop shut. "You have no idea what it was like there for someone like me. I'd had enough. That play was the final straw—I *knew* I was good enough, but I was passed over again, as I had been all my life. Why shouldn't I be given the chance to start somewhere new? Why did everything good always go to everyone else? I realized it was my last chance to have the kind of life I wanted, and I took it."

"Yes," Jinx replied, "and you didn't care who you took down while you did so, did you?"

"No, I didn't," Stella hissed. "*You* don't know what it's like to be always passed over, always ignored. It wasn't even as if they laughed at me—I might as well not have been there for all the notice they took of me.

"Yes, I lied about McGregor, and why the hell shouldn't I? He was one of the worst, always looking after his favorites and ignoring everyone else." Stella shook her head. "Who told you all this, anyway?"

"I had a very interesting chat with Jennifer Lewis when—thanks to you—I was suspended last week. She's an old friend."

Stella looked furious. "That bitch was one of the worst. I might have known she'd be a friend of yours. You all stick together, don't you? You just can't help yourselves."

"If you'd bothered to take the time to get to know us, Stella," Jinx said, very calmly, as she definitely didn't want to be kicked out before she'd had the chance to put her plan into action, "you'd have realized pretty quickly that Stagmount is nothing like Bedales. We don't ignore people unless they deserve it. We were totally prepared to be friends with you when you arrived, but you've done nothing since you got here to make us think you're worthy of it."

"Don't make me laugh, Jinx," Stella said, half closing her eyes and glowering at Jinx. "*You* tried to humiliate me from the word *go*. Whatever's going on here is only what you and your stupid cronies deserve."

"What?" Jinx exclaimed, truly shocked by the accusation. "I didn't do anything to you. You're a raving lunatic."

"Oh, yeah?" Stella said, swiveling round in her chair and fixing Jinx with an evil stare. "Well, how else would you explain dissing me in front of the whole class on the very first day I arrived?"

"No, I didn't," Jinx replied, racking her brains but coming up with nothing. "You're making it up, Stella, you really are."

"What was it? What was it?" Stella said sarcastically, drumming her fingers on the desk. "Oh, yes, I remember. 'How old are you, Stella? Are you sure you should be in the lower sixth?'" She spun round and glared at Jinx again, as if daring her to disagree.

"Whaaaaat?" Jinx sighed and shook her head. "You really are mad. I can't believe you've held that against me all term. It was a joke. That's J.O.K.E.—you're obviously not familiar with the term."

"Come off it, Jinx, you wanted to humiliate me in front of

everyone." Stella smiled. "And it didn't work, did it? No, once I realized the kind of girl you were, I decided to play you at your own game. And it looks like I've won. Your J.O.K.E. has back-fired. I hope you've found it *funny*."

"Look, Stella," Jinx said, "I didn't come up here to argue with you, and I'm sorry—really I am—that you took that stuff I said to heart, but you took it the wrong way. You totally overre-acted, and look what's happened. And if you had such a prob-lem with me, why the hell didn't you just say something?"

"Shut up," Stella spat back. "I don't have to listen to any-thing you've got to say. What do you want, anyway? Spill it or get out. I was perfectly happy to be friends with you at the beginning, but you ruined it, and I've had almost as much as I can stand of The Great Jinx Slater."

"Okay. I just want a few answers, that's all, and then I'll get out of your hair. What happened to Mr. Morris?" Jinx jiggled her hand in her pocket to make sure the recorder wasn't jammed against her leg and would pick everything up. Stella sat in silence, but a glimmer of a smile began to play about her face. "You just couldn't stand being told off by him, so you played the same game with him, didn't you?"

"Yes, I did." Stella leaned back in her chair. "And what are you going to do about it?

"Oh," she crossed her legs and smiled triumphantly. "I forgot—there's nothing you *can* do, is there? Yes, in my experi-ence people have a habit of taking these things pretty seriously. In fact, I'd say it's pretty damn unlikely you'll ever see your beloved Mr. Morris again.

"So, when all things are considered, it's pretty irrelevant what you think, isn't it, Jinx? No one's going to believe you over me. And even if they did suspect you were telling the truth, you've got no way of proving anything." She stood up and stretched. "What an interesting chat this has been. Liberty and I are planning an early-morning gym session, and I need to go to bed."

Stella stood up and held the door open. "Night, then," she trilled sarcastically. "Sweet dreams."

"Night, Stella," Jinx said, backing out of the door, her hand placed protectively over the front of her jeans. "It *has* been an interesting chat. Very illuminating indeed."

Jinx ran down the corridor and took the stairs two at a time, not bothering to tiptoe. She dashed into her room, wedged the chair under the door handle, and removed the tape recorder from her pocket. She placed it reverentially on her desk and admired the blinking red record light before carefully switching it to off. She rooted around at the back of her desk drawer, found the tuck box key she rarely used, except when she had a bag of weed and needed a safe stashing place, put the recorder in there, locked it, and went to sleep gripping the key in her hand.

Jinx turned up to the daily dress inspection with the key in her pocket but didn't bother going to chapel. Stuff the consequences, she needed the precious time. Given that she wasn't in the best of books with Mrs. B right now she knew she had to plan carefully what she was going to say to the head about all of this. There was no way she could just rock up at the head's office without a clear idea of exactly where she wanted this conversation to go. If it went wrong, Jinx dreaded to think what damage Stella might inflict next—she absolutely had to make Mrs. Bennett see there was no alternative but to get rid of her; this was her one chance, and she couldn't risk being kicked out or not listened to.

Since Gunn was more than likely prowling the house looking for chapel-dodging miscreants, Jinx didn't dare smoke her usual morning cigarette out the window but decided to have it in the bike shed instead. She'd copied a key years ago, and walked over there chewing the inside of her lip and wondering what the fallout from this particular mission would be.

Mrs. Bennett would surely get rid of Stella—she couldn't keep her at Stagmount after something like this. Liberty would *have* to see that she'd been duped. Mr. Morris would be reinstated before Ms. Gunn got too comfortable, and things would go back to normal. Jinx grinned.

As she stood outside the lockup and removed her duplicate key, she thought she heard rustling from within. None of the juniors would be skipping chapel—they had tutor group beforehand and were walked there by their form teachers, who sat at the end of their rows. None of her year would be in there thanks to Gunn's new regime, and anyway, as far as she knew, she was the only pupil who had a key. She pressed her ear against the door and heard a distinct moan. Who the *hell* was in there, and what were they doing?

She decided to fling the doors open and confront whoever it was, if necessary claiming she'd been given the key by one of the gardeners to get her bike out. Jinx quietly put the key in the lock, wiggled it around, and felt it click. She flung open the door and gasped as her eyes adjusted to the dim light. She couldn't believe the sight in front of her.

Ms. Gunn was on her knees on the dusty ground, her vast bottom facing the door. She was wriggling about and groaning in front of . . . oh my *God* . . . it was The DICK! The Dick was lying against an old milk crate. Her check skirt had ridden up to expose incredibly pasty and much-veined legs wrapped around Gunn's huge waist. Her white arms were flung with careless abandon around Gunn's neck, and her bright orange hair was only just visible behind Gunn's massive head. The pair of them were sucking on each other's lips, moaning and groaning all the while, obviously having the time of their lives.

They were so involved in each other that neither had noticed the door opening or Jinx coming in. "Dick, dick, DICK!" heavy-breathed Gunn, pumping herself forward in ecstasy.

"Patricia, I want you!" responded The Dick, tightening her legs around Gunn's midriff and exposing even more thigh.

Jinx was torn between hysterical laughter and the very real feeling that she might actually be sick. She reached in her pocket for her mobile phone and set it to video. No one would believe her if she didn't have documentary evidence. This was going to be the best video footage *in the world*. Jinx lit her cigarette and trained her phone on the grunting pair.

Gunn was the first to turn around. When she saw Jinx, her eyes disappeared so far into the folds of fat above and below them that she looked like one of the brains in the jar in that Steve Martin film. "Slater!" Gunn looked absolutely horrified. "What the *hell* are you doing here?"

She somehow managed to turn herself around to face Jinx while still protecting The Dick's modesty—fragile as it was at this stage. "How did you get in here?" she blustered. "I can assure you this is not what it looks like. Mrs., er, Dickinson had something in her eye, and I, er, was—"

"Don't bother, Ms. Gunn." Jinx smirked. "I've got two brothers. I've heard it all before. And anyway"—she tapped her phone—"I've got it all saved in here. *Very* interesting it is, too. The Dick and The Gunn...who'd have thought it!"

"Jinx . . ." The Dick had managed to pull her skirt down to where it belonged, had stood up, and was staring beseechingly at her. "Please—I *beg you*—don't show anyone that. I know we've not always got on in the past, but I do think you are a very warmhearted girl and not at all bad at French."

Jinx laughed so heartily at this that she had to steady herself against a stack of bicycles leaning against the wall.

"Don't make me laugh," she snorted. "You *hate* me. I've never heard anything more pathetic in my life. Now I hope *you're* not going to start telling me how much you love me," she giggled, pointing at Gunn. "That really would be the icing on the cake."

"What do you want, Slater?" Gunn growled. "Come on— out with it. We'll never be able to work at Stagmount if this gets out. The girls would have a field day."

"Never a truer word spoken," Jinx agreed. "Well, not out of *your* mouth, anyway."

As The Dick squeezed out a few tears, Gunn put a meaty arm protectively around her shoulders. Jinx stared at them. What *did* she want? It didn't take her long to decide.

"Right," she said, one hand on the door in case they tried to rush her. "Here's the deal. You two have made Stagmount

girls' lives an absolute misery for far too long. You've been positively evil, and—let's face it—you're both near retirement age
anyway.

"My terms are as follows," Jinx unlocked the door and prepared to make a run for it. "I will destroy the evidence and
swear never to breathe a word about this . . . um . . . incident if
the pair of you tender your resignations immediately."

"You"—she pointed at Gunn, who'd drawn a sharp intake
of breath—"will take back all the unfair punishments you have
dished out to the lower sixth since you arrived at Tanner,
rescind all those ridiculous rules, and spend the next week and
a half keeping a very low profile. And you"—she turned to face
The Dick—"will see out the end of term at home due to your
head injury. Frankly, Mademoiselle Dupont does a far better job
than you anyway. *She* has a sense of humor."

"Slater," Ms. Gunn snapped, "watch your mouth."

"On the contrary, Ms. Gunn." Jinx smiled as she spoke. "I
think you'd better watch *yours*. Don't forget, I hold all the cards
here. There's really nothing you can do but accept my terms."

The teachers looked at each other. They knew that if they
didn't, their lives wouldn't be worth living anyway, and if they
did . . . well, they could then perhaps realize their dream of
moving to a country cottage within easy reach of Devil's Dyke,
living in bliss together and growing their own vegetables.
Slowly, and in unison, they nodded their agreement.

Jinx smiled to herself, thoroughly delighted as she walked
out the door and headed for main school. What a day! She

could hardly believe her luck in catching the evil pair in fla-
grante delicto like this. She laughed out loud as she looked at
her phone—it had been too dark in the shed for the bloody
video to work. The only thing visible on the screen was flickering shapes and—if you listened really carefully—a couple of
indistinct moans.

40

Jinx stood by Jo's desk waiting to see Mrs. Bennett, glancing over her shoulder at the ringed pictures of celebrities' armpit sweat stains in the new *Heat* magazine. Jo had tried to fob her off with an appointment for later in the day, but when Jinx had insisted and said it concerned Mr. Morris, she'd miraculously magicked up a free slot in the diary then and there.

Jinx sat down in the chair she seemed to have spent an inordinate amount of time in this term and glanced out the window at the raging sea before opening her bag, removing the tape recorder, and placing it on the desk between her and her headmistress without saying a word.

"Well? What is it Jinx?" Mrs. Bennett tapped her pen against the side of her computer and raised her eyebrows to the ceiling. "I'm very busy today, and I certainly don't have time for any of your games."

"Just listen to this, Mrs. B." Jinx switched on the tiny machine. "And then I promise I'll get straight out of your hair."

As the sounds of Stella and Jinx's discussion filled the air, Mrs. Bennett sat stock-still, listening intently. She didn't move a muscle, not even to push her glasses up her nose when they slipped down. Jinx stared out the window the entire time, wondering how long it would be before Mr. Morris was reinstated and what, exactly, would happen to Stella. Not that she cared, particularly: she just found it interesting.

"Right." Mrs. Bennett stood up when the tape finished playing and started pacing back and forth behind her desk. "Right."

Jinx didn't say a word. She was panicking, wondering what she'd do if Mrs. Bennett told her to take a hike. Why wasn't the woman saying anything? What if she still didn't believe her?

"Jinx Slater," Mrs. Bennett said eventually, pushing her glasses up her nose, staring a very nervous Jinx in the eye and smiling, "I've told you before that you're a credit to this school, and today you've proved it. I am *incredibly* proud of you. Not only have you saved two innocent men from a lifetime of suspicion and unemployment, you've proved yourself a true Stagmount girl."

Jinx blushed and turned to look out the window again. She loved Mrs. B and everything, but really, this gushing was a bit much to deal with. She blushed even harder when the headmistress enveloped her in a huge hug, and practically stopped breathing when Mrs. Bennett asked her if she would consider being Stagmount's head girl next year. It was nice and everything, but Christ, she did have her reputation to consider.

There was one thing she needed to ask before she left the office. "Mrs. Bennett," said Jinx, "I just don't understand one thing."

"What is it, dear?" Jinx had a feeling Mrs. B would have kissed her feet if she'd asked her to.

"Well . . ." She paused—she didn't want to ruin the good mood, but she needed to know. "Why did you take her in the first place? I mean, you obviously *knew* why she'd left Bedales, and they must have had their suspicions about her, right?"

"Yes, Jinx, you're exactly right of course." Mrs. Bennett sighed. "I was dead against it from the start. In fact, I'd put my foot down and said no. The bursar had other ideas. When Mr. and Mrs. Fox offered to make a generous donation to his roof fund, he forced my hand, I'm afraid. I wish I'd stood my ground, but he really can be *very* insistent."

It was obvious that Mrs. Bennett needed to get on the phone and sort stuff out, so Jinx decided she'd deal with the head-girl issue later—it *was* two terms off, after all, and anything could happen between now and then.

"Just one thing, Jinx," Mrs. Bennett said, looking up and grinning slyly. Jinx turned round, her hand on the door handle.

"Where did you get the recording device?" Jinx blushed and desperately tried to think of something, *anything*, but her mind remained resolutely void of excuses.

"Actually," Mrs. Bennett said, tapping her forefinger against the side of her nose and winking, "forget I asked that. Something tells me I don't want to know. Off you go!"

Jinx slunk into double French an hour late and explained to Mademoiselle Dupont that she'd been with Mrs. Bennett. She didn't look at Stella but noticed Liberty staring quizzically at her. As she sat down in her front-row seat, she felt the enquiring glances of her entire class and wasn't surprised when a sharply folded note flew through the air and landed with great precision in the middle of her textbook. It was from Liv, demanding to know where the hell she'd been all morning, and signed off with her usual *don't get it twisted*. Jinx wrote, *Later, Liv,* and then, giggling to herself, added, P.S. *Twisted doesn't even come close to* THIS, on it, flicked it back to her, and settled down in her seat, wondering how long it would take for Mrs. B to summon Stella.

She didn't have to wait long. Five minutes later, and just as Mademoiselle Dupont was really getting to grips with the past participle, Jo knocked on the door.

"Stella Fox?" she said, looking round the room with a stern expression on her face that none of the girls had ever seen before. "Mrs. Bennett's office. Now."

Jo waited in the doorway, arms folded, as Stella gathered up her books and made to follow her out. As they turned to leave, she waved at Liberty as if she didn't have a care in the world and mouthed, "See you later, save me a seat at lunch."

Liberty nodded and Jinx felt a pang for her friend. But not too much of one—Liberty would realize what a snake that girl was soon enough.

At the end of the lesson they raced down the "up" stairs toward the dining room, with Jinx fielding question like they were balls being flung out of one of those tennis machines. Only Liberty hung behind, walking sedately down the "down" stairs, obviously with no idea that Stella's days were numbered and still wanting nothing to do with anyone else. "Will you all just shut up!" Jinx giggled. "I'll fill you in over lunch, when we're all sitting down in the same place at the same time." Needless to say, they made it to lunch in record time.

"Lib . . ." Jinx walked over to where she was sitting on her own at the end of a table of second-years, pretending she was oblivious to what the lower sixth were doing. "Will you come and sit with us? Please?"

Liberty suddenly seemed to take a great interest in the contents of her shepherd's pie, pushing it around her plate and refusing to look at Jinx.

"Come on, Lib." Jinx knelt down, put a hand on Liberty's knee, and squeezed it. "You know how much I love you, and I'm sorry—*so* sorry—that I've upset you. Look, even if you're still furious with me, I promise you don't want to miss this. Honestly, you've got to hear it."

"Fine." Liberty stood up and picked up her tray. "But I'm still cross with you. And me coming over there doesn't mean I've forgiven you."

"Okay, sweetheart." Jinx raised her eyebrows and picked up Liberty's bag from where she'd left it under the table. "Totally understood. I've got your bag, by the way."

When Jinx had finished speaking, all the girls, even Liberty, were staring at her openmouthed. If a stranger had walked into the dining room right then, she'd have thought this lot were Stagmount's own village idiots, shunned to a separate table by their cleverer peers.

Liberty was the first to break the silence. "But why didn't you *tell* me, Jinx?" she whined, flicking her hair, still undecided as to whether she should continue the feud or not. "If you'd *told* me all this stuff, I wouldn't have hung around with her, would I?"

"I tried, darling." Jinx sighed. "But she had you wrapped round her beautifully manicured little finger, didn't she?"

"And also, Lib," said Chastity, "Jinx didn't *know* everything until last night, did she? She couldn't have told you everything she's just told us now."

"But I thought she was so, like, *sophisticated*," Liberty moaned, clearly in shock, "and, you know, *cool* and down with it and everything."

"And"—Liberty grabbed Jinx's hand across the table and squeezed it hard—"I thought you lot were jealous of me having such a great new friend. But the thing that upsets me most is that I believed her over you guys—my best friends in the world. I'm so sorry—I've been as bad as her. Forgive me?"

"Of *course* we will!" they all yelled at once, pushing and shoving each other to ruffle her hair and pinch her cheeks until she screamed for mercy.

"Yeah," Liv agreed when they'd all sat back down, looking rather more flushed than usual. "We should just draw a line under it from here on. Let's not get it twisted. And face it—it's not like she's going to be here much longer, is it? There's no way Bennett will let her hang around to poison our pure little minds any further—I wouldn't be surprised if we never see her again."

Liberty seemed to agree, and it was a far happier crowd who traipsed down the drive back to Tanner House to watch *Neighbors*. Even the sun was shining. As they approached the front door, they saw Ms. Gunn striding through it, and all of them apart from Jinx shrank to the other side of the path.

"Has she gone fucking mad?" hissed Liv to Charlie as Jinx gave Gunn a jaunty wave and enquired after her health in a decidedly breezy manner. The rest of the girls were even more appalled when Gunn grunted a response and didn't say a word about the fact that they were not—as per her new rules—allowed back to the house during the day unless they were at death's door and had a note from Mister S to prove it.

"I don't know, love," replied Charlie. "Maybe it's Gunn who's gone mad." Jinx just smiled. That was one confidence she'd sworn to herself she was never going to break.

As they entered the house, they saw Stella sitting on the sofa in the foyer. There was a huge suitcase and a boxful of books on the floor next to her. She was talking in a very tight voice into her phone, demanding to know where her taxi was.

"Taxi for one to the station," hummed Chastity, and the others giggled as they floated past her without a second glance. Only Jinx hung back.

"You think you're so fucking clever, don't you?" sneered Stella. "Well, I'm going to have the last laugh, you just wait."

"Whatever, Stella, *whatever*," Jinx said, making the W sign with her thumbs and forefingers. "Oh look, how convenient. There's your cab. See ya, wouldn't wanna be ya!" She laughed to herself as she followed the others to the common room. What a day.

41

The girls were lying on the floor, scoffing a bumper packet of Jaffa Cakes, and totally engrossed in *Days of Our Lives* when they heard the unmistakable hum of a helicopter hovering above the games pitches through the open window. "Ignore it," yelled Chastity. "He's about to tell her about his affair!"

They tried to zone it out, but the sound was getting louder and louder. It was obviously about to land. Jinx jumped up to shut the window but felt a shiver trail down her spine when she recognized Harrods's unmistakable green-and-gold livery plastered all over its sides. She only knew one person who hired that thing to fly to Stagmount.

"Guys!" she said urgently. "Fuck the TV. Come here and check this out."

They extricated themselves from the cushions they were

spread out on and came, grumbling, to the window. "So what?" Chastity loved *Days* more than anything. "It's a helicopter. Big fucking deal. It's probably some first-year's parents or something. I don't know what you're making such a fuss about."

Liberty was rooted to the spot as they watched the chopper make its landing. As the occupant jumped out and ran, bent low, to the safety of outside the landing square, she turned to Jinx. "Shit," she whispered, gripping Jinx's arm so tightly it hurt. "It's *Dad*."

"Your dad?" Charlie was confused. "What the fuck is he doing here?"

"We don't know," said Jinx grimly, "but I've got a terrible feeling we're about to find out. And somehow I don't imagine he's here to take us out to tea."

As they watched, Mrs. Bennett flew down the steps by the ice cream shop before running elegantly down the gentle slope toward Amir Latiffe. She held out her hand in greeting, but he seemed to refuse to take it. She stepped backward as he began gesticulating wildly about, waving what looked like a large brown envelope for emphasis.

"He looks mad about something," murmured Liv, "that's for sure."

After what looked like a lot of persuading and peacemaking on Mrs. B's part, Amir eventually began to walk with her up the slope toward the path that led to the main-school front door and her office.

"Lib . . ." Jinx put her hands on a transfixed Liberty's shoulders and shook her gently. "We've got to deal with this. Whatever he's doing here, it's obvious he'll want to see you sooner or later. Shall we bite the bullet and go up there now?"

"I think you should," Liv put her arm around Liberty's waist and squeezed her. "If he thinks you've done something wrong, then at least this way you'll look like you're behaving like an adult."

"But she hasn't *done* anything," said Charlie. "Has she? None of us has—not for ages."

"No," Jinx agreed. "He's probably got mixed up about something. Or he was probably in London and decided to pay a flying visit at the last minute. We'd know if it was anything else."

Liberty didn't look convinced, and, to be honest, neither was Jinx, but she eventually agreed that they should be seen to be behaving innocently, if nothing else.

They all agreed that only Jinx should accompany Liberty. None of the others really knew Amir, whereas he'd known Jinx since Liberty started at Stagmount.

As they walked up the drive arm in arm, Jinx prattled on about Stella and how nice Mrs. Bennett had been to her that morning. She said anything, in fact, that came into her mind apart from what possible reason Amir could have for turning up out of the blue like this and in such an obvious mood about something. Liberty's face was set in a frozen mask of terrified anticipation, and she only murmured yes and no answers in response to Jinx's nonstop nervous chatter.

They stood outside Mrs. Bennett's office, next to a shell-shocked-looking Jo, who didn't ask them what they wanted but motioned for them to join her in leaning close to the outside of the door. At the sound of her father's voice, Liberty immediately turned white and began shaking like jelly. What they heard sent a shiver down Jinx's spine.

Amir, obviously in the middle of a marvelous raging rant, was screaming and yelling about decency and propriety, and Mrs. Bennett was using her most soothing voice in what was clearly a vain attempt to calm him down.

"But *how* do you explain this, Mrs. Bennett?" he screamed. "You *can't*, that's what! I pay a fortune to send my firstborn to this school, believing you will look after her, and then I see *this*." There was the sound of something being smacked down on a desk and then silence.

"I can see why you are upset, Mr. Latiffe," began Mrs. Bennett, "and I can assure you . . ."

"You can assure me of *nothing*, Mrs. Bennett, *nothing!*" Amir shouted. "For a long time I have wondered about this Stagmount, and this is the final stick. This has broken my donkey's back. I remove Liberty now, at once and forever."

"But Mr.—" Mrs. Bennett was using her most soothing voice.

"But *nothing*," Amir interrupted. "Shut up, woman. Where is my daughter? I want to see my Liberty now. *Where is she?*"

"Hi, Dad," a quaking Liberty said, walking into the office, closely followed by Jinx. "I saw you land. What's up?"

Amir spun round and stared at Liberty with a look of such

fear and loathing and unreconstructed hatred that Jinx wanted to grab her hand and run, run all the way down the drive, past the marina and beyond. To Hampshire. To London—to anywhere this terrible man wouldn't be able to find her.

"You dare to ask me what is up." He threw himself to the floor, conveniently landing smack-bang in the middle of Mrs. Bennett's Bokhara rug, thereby saving his knees, and held his head in his hands. "Like a filthy American. Like your *mother*." He started crying and smacking his head with his hands. Jinx thought she might collapse into hysterical nervous laughter but managed to stop herself for fear of what the man might do next.

"It is over, Liberty," he said, his eyes suddenly dry and hard. "I have—how do you call it—tough evidence that you have been bringing shame to the good name of Latiffe, and you leave with me now, this minute."

"But Dad," Liberty said, stretching out a hand and moving closer to him, "I don't understand what I'm supposed to have done."

"I show you." Amir leapt to his feet and grabbed the brown envelope from Mrs. Bennett's desk, shaking it so that a collection of photos spilled out all over the floor. "*This*! This is what you have done. And it stops here."

Jinx looked at the images spread out on Mrs. Bennett's floor. At first glance they looked like any of the photos tacked up on their bedroom walls all over Tanner House and teenage bedrooms all over the country. Girls and boys holding up beer bottles and glasses, their arms wrapped around each other, smiling broadly for the camera. On closer inspection, she real-ized they showed Liberty and other people she didn't know laughing and obviously having a good time in a club she didn't recognize.

As she leant forward to study them more intently, she real-ized the blond girl with the massive toothy grin and heavy makeup who appeared in all the pictures was Stella. Both Stella and Liberty had a reddish tint to their eyeballs and seemed to be sweating. In truth, they looked absolutely wrecked. Jinx was confused. How the hell had Amir gotten hold of these? Had he been having Liberty followed or something? She caught Mrs. Bennett's eye and raised her eyebrows in a silent question. Mrs. Bennett shook her head before inclining it to where Liberty was staring at Amir with a hunted look on her face.

"But Dad," she said, her voice quavering, "I haven't done any-thing wrong. So I went to a club with my friends. So what? That's what kids do. They hang out with their friends and they have a nice time. I love you and I'm sorry if you think I've let you down. But please be reasonable—I went clubbing, that's all! It's not shameful, it's not dirty, and it's no reflection on your reputation."

Amir stared at her and shook his head. "I don't care what you say," he said in a terrifyingly harsh voice. "I am not listen-ing to you anymore. For nearly four years you have persuaded me to let you stay here to finish your education, and today it ends. It stops. You come back to Saudi."

"Dad," said Liberty, who looked near breaking point, "how did you get these?"

"I was sent them in an e-mail. I got them this morning, and it so happened I was in London on business." Amir smoothed his beard, looking very pleased with himself. "Yes, it seems that not all Stagmount girls are like you. *Some* of them have a sense of moral decency and know the difference between right and wrong. What was her name?" Amir scratched his head. "Ah yes, it was like a star and an animal. Stella Fox. She was most informative. She said she thought it was time I knew what kind of company you were keeping and what you get up to behind my back. She wrote that she'd heard I was a decent man and most concerned about my daughter and she wanted to help me out. I am very pleased with her indeed."

Jinx thought she might throw up. She *had* to make Amir see reason. "Mr. Latiffe," she said, a very grave expression on her face, "I'm so sorry that you think Stagmount has let you down, but it certainly hasn't let Liberty down. Look at her. She's beautiful and kind and she's doing so well in her lessons this term. She's got so many friends here, and we all love her so much. We'd never let anything happen to her—"

"Jinx . . ." Amir interrupted and bowed slightly to her. "I always liked you, and I liked your parents, too. I thought you were a good friend to Liberty, and in your own way you probably were, but I cannot have this. Liberty is bringing shame on her family, and none of you can understand that. I'm sorry, but she's coming back to Saudi with me today, and that is the end of it."

"Come on, Jinx." Liberty put her arm round Jinx's shoulder but leant in to her friend as if she couldn't quite manage to stand up unsupported. "It's no good. His mind is made up. Come and help me get my stuff."

"No." Amir folded his arms. "You come with me now. Right now, this second. No stuff, no bags, nothing. That will come later. We leave now."

"But . . ." Liberty's eyes had filled with tears, and if Jinx hadn't put an arm round her waist, she might have fallen over.

"No buts," he said, gathering up the photographs and stuffing them back into their envelope. "I say now and I mean now."

Jinx took Liberty's right hand in her left and wrapped her right arm around Liberty's waist. They walked like that, crying and telling each other how much they loved each other, all the way to the H-pad in the middle of the hockey pitch where Stella had smashed her ball into Liberty's head on her first day.

Amir didn't say a word to Jinx or Mrs. Bennett as he helped Liberty climb into the back of the ostentatiously branded Harrods chopper. She pressed her face against the window and stared at them with huge tears rolling down her cheeks as Amir jumped in the front and the pilot prepared for takeoff. Mrs. Bennett put her arm around Jinx's shoulder, but there was no consoling her. The two of them stood and watched as the helicopter circled the pitches twice before disappearing over the sea. They stood there until they could see it no more.

"I know this looks bad, Jinx," Mrs. Bennett said, tenderly smoothing a flyaway strand of curly blond fringe back behind Jinx's ear, "but I want you to promise me you won't worry yourself sick about it—you've had quite enough to deal with over the past few weeks. Rest assured I will try my very best to make Mr. Latiffe see reason. I'm going to give him a couple of days to calm down and then I shall employ all my powers of persuasion and do whatever's necessary to make the man come round."

Jinx smiled weakly, but she wasn't entirely convinced Mrs. B would be able to do anything. She'd seen Amir in some right old strops before, but never in such an all-consuming rage like this. She refused Mrs. Bennett's offer of a cup of tea and a chat, saying she'd prefer to be alone. They parted company by the ice cream shop, and Jinx began her solitary trudge down the drive to Tanner House. She felt numb to the core, so shocked she couldn't even think about what had just happened. She couldn't remember feeling this miserable ever before and doubted she would again.

42

Thankfully, no one was sitting around in the foyer, so she didn't have to deal with any stupid questions about Stella or fake interest in the results of someone's maths test or most recent row with her boyfriend. She collapsed on her bed facedown and wondered whether she would ever see her best friend again. She couldn't believe the nerve of Amir, turning up out of the blue like that. She supposed, if she was really honest, he'd been looking for a reason to take Liberty out of Stagmount pretty much since she'd started. The one thing she'd never been able to understand was, since he so obviously hated liberal western culture, what on earth had possessed him to send her here in the first place.

As she lay there, Jinx began to wonder if it was in fact *her* fault that Liberty had been dragged off like that, especially given the Stella debacle. If she hadn't taken that recording to Mrs. Bennett, who'd then got rid of her, Stella would still be here and not desperately seeking revenge.

Someone knocked softly at Jinx's door and she groaned. It was bound to be Chastity or one of the others wanting to know what had happened and why Liberty had been flown off like that at a moment's notice. She supposed she'd have to tell them at some point and, much as she didn't feel like it, it might as well be now. She got up off her bed and opened her door.

Fanny Ho was standing there on one leg. She was rubbing the other up and down the back of her calf, chewing her lip, and was clearly bothered about something.

"Hi, Fan," Jinx said, smiling even though she felt like crying. "What do you want? More Vaseline?"

"Um, no." Fanny looked close to tears as well. "I need to ask your advice about something. I've got a real problem and I don't know who else to talk to."

"Okay," Jinx said, so surprised she forgot about Liberty for a second. She and Fanny had always got on, but they'd never exactly been bosom buddies, because Fanny normally kept to herself. "What is it?"

"Well, it's actually easier if you come into my room, Jinx," said Fanny, gesturing across the corridor. "I can explain it better in there—and I really appreciate this, I really do."

"It's fine, don't worry about it," said Jinx, slipping on her white havianas and following Fanny, now feeling very curious.

Fanny flung open her door, strode into what Jinx could

immediately tell was a very clean room, and sat down on her bed. Jinx followed her in and looked around before doing a massive double take. Sitting next to Fanny on the bed was another Chinese girl. She was wearing a gray Y-3 T-shirt, baggy black maharishi trousers, and retro Nike trainers. If Jinx hadn't just seen Fanny in the corridor wearing a bright pink Paul Frank top, she wouldn't have been able to tell them apart.

"What the fuck?" Jinx was staring at them. "Am I seeing things, or are there are *two* of you?"

"Jinx," Fanny said, putting her arm around the other girl and squeezing her shoulder reassuringly, "this is my girlfriend, Maureen Mo."

Jinx stared at them for another long minute before collapsing to the floor, where she rolled around crying with laughter. "I knew it!" she spluttered through her tears. "I totally KNEW it the whole time, but I've been so engrossed in all the stuff with Liberty and Stella that I haven't been thinking straight."

"I know," said Fanny. "You've given me so many strange looks I was *convinced* you'd figured it out. But I'm thrilled you didn't give us away. It's great—and exactly what we wanted! We didn't look that alike to start with, but we got so many funny looks from you lot, we quickly realized we'd have to change our hair and start wearing all the same clothes and huge hats if we didn't want our game to be up pretty damn quick. It's been a mission, that's for sure. We've practically had to clone each other—but for one result. It's been fun up till now."

"All term," Jinx snorted, "all freaking term we've thought

Fanny had the biggest wardrobe in the western world . . . and the best hairdresser."

"I know." Fanny grinned. "And Maureen said she called you Liberty once by mistake. I thought the game was up then."

"No!" Jinx cried. "I thought you'd gone mad. And what about when I saw you with that massive takeaway? That was for both of you, wasn't it? God, Fanny, I'm sorry—I thought you were *such* a pig. And I knew you looked totally different that night—you didn't have your hat on, did you . . . Maureen?"

"No." Maureen smiled. "I thought you'd definitely suss us out, but you were so drunk you obviously thought you just couldn't see clearly."

Jinx laughed again. She couldn't believe the nerve of it all—who'd have thought quiet old Fanny Ho could orchestrate and carry out an extreme prank so successfully? Jinx was well impressed.

"Don't worry about it, Jinx." Fanny smiled. "If anything, I should apologize to you. You've probably thought I was being really off and rude all term, but Mo and I decided we couldn't get involved in any long conversations with anyone, as we couldn't afford to draw attention to ourselves. That's why I've practically run away every time you've tried to speak to me—if we'd been friendlier, you lot would *definitely* have noticed."

"But Fan," Jinx said, when she'd collected herself sufficiently from her latest fit of hysteria, "I don't understand— you've got away with it for so long, and I certainly won't tell anyone, so what's the sudden problem?"

Fanny bowed her head and looked very concerned. "The thing is, Jinx," she said, "Maureen is not actually a pupil here. I smuggled her here from Hong Kong."

"*What?*" Jinx could hardly believe what she was hearing. "You're telling me Maureen's not registered at Stagmount? I thought she must be a fifth-year from one of the junior houses or something. How the fuck—?"

"I know," Fanny said grimly. "It's been fine all term. Maureen's been coming to breakfast, lunch, and dinner every day. The occasional assembly—even a couple of maths lessons when I was studying loads and couldn't be back here as much as I liked."

"It's true," chipped in Maureen. "I even sat in on a couple of your tutor group lessons with that weirdo Mrs. Carpenter when Fanny was too tired to get up in the morning."

"Mr. Morris has even seen us together a few times," added Fanny. "He didn't notice anything out of the ordinary at all. I guess he assumed the same as you—that Maureen was a friend of mine from another year or something. He's become quite accustomed to seeing her around the house."

"So . . ." Jinx couldn't see what the problem was.

"So," said Fanny, "he's gone now, hasn't he? And that terrible Ms. Gunn has stormed in with all her registers and inspections, and she keeps wandering into our rooms to root about and see what we're hiding. It's all well and good for you lot," she sniffed, "with the odd bottle of vodka or packet of cigarettes, but I'*m* harboring an illegal immigrant. What the hell would she do if she found Maureen and realized she didn't belong here?"

"Yep," agreed Maureen. "Fanny and I walked past her going down the drive this morning, and she gave us a very funny look."

Jinx collapsed in tears again. She wasn't sure if she was laughing or crying anymore, but one thing was for sure—she couldn't *believe* what she was hearing. This was absolutely priceless. She decided then and there that she would swear Fanny and Maureen to secrecy and break Gunn and The Dick's confidence just this once. Poor Fanny looked so frightened, she had to put her mind at rest. Anyway, there must be some sort of honor amongst lesbians, mustn't there?

Jinx settled herself comfortably against an offensively pink Hello Kitty–branded beanbag—she'd never understand the attraction of that stuff: all the Chinese girls were mad for it— and began to fill them in on everything she'd seen in the bike shed that morning. She was just explaining the bargain she'd struck with the evil pair and saying that so long as Maureen kept a reasonably low profile for the rest of term she'd be absolutely fine when there was a tap at the door.

"Ah, hello, girls," a beaming Mr. Morris said, lounging in the doorframe. "I thought I heard Ms. Slater's dulcet tones coming from in here."

He looked around and smiled. "Afternoon, Fanny; afternoon, Maureen," he said, putting his hands in his pockets and looking genially at them. "Your housemistress must spend most of her time wondering where you are, Maureen."

"Hello, Mr. Morris," Maureen said brightly, cool as a cucumber. "It's great to have you back. We've missed you."

"Don't worry, girls—your secret's safe with me." He smiled his goodbyes and winked before bumbling off.

Jinx lay back against Hello Kitty's wide, smiling face and convulsed again, still not sure if she was laughing or crying. When she'd pulled herself together enough to stand up and get back to her own room, she peeled the Polaroid of her and Liberty on the first day they'd met off her wall and collapsed onto her bed, staring at it. Fat girls were indeed harder to kidnap. If Liberty had been uglier and friendless, maybe this would never have happened. Her phone rang and she answered it with a sob, hoping against hope it was Lib.

"Hi, darling," Caroline Slater's cheery voice said at the other end. "Dad and I haven't heard from you for ages. Is Liberty coming home for Christmas this year?"

Jinx sighed and turned her stereo down. "Mum," she said, her voice breaking, "I've got so much to tell you. I can't wait to come home."